Christmas Proposal

by

Pam Binder

Christmas in the Castle Series

Christmas Proposal

Cover Art by *Lisa Dawn MacDonald*

The Wild Rose Press, Inc.
PO Box 708
Adams Basin, NY 14410-0708
Visit us at www.thewildrosepress.com

Publishing History
First Edition, 2023
Trade Paperback ISBN 978-1-5092-5260-2
Digital ISBN 978-1-5092-5261-9

Christmas in the Castle Series
Published in the United States of America

Dedication

To my mother, Irene Louise.
Thank you for teaching me
the power of love, family, and forgiveness.

"I am determined that only the deepest love will induce me into matrimony."

~from *Pride and Prejudice* by Jane Austen

The door banged open. A woman, with hair that cascaded down her back in crimson waves, burst through the door, holding a pistol. She had removed her traveling coat and wore a high-waisted, ice-blue frock that flowed over her curves like silk. His breath quickened. He recognized her instantly. She was the woman from the carriage—the Lady in Green—and more lovely than he had remembered.

The room stopped spinning as he drank in her beauty.

She glanced toward him as though in slow motion, her eyes widening in recognition. Then she looked toward Devonshire and Lady Montgomery as though assessing the situation.

She seemed to have made a decision, and instead of lowering her weapon she kept it focused on Devonshire. "Drop your weapon." Her voice was steady and her grip on the pistol confident.

"Who are you to order me about?" Devonshire said, with an arrogant lift of his chin.

"I am a person who never misses," she said, her voice as cold as steel. "That is who I am."

Robert saw the determination in his cousin's expression falter. But war had taught Robert a valuable lesson. When an enemy was cornered, they were unpredictable. Devonshire would shoot the lady who Robert now regarded as his rescuer, then turn his weapon on Robert to finish the job. Devonshire was a viscount. His power and position would protect him, and with both the woman and Robert dead, no one would dispute the story, as there was no certainty of being able to rely on Lady Montgomery.

Chapter One

Boston, 1814

"What a bumblebroth I've made of things."

It was not the first time Miss Madeline Louise Mercer had made that comment in the last twenty-four hours.

Gas lamps spread ribbons of cream-colored light on the street as Madeline stepped from the carriage that had transported her from Bradford Academy to the back entrance of The Feathers, Boston's most notorious brothel. She wore the latest fashion, a traveling ensemble of warm green velvet, with lace-and-satin-trimmed sleeves and a matching bonnet.

She paid the driver handsomely, assuring him he had indeed transported her to the right address, then left the worried man and entered a world she had hoped she would never see again.

The back entry's waiting room walls were wallpapered in red velvet. Paintings of half-naked men and women frolicked in meadows, above a marble bust of Bacchus, the Greek god of wine, and nude statues and busts of Greek and Roman gods and goddesses. A gold and crystal chandelier hung from the ceiling. Mahogany tables were polished to a high shine, and chairs and sofas were upholstered with red, black, and gold silk. The entry was a mere sampling of the opulent and decadent atmosphere that awaited an exclusive clientele. Her fellow students at the academy would be scandalized if they knew she was here. They judged without knowing. Her feelings were tumbled and confused, for this was home…the only one she had ever known.

Madeline removed her gloves, set down her satchel, and braced for a world she hadn't seen in over ten years. On the eve of her fourteenth birthday, her mother had sent her to boarding school at Ursuline Academy for girls in New Orleans. She had excelled and moved from there to more advanced courses at Bradford Academy, in Massachusetts, with instructions to keep this part of her life a secret. After her mother had made generous donations to Ursuline Academy and then Bradford, the administrators were willing to accept the story that her mother was the wealthy widow of a railroad tycoon. Once again, Madeline thrived and made friends.

But nothing lasts forever.

She had had an offer of marriage from the son of one of her professors, which she had declined. She was fond of him in the way a person was fond of a brother or a cherished cousin. She was not in love with him, nor was she seeking love. Her mother had lectured her on its follies and pitfalls. Madeline's father had abandoned her and her mother before Madeline was born, confirming that, for women, love came at a price at times too dear to pay.

Then an offer of a different sort from a married professor was made, and this time it came with threats. The threat was straightforward: accept his offer and become his mistress or he would reveal her mother's profession. For additional inducement, he promised he would recommend her for a teaching position at

Bradford. She did not trust him any further than she could toss his pear-shaped hide.

Madeline had stalled, asked the professor if she could consider his offer for a fortnight, and then, needing her mother's advice, she had hired a carriage and returned home. Her mother was many things: the successful owner of an establishment too exclusive to be considered as a brothel, wise in managing her wealth, kind and generous with her employees, and above all, a loving mother. Her mother would also know how to handle the professor.

Madeline heard a commotion in the hallway: a heated argument between a gentleman and a lady. Then Madeline's mother's voice, lifted, strong and clear above the shouts and accusations, demanding that the gentleman leave at once or be tossed out on his ear.

Memories flooded back, rooting Madeline's feet to the thick carpeted floor.

Her mother had created a safe place for her girls, employing a physician to assist with pregnancies and diseases, hiring maids and cooks to assure the house was clean and the food of the highest quality, as well as loyal guards to protect the girls if her clientele became violent. The violence was the ugly side of her mother's business, and though her mother was reluctant to send Madeline away, she had felt she didn't have a choice.

Another reason for sending Madeline to boarding school was that there could be little hope of securing a suitable marriage for her if gentlemen, and their marriage-minded mamas, knew of her mother's occupation. In many ways, Boston's wealthy elite were not that different from England's *beau monde*.

Angry voices grew louder. More insults. More

threats. Madeline heard a slap. A woman cried for mercy, prompting Madeline to wonder why a guard had not appeared. Perhaps he had been overpowered.

Worried for the safety of both the woman and her mother, Madeline scanned the area in the entry for something to use as a weapon. She reached for a bust of Zeus and ran toward the sound of her mother's voice.

The front room was dimly lit. In its center, a middle-aged man had his back turned toward Madeline. He hurled insults at Madeline's mother as he towered over a woman kneeling on the ground. The man was well-dressed, in a somber black coat and breeches, with tight, pumpkin-orange hose—his legs reminded Madeline of a pair of stuffed sausages.

"I do not want my money returned. I want the baggage in my bed."

Her mother, in her signature red velvet evening gown, spoke soothingly, her countenance composed, as she helped the frightened woman stand. "You know the rules of my establishment: chief among them is that you do not hit a woman. I have asked you to leave and never return."

"I will ruin you! I will shut you down, but first…" He reached for a sidearm.

Madeline saw the danger and did not hesitate. She swung the plaster bust and smashed it over the man's head. His mouth gaped open like that of a beached whale, and he slumped to his knees.

A large man, his mop of black hair falling over his forehead and almost to the bloody gash under his right eye, rushed down the stairs. "Apologies, madam. Taking care of a congressman deep in his cup and wielding a knife. Had to tie him up before he caused harm. The girls are watching him." He took in the situation. The middle-aged man on his knees, a woman with a bruised eye, and Madeline holding what was left of the bust. He nodded toward Madeline's mother. "Want me to finish him off?"

"By all means, Liam. Do what you do best."

Liam balled up his fists and hit the man squarely in the nose, to render him unconscious, before he scooped the man up in his arms and slumped him on his shoulders like a bag of potatoes.

Her mother glanced toward her daughter. "I see you haven't lost your grit. You were always the first one to leap into the fray."

"You were a good influence."

"I'll have this lowlife returned to his manor," Liam said. "There will be calls to shut us down."

"There always are," her mother said, almost under her breath, rubbing the back of her neck as Liam headed toward the back entry. "The women in the Temperance League will launch a new campaign. No matter that it is the men who need temperance, not us. But that is the way of the world."

Her mother was in her early forties, still trim and lovely, but for the first time Madeline noticed the dark circles under her mother's eyes. "Mother, are you well? Were you harmed?"

Her mother waved away Madeline's concern. "Madeline, what did you use to hit the judge with?"

Madeline held up a section of plaster that had once been a bust of Zeus, eyeing her mother more closely. Her mother's shoulders were rounded as though she carried a heavy burden, Madeline wanted to lift that burden, but she didn't know how to begin. Her mother was independent and prided herself on not needing anyone's help.

"I apologize," Madeline said absently, her concern for her mother growing. "It was the only thing I could grab to use as a weapon. Was it expensive?"

"It was a gift, but I never liked it. Zeus' expression seemed judgmental. I'll have Cook make us tea and add a little whiskey to the brew. I have a feeling you are not here because you missed me. Would your visit have anything to do with the Bradford professor with his wandering hands?"

"How did you know?"

"Call it a mother's intuition."

"And you have spies at Bradford."

Her mother grinned. "And I have spies at Bradford and other places. The incident with the judge and the congressman, with the ruckus they will cause, only solidifies what I have been pondering for a while. Men like them will seek retribution. Your professor discovered our connection, and more will follow. Men like the judge will get to me through you. We have received an offer we must pursue. No, do not argue," she said when Madeline offered a protest. "I have made my decision. We leave at high tide in a sennight and should arrive in London in time for the Christmas season."

Chapter Two

In the shadow of Conclarton Castle in England, snow spread a thin blanket over the graves in Robert Oswyn's family cemetery. Icicles hung like prisms from the trees, catching the pale light of the afternoon sun. The secluded location was quiet, serene, a place for reflection and prayer. But Robert, the eighth Duke of Conclarton, felt only anger and helplessness. His father and brother were buried here, and although both deaths were declared accidents, Robert had his doubts.

He tied the reins of his horse, Trinity, to a fir tree a short distance from the road and scratched the animal behind its ear. "I will not be long," he promised.

His family's mausoleum stood in the heart of the cemetery. It was made from white Italian marble, with Greek-style columns, and housed his ancestors. Robert shuddered. His father's and brother's bodies rested inside. The mausoleum overlooked a valley with a winding stream, with the intent that those buried here would appreciate the peaceful setting.

But the location was not to bring peace to the dead but to impress the living, he thought with more than a twinge of bitterness. No such consideration had been given to those who died on the battlefield.

Robert stood, as still as a sentry, as the winter wind chilled him to the bone. At the time of their deaths, he had been a captain in His Majesty's Army, fighting

Napoleon's troops. It had taken six months for the news to reach him. Then another three to recover from wounds he sustained while rescuing soldiers from his regiment. Finally, he was released to travel. In his mother's letter, she had insisted Robert meet with his father's solicitors in London before returning to the castle. And like a dutiful son, he had complied.

He was now the Duke of Conclarton and had petitioned the House of Lords to take his father's seat, only to be attacked in an alley near his hotel.

He rolled his shoulder, easing the pain of the injury he had sustained in the fight with the men in the alley. He'd given more than he got, but his assailants had escaped, and the police pronounced the attack a random attempted robbery. He did not believe in coincidences, which was why he was having trouble reconciling the deaths of his father and brother.

He shut his eyes against the glare of the marble columns on the mausoleum. His father had believed it a great honor to be a member of the House of Lords. Signing the petition had made it real that his father was truly and forever gone.

"Bloody hell."

The curse rolled off Robert's tongue with more frequency these days. An unexpected consequence, he supposed, from spending the last three years commanding a regiment in his Majesty's Army during the Peninsular War. They had defeated Napoleon Bonaparte, resulting in an armistice. Napoleon had abdicated as emperor and had been sent into exile on the island of Elba.

It was over.

Why then did Robert feel ill at ease? Had he left one

war behind only to become embroiled in another? The answer lay with the mysterious deaths of his father and elder brother and his mother's demand that he marry his elder brother's fiancée.

While in hospital recovering from battle wounds, he had received his mother's missive, announcing that his father and brother had died in a hunting accident. The missive looked tearstained and his mother's handwriting shaky. She had always been as solid as their castle walls. His father had nicknamed her their family's rock. Viewing the emotion expressed by his mother in the letter made it all too real. How could a person recover from such a loss?

His father had fallen from his horse and broken his neck, and his brother had been gored by a wild boar. Both plausible accidents, perhaps, though hardly likely for an excellent rider and an experienced huntsman. It was not very plausible that they had died on the same day.

None of what he had heard made sense.

He pushed his hair away from his forehead and headed back to the road. Once he passed through the gates of Conclarton Castle, he would assume the role of the Duke of Conclarton. He huffed out his frustration. He hardly looked the part. He needed a haircut and to shave his beard before he met with his family, let alone the stranger his mother wanted him to marry. In London, no one had commented on his unruly appearance other than to raise a disapproving eyebrow. He knew he looked more like a hardened soldier who did not give a farthing about his appearance rather than a member of the pampered *ton*. But, somewhere on a battlefield in France, Spain, or Portugal, he had lost the ability to care what others thought of him.

His mother, however, would not be so understanding.

Whatever the reason for his unsettled feelings, he had returned home and vowed he would approach his duties and obligations in the same manner as he had prepared to lead his regiment into battle. "Hope for the best outcome and plan for the worst" had been his father's advice the day Robert left for war. The advice had proven sound.

He would need that advice to manage an estate the size of Conclarton. He had never expected to become the duke. Nor had he wanted the title. That title belonged to his elder brother, Donald. Donald was the heir and Robert the spare. He had a slightly younger brother, William, and twin sisters, Sophia and Lydia, who would turn twelve in a few months. He wondered if they still wanted to marry a prince. Thank God they were too young to be presented into society just yet.

Robert heard the sound of carriage wheels and the muffled clip-clop of horses' hooves over the snow-packed road below the cemetery. He and his childhood friend, Lord Jeremy Dumont, who had met him in London to welcome him and accompany him home, had remarked about the steady caravan of carriages they had encountered. Jeremy had speculated that one of the nearby estates must be holding a ball to celebrate the Christmas Season.

He swore again, this time loud enough to chase birds from a snow-covered tree and elicit a questioning glare from his horse. As duke, he would be required to attend balls and what not. The *ton* expected a nobleman to keep a stiff upper lip and rise above inner turmoil.

Doubt and guilt warred within Robert in equal measure. The last words he and his father had spoken had been in anger, with his elder brother, Donald, as mediator.

His father had not approved Robert's decision to fight for God and country and claimed that Robert courted danger with as much enthusiasm as most men courted women they intended to marry. Why couldn't Robert, his father had argued, be more like Donald, who was steadfast and reliable? How could Robert explain that he needed to get out from under the shadows of his father and brother? Whenever he tried, his explanation sounded disrespectful. The easier path was to leave home for a while.

Before Robert's brother Donald had turned eighteen and the weight of being his father's heir bore down on him, they had been like peas in a pod. Neither could sit still and had driven their governesses and tutors mad with their constant need to explore the woods, climb trees, or race horses through their mother's gardens. As they grew older, they grew distant and rarely spoke beyond the required pleasantries.

Grief closed like a fist around Robert's heart. He regretted the words he had spoken to his father in anger and that he had not made more of an effort to understand the weight of responsibility his brother carried as heir. Most of all he regretted that he hadn't stayed. If he had, maybe they would both still be alive.

A winter breeze rustled through the brittle limbs of the trees, rattling them like bones and chilling the air as Robert neared his horse. Clouds darkened and moved to blanket the sky in shades of gray.

Trinity tossed his head and whinnied as though in

response to the team just passing.

He smoothed the gelding's mane. "Have no fear, old friend. It is just the wind. You have been patient and, yes, it is time for us to leave. We both could use a warm meal and a roof over our heads."

Robert gathered the reins of his horse and led him from the cemetery knoll to the road, awakening the aches and pains of traveling a long distance in a short span of time. It was time he joined Jeremy on the road or risked being caught out in the elements after dark.

Jeremy was the second son of the Earl of Chelsey and had inherited the stocky build and ginger hair common in his family. He had considered joining Robert in the fight against Napoleon, but he had fallen in love and married, so the notion was unthinkable. The idea was made even more remote since his elder brother was not in a hurry to find a bride and start a nursery, and someone had to provide an heir for the title and estates.

Sharp pain shot up Robert's leg, a souvenir from the Battle of Paris, as he limped to the road. The doctor had advised him to stay longer in hospital, but Robert knew he was needed at home.

A carriage drawn by a team of four horses was parked along the roadside as Jeremy helped a woman inside. The slender lady was dressed in a green brocade traveling coat, her profile hidden under a matching bonnet. The quality of her garment and carriage suggested wealth and privilege. Had the lady stopped to ask for directions?

Jeremy's expression looked confused as the carriage drove away. "The lady stopped her carriage to give me this bag of coins," he said as Robert approached. "While you were paying your respects to your father and brother,

I had dismounted and sat down to rest against the trunk of a tree. The lady ordered her carriage to stop and asked me if I was well. I assured her I was, but she gave me a curious smile, and handed me the blunt, nonetheless. I am aware that I'm in need of a shave," Jeremy said handing Robert the coins, "and my clothes are covered with the grime and filth of the road, but I did not believe I looked like a beggar."

Robert tested the weight of the purse in his hand, untied the cord around the bag, and peered inside. He drew back in surprise. "It is filled with gold crowns. A small fortune." Scratching his full beard, he followed the direction of the carriage as it rounded a bend in the road. "Did you tell her you are a lord and in no way in need of her charity?"

"I did, but as I mentioned, I do not think she believed me. In her defense, I was not my usual, glib self. I was asleep, dreaming of my wife, Molly, and the next thing I remember was a lady standing over me, asking if I was all right. Still groggy with sleep, I was unsteady as I stood, and my words garbled." Jeremy glanced toward Robert: his eyes wide. "The lady made me vow to use the blunt for food, a warm bed, and clean clothes. When I nodded, she bid me help her into the carriage and said good day."

Robert looked after the carriage again, struck by the unexpected generosity of the lady who had given Jeremy the bag of coins. He had seen too little of that type of goodwill in the past few years and had lost faith that it still existed outside a church.

"I must thank the lady for her kindness and return her blunt."

Without waiting for Jeremy's response. Robert

mounted his horse and chased down the carriage. Its speed was impressive, but not a challenge for Trinity. Robert knew this forest well. He and his brothers had spent their youth exploring every path, bend in the road, and hillside. He gave Trinity his head and the horse lengthened his stride, gaining ground. When Trinity galloped alongside the carriage, Robert leaned toward the open window for a better view.

In the dim interior light, two ladies sat on opposite sides of the well-appointed carriage. On the far side sat a lady dressed in deep purple, the shade often worn by widows. The lady one by the window sat against the tufted, velvet cushions dressed in green.

"Ladies," Robert shouted, as he kept pace with the carriage. "Thank you for your kindness."

The lady by the window rested her embroidered green glove on the sill and leaned toward him. She had removed her bonnet and freed her hair from the pins women often wore to hold their hair in place. It tumbled over her shoulders like flames over wood logs in an evening fire, framing a heart-shaped face in which her full lips radiated warmth and her eyes held him in their gaze.

Robert couldn't determine if her eyes were blue or green or some combination of the two. The notion that it was a mystery he wanted to solve caught him by surprise.

She said something under her breath to the lady in purple who then shouted for the coachman to slow down.

When the carriage slowed to a comfortable pace, she turned toward him again. "There is no need to thank me, sir, but you are most welcome." She then reached into her reticule, withdrawing a velvet bag with drawstrings. "My apologies. I thought there was only one gentleman on the road. I have more to give."

He was lost in her smile and the musical accent of her voice. It was an accent he couldn't quite place. He cleared his throat. "You misunderstand. I wish to return your coins. They are not needed. But I thank you for your generosity."

She held up her hand and shook her head when he extended the purse. "I will not accept its return. Your pride might rebel against charity, sir, but your belly will thank you for it."

He heard her grit and determination. Most women he had encountered would consider a man's wishes above their own. The lady in green did no such thing. She believed he and Jeremy needed help, and she would not be deterred. Extraordinary. And then he recognized her accent.

"You are from the Colonies."

Her laughter reminded him of wind chimes. "The United States of America," she corrected.

He smiled in response. "Of course. Please accept my apologies, milady. "What is your name?"

But at that moment the driver ordered his horses to speed up, and the team and carriage clattered over a bridge too narrow to accommodate both his horse and the vehicle. Robert pulled back on the reins to let it pass as the lady leaned out the window and waved.

When she smiled it felt as though the sun had ventured out from the clouds and showered the forest with light. She was the loveliest creature he had ever seen, and those eyes...

Jeremy had once said that when he first met his wife he lost all interest in anyone else. Internally, Robert had dismissed the romantic notion of love at first sight.

Jeremy had been in the market for a wife and Molly's attributes were flawless. Nevertheless, Robert had been happy for his friend. The Lady Molly Todd was known for her generous spirit and quiet nature, and Robert had speculated that the two would make an amiable pair. His speculation had proven correct.

He had told his friend that he wasn't looking for love. That statement was truer now than it had ever been. He did not have time to look for love. He was the Duke of Conclarton. He must marry a woman of impeccable breeding and character and set up a nursery.

The lady in green waved again as the carriage crossed the bridge and, reaching the other side, sped away on the road beneath a canopy of trees. Her unexpected gesture and smile stole his breath, and for a moment he believed he was incapable of drawing another.

"Love at first sight," he said aloud.

Jeremy drew his horse alongside Robert's, a grin plastered on his face. "The Lady in Green has made the skeptical Duke of Conclarton a believer in love. Extraordinary." When Robert shot him a murderous stare, Jeremy laughed softly and shook his head as they continued over the bridge. "What did the lady say to you?"

"She mentioned that she hadn't realized there was another man on the road and offered to give me blunt as well. The Lady is from the Colonies—er, the United States," he corrected.

Robert tucked the coin purse into an inside pocket, feeling its weight press against his heart. "You did not tell me she was beautiful," he said as they headed under the trees in the same direction the carriage had traveled.

"She wasn't beautiful," he amended. "She was more."

Jeremy eyed his friend. "Ah, so that is how it is. We have known each other since we were both in leading strings, and I have never seen you react this way to a woman before. Yes, she is a tempting armful, to be sure. But the ladies you have been acquainted with in the past were lovely, as well."

"The lady in the carriage is…different."

"Different," Jeremy said as though measuring the meaning of the word. "It has been my experience that when it comes to women, being different is more powerful than being beautiful."

"That is nonsense. Besides, I will never see the lady again."

As they rounded a bend in the road, Conclarton Castle came into view near the White Cliffs of Dover, an enduring symbol of power against all odds. It had endured centuries of battle and political intrigue. Closer inspection would expose its flaws, but from a distance it rose like a beacon of strength and beauty. Light bloomed from the windows, torches flickered from the turrets in the winter wind, and music rode the breeze, announcing a ball or some sort of soiree was in progress.

"It has been over nine months since your father and brother's deaths," Jeremy said breaking the silence. "I assume your mother will hold a ball during the Christmas Season to end the mourning period, and I wager that half the *ton* will be in attendance. They will want to meet the new Duke of Conclarton."

Robert ducked under a low-hanging branch and winced. He had not shared his misgivings with Jeremy regarding the title. But Robert suspected his old friend knew. They were as close as brothers. "I agree. My mother has always said this is her favorite time of year and Christmas her most cherished celebration."

"You mentioned your father's solicitor said your family wasn't the only one in the area concerned about their family's dwindling assets. Is it possible your mother will invite wealthy heirs and heiresses from the former Colonies—for example, the United States—with the purpose of helping your family as well as others find suitably rich wives and husbands for their sons and daughters? If the Lady in Green is headed toward your estate, which I believe she is, it is my opinion she will have more than one suitor vying for her attention."

Robert gritted his teeth. "Bloody hell."

Chapter Three

Robert and Jeremy had parted ways, Jeremy to his estate and Robert to his. But Robert wished Jeremy had stayed, at least long enough that he might have asked Jeremy why the condition of the road leading to Conclarton Castle was worse than Robert remembered. Or was he just not remembering correctly?

His commanding officers had said it was normal, when surrounded by cannon fire and bullets, to embellish memories or mask realities in gold and glitter. That way they helped a man get through the blood and death on a battlefield.

Perhaps the roads had always been thus, and he had ignored their condition as beneath his worry. He had been an arrogant, indulgent fool in those days before his commission. God willing, he hoped he had changed.

He was the second of three sons, and his parents were insistent even then that, as a man of means, he should forsake the single life and choose a suitable woman from the *ton*. He knew going to war merely delayed the inevitable, but he had thought he would have more time. His mother reminded him in her letter that his time had run out. He was to marry his brother's betrothed. It had been his brother's dying wish.

He reached into his saddlebags for the miniature his mother had sent to the solicitor to give to him. Lady Elizabeth Montgomery was described by his mother as a true Incomparable—slender, graceful, well spoken, and educated to the standards needed as the wife of a duke. Her blonde hair looked almost white against the black mourning dress she wore and framed an oval face. His mother had mentioned that his brother and Elizabeth had loved each other. How, then, could Lady Elizabeth consider marriage so soon? Had anyone bothered to ask her?

He returned the miniature to his saddlebags and led Trinity over the drawbridge and through the open gates. Carriages of every size and shape crammed the courtyard. Footmen, wearing powdered wigs and dressed in the Conclarton colors of red and gold, bustled about helping guests descend from their carriages. Robert did not recognize any that resembled the vehicle in which the Lady in Green had been riding. Evidently, she had not been bound for Conclarton Castle after all.

He dismissed the sudden twinge of disappointment as the result of a long journey.

"Who goes there?" A man, gray at the temples, wearing a formal butler's jacket embroidered with the Conclarton crest, approached with the stride and authority of an admiral. Like the footmen, he wore a black armband out of respect for Robert's father and brother.

"State your purpose, sir, or I will be forced to have you arrested."

Robert smiled at the man who had been more father and friend than butler to him. "Winfield, it is I, Robert."

"Is that really you, Your Grace? We had heard troubling news…" His lips stiffened and he bowed again. "A mistake, of course. I did not recognize you. The beard and long hair and your clothes… You look older, and broader in the shoulder. More man than boy. Your mother will be pleased you are home at last and order the cook to prepare all your favorite meals." Winfield cleared his throat. "I am most pleased to see you. My apologies again for not recognizing you at once. It was inexcusable."

"No need," he said, frowning. He had only half heard what Winfield had said. Winfield had referred to him as Your Grace, the title that had belonged to his father and should have been his brother's.

"Being called Your Grace will take some time to adjust, I fear. I left a young man and returned a weathered soldier with the scars to prove the journey. I fear I look worse than my father's hunting dogs after an afternoon romping in the woods and lakes, and no doubt have twice the lice. What I need is a hot bath. I would first like to see my mother, if she is available."

Winfield nodded with a slight bow. "Your mother is with guests. Quite a few, actually. She could not wait for the marriage season's round of balls this spring, and when the proper mourning period of no entertaining ended, she took it upon herself to get a jump on it. I believe those were her exact words. She has invited wealthy heirs and heiresses from the former colonies to stay with us until after the New Year. I will send word that you have arrived. She will want to see you straight away. Might I suggest the Gold Room?"

Robert heard the hesitation in Winfield's voice and the emphasis he placed on the words "wealthy heirs and heiresses." The solicitor was correct. Robert had not concerned himself with the running of the castle and its lands. That task had been his father's and brother's. He assumed in his absence his mother would have hired someone to take over until he returned.

He lifted his gaze toward the castle. The double doors were held open, allowing a constant parade of guests. Twin mourning wreaths hung over the open double doors, and Robert felt a tug in his heart. Their presence, and the black armbands, reaffirmed that all was not well. The flags were faded and torn, and not all of the torches were lit. When his father was alive, neither flaw would have been tolerated. It was as though a shroud had been draped over the castle.

He cleared his throat, forcing his attention to the present. "Winfield, would you have a groomsman see to my horse? Trinity has had a long journey and, like me, longs for good food, a dry bed, and the prospect of a quiet night's rest."

"Most assuredly, sir," he said handing the horse's reins to a footman who had appeared beside him as though out of thin air. "We will make sure Trinity is well cared for."

"Robert!" His mother stood by the double doors and cried out his name again. "We heard you were dead."

"Not yet, though many seem to try."

His mother wore a black crepe mourning dress. Except for a few more gray hairs laced in with her chestnut brown, her eyes were bright and her smile warm and welcoming. He was pleased that some things had remained the same.

She rushed to gather him in an embrace, then seemed shocked by her sudden display of affection and drew back. "Winfield, my son and I will be in the Gold Room. Please bring refreshments."

Robert followed her inside, a little shocked at her public display of affection. He knew his mother loved him. She loved all her children. But she had rarely shown any signs of affection in public. She, like his father, had kept her emotions under tight control.

There were exceptions, of course. There was the time he had fallen from a tree and broken his arm. She had not left his side until the physician had declared him safe enough to be moved downstairs for a turn in the garden. Then there were the times his sisters had come down with influenza, or his younger brother, William, with the case of a bellyache, which proved to be caused by overeating.

His older brother Donald on the other hand, seemed to have lived a charmed life, which had made the incident with the wild boar all that much harder to swallow. Other than that, his father had instructed that the care of his children should be left in the hands of tutors and governesses.

The entry room of the castle, with its tall ceilings and walls covered with portraits of pinch-faced ancestors, was a blaze of light. Boughs of cedar, pine, and holly wove around doorways and the banisters leading to the second-floor wings. Music and laughter drifted from the direction of the grand ballroom, and guests, dressed in their finest, milled about the room, casting wary glances his way.

He could almost read their minds. They wondered why a man dressed as he was, and looking and smelling more like a vagrant, footpad, or cutthroat than the lord of the manor, had been allowed entrance. He could, of course, have set them straight on all accounts. For now, he kept silent on the matter. He had lived in the spotlight all his life, his every gesture, word, and deed judged. It occurred to him that he relished anonymity.

Once inside the Gold Room, a room that overlooked her rose garden, his mother folded her hands in front of her. "You walk with a limp."

"It is nothing. You are looking well, Mother."

"Of course, I am." She waved away the compliment. "How can you say it is nothing? You limp."

"A bullet wound from battle. A souvenir from the war against Napoleon's armies."

"Do not joke. I will not have it. Will it heal?"

"In time, or so said the head leach at hospital."

She lifted her chin. "Well, you look terrible. And that beard… Most unbecoming."

He gave her a mischievous grin as he scratched his beard. "I do believe I am infested with fleas and nits. Mayhap I should sleep with my horse."

She cuffed him on the shoulder as the corners of her mouth edged up in a smile. "Do not tempt me. You will stay in the house like a proper gentleman. You should be ashamed, jesting with your dear old mama." Her lips trembled. "I have missed you. Your father and brother were so proud of you. They would have…"

"I am sorry… I should have been here."

She placed her hand on his shoulder and gave him a slight squeeze. "You were fighting for your country. Your father and I both agreed there was no better cause. Off with you. You need a bath and a meal. Tomorrow will be time enough to meet with your young brother and sisters and offer me no end to worry. I have planned a Christmas Eve Ball, and now it will be a celebration for your return as well. I have missed you."

Robert leaned over and kissed his mother on the cheek. "It is good to be home, and you already said you missed me."

"Well, it bears mentioning again. Before you leave, however, I would like a full accounting of your experience fighting Napoléon before he was captured. Is it true he is exiled and considers himself the Emperor of Elba?"

"All true. Mother, I am impressed. I was unaware you were interested in such things."

"Ah, our tea and refreshments have arrived. Son, there are many things about your mother you do not know."

Chapter Four

Madeline braced her hands on both sides of the inside of the coach as the team of white horses jostled around a bend in the road toward Castle Conclarton, splashing mud in through the open windows. The coach sped at a dangerous speed to make up time. They had visited the nearby village of Conclarton, as her mother insisted they needed new bonnets.

The village was charming and the people friendly, but Madeline noticed a few of the shops were boarded up and others were in need of repair. When they returned to the carriage with their new bonnets, the driver assured Madeline and her mother that they would reach their destination before dark. As far as Madeline was concerned, she would have preferred for them to turn around and book the first available boat back to America.

Maybe her mother was mistaken, and the judge would reconsider his boast of revenge by closing Feathers. If the judge did make good on his promise, how could her mother's scheme prevent it from occurring?

Madeline dabbed at her mud-splattered face with her handkerchief, worrying about the smudge, then sighed. She would need more than a flawless complexion to attract a man with a title. She would need a miracle. She had never felt so out of place in all her twenty-four years, and she had been born in a brothel and attended boarding schools where students boasted of their fine homes, servants, and impeccable lineage.

Her mother dozed across from her, as content as a well-fed cat. Madeline believed this wild scheme was doomed to fail. Or worse, get them tossed into the Tower of London for impersonating an heiress. Madeline had been seasick for most of the voyage from New York to England, kept her mother calm when they landed at London's rat-infested docks, and procured the carriage and directions to Conclarton Castle. The only thing that kept her going was knowing that this was important to her mother.

The coach and four sped around another bend in the road and Conclarton Castle loomed in the distance, highlighted by the setting sun. Torches flanked the stone towers on either side of the iron gate like watchful guards who knew the secrets of all who entered. Madeline shuddered. She hoped not. Secrets should stay buried and protected.

She pulled back from the open window and resumed working on her drawing. She had been sketching to occupy her time along the journey from America to London. It calmed her and gave her a respite from the never-ending lists of details her mother required her to memorize.

"That is a fair likeness of that poor soul you gifted with coins on the road a while back," her mother said, stretching as she awoke from her nap. Her mother's dress, like Madeline's, was the height of fashion with its high waistline and Greek-style silhouette. Her mother had exchanged her signature red color for the demurer shade of purple, while Madeline had chosen dark green.

"You view the image upside down. How can you possibly know that it is a fair likeness? Besides, it's only a rough sketch, thanks to the way this carriage bounces."

"But I know talent and my daughter's skill," her mother said with a confident air. "Have you forgotten that many of my patrons gifted me with masterpieces? One in particular from the female Belgian artist Michaelina Wautier, the *Triumph of Bacchus*, is one of my favorites."

Madeline smiled. "A nine-foot-high and twelve-foot-wide portrait of near-naked men surrounding the god of wine, which you hung in the main room of your establishment. How could I forget? The women in Boston called it scandalous."

"Ah, yes, and yet they visited my establishment often to view the painting and comment on its inappropriateness. As a child you tried to copy Wautier's skill, sketching little drawings of our cat, bowls of fruit, or vases of flowers. That is when I realized your interest in painting."

"I am grateful you encouraged me and hired tutors, but I fear I lack Wautier's gift." Madeline examined her drawing of the horse and rider who had chased down the carriage.

Growing up in America she had ridden since she could walk. As a result, she recognized a skilled horseman. The man chasing the carriage looked as though he were born on a horse. Horse and rider moved as one in her direction. Hooves dug into the mud, splashing water and clouds of dirt.

Heart racing to the beat of the thundering hooves, she silently urged them closer. Unlike the clean-shaven men on the ship and those she had encountered in London, the rider had a full beard and long hair that flew behind him untethered. "Wild and free as the wind" had been her first impression. "Dangerous" her second.

"I particularly like the man's eyes," her mother said. "Silver."

Jolted back to reality, she realized her mother was commenting on her sketch. Straightening on the carriage's bench seat, Madeline nodded. "His eyes are not silver. They are the shade of the ocean on a stormy day. I much prefer people to bowls of fruit. But I am not satisfied that I captured the expression in his eyes. They were unexpected. Wise, and yet sad, as though he carried the weight of the world on his shoulders."

"He wore a military uniform that was threadbare and stained, although his companion was in common clothing. The uniform was like that of a man who has seen battle. An honorable men who faced death so that others could live. Unlike those who avoid the messiness of war yet strut like peacocks in uniforms with polished boots and shiny buttons. I am pleased you helped those men."

Madeline traced the jawline of the man she had sketched. "I wonder what he looks like under the beard."

"Or naked," her mother said with a wiggle of her eyebrows. "Broad shoulders, with a commanding hold on his horse, and the way he sat the saddle reminded me of…"

"Mother!"

"Oh, do not give me that false look of indignation. You saw exactly what I saw and blushed scarlet when he rode after our carriage. For what it is worth, he has the look of a man a woman can trust."

The carriage jolted from side to side over a pothole as Madeline tucked her drawing between the pages of a book and placed it in her valise. "How can you make that assumption? You caught only a glimpse."

Her mother leaned against the back of the seat. "You forget. It is my business to understand men."

"I offered him more, but he declined."

"Oh, dear, no wonder you look smitten."

"You realize that you are the most inappropriate of mothers. The young women at my boarding school said that their mothers only discussed fashion and the importance of marrying well."

Her mother rolled her eyes. "It is no wonder those kinds of mothers visited Wautier's painting. But I share one characteristic in common with those mothers. I, too, wish my daughter to marry well."

"Are you sure our plan will work?"

Her mother squeezed her daughter's hand. "I am sure of it." Her mother had applied more makeup than usual to hide worry lines and the dark circles under her eyes. Madeline and her mother had slept little on the voyage across the Atlantic, and blamed it on the storms and waves, rather than on worrying if they would succeed.

Madeline offered a half-hearted smile and a nod regarding the words she had heard daily. She had argued against this plan as far too risky, but she had not prevailed.

"Do not worry," her mother said. "Lord William Conclarton is the younger son, and his mother wants him married and settled. His mother assures me that he is a good man. The father and the eldest son died recently, and the second son inherited the title and is engaged. So, you will set your cap for the youngest son. He will fall in love with you the moment he meets you."

"What if he doesn't?" Madeline's words hung in the

air like storm clouds. She let them settle before continuing. "I am not the only heiress vying for his attention, nor am I under the delusion that I am the prettiest."

"We have what the others do not. With what I learned from one of my clients in Boston, and the information from the loose-tongued gossips on the ship from New York to London, I know the type of woman men like Lord Conclarton desire."

"You are talking about a list of the *ton's* tedious requirements for a bride. I am never to raise my voice above a modulated whisper. I must possess proficiency in needlework, the pianoforte, and singing. I may draw but not well. I should never offer an opinion that clashes with his. My manners must be flawless and my clothes fashionable and alluring yet not provocative. The list is endless. I will never remember them all."

"You must. You have a kind heart, and some would say that you care too deeply for the plight and misfortunes of others, as evidenced by what you did for those men along the road. Lord William would be a fool not to fall in love with you."

"And what of me? Am I not to marry for love?"

"It is more important that you are safe and secure. You have witnessed the precariousness of my life and livelihood because I am not under the protection of a husband. We are welcomed here because people believe we are wealthy. But wealth is not enough for the *ton*. They expect, if not flawless respectability, at least its façade. We have assumed the identity of the widow of a rich railroad magnate and his daughter. Fathers want their sons to marry brides with large dowries because generations of idleness rendered them bankrupt and in debt. Their wives want to brag to their friends on the pedigrees of their son's wives."

"They have titles to sell."

"It is not just a title we want to buy, but what it represents." She reached over and drew Madeline's hands into hers. "I am a successful businesswoman. What I lack is respectability and security. I am not ashamed of what I had to do to keep food on our table and a roof over our heads. Nor do I give a farthing about what people think of me. But the world in which we live is cruel. They will judge you for my decisions. When you are a lady, your high position will protect you. If the *ton* learns our secret, they will keep their silence for fear of retribution."

Madeline glanced out the window. The carriage slowed as it traveled over the castle's drawbridge and under the arched stone gateway. This was an old argument between her and her mother that ran in a circle. Madeline was aware of the cruelty of those who considered themselves better than those less fortunate. Her experience at the posh boarding schools had not gone without conflict. There had always been rumors about her mother's source of income. As a result, students kept their distance. Instead of bemoaning the lack of friends, Madeline studied harder, and when she wrote to her mother, she kept the truth to herself.

"I expected the castle to be decorated for the Christmas season," Madeline said, changing the topic. "It is so drab and gray."

Her mother nodded. "I am surprised as well. It is grand indeed but worn down by war and neglect. Oh, my." She paused to straighten her hair. "Those footmen running over to open our doors are tall, handsome, and trim. I heard men in England looked like potbellied stoves. I worried I would have nothing to do while you found a titled husband. I was mistaken."

"Mother, we talked about this."

"It was not a discussion, as I recall, it was a lecture. I will be discreet. I learned that widows in England are allowed their entertainments."

"You were never married."

"Technicality."

The door opened, and as Madeline's mother had just described, two handsome young men, of about the same height and appearance, advanced toward the carriage. They wore matching powdered wigs, gold-braid-trimmed red coats over waistcoats, and knee-high breeches with white stockings.

The taller of the two, by only a fraction, opened the door as the other man set the steps in place and announced that someone would escort them to their rooms in the west wing.

"I feel as though we are headed to the guillotine," Madeline said under her breath.

Her mother chuckled. "A wise comparison. If men in England are all this handsome, we could both lose our hearts as well as our heads before this journey ends."

Chapter Five

Robert was bone weary as he left his mother and headed toward his rooms in the west wing of the castle. Winfield indicated that as the duke, Robert was now entitled to occupy his father's quarters. Robert firmly declined. That would take getting used to. For now, he was content with the rooms he had occupied before he had joined the military. They were in the same wing as his brothers and father.

His meeting with his mother had taken longer than anticipated. She had wanted a full accounting of the time he'd spent fighting Napoleon's army. He spared her many of the details, as they would have frightened and worried her needlessly. He stressed that he had survived and had returned to assume his duties as heir. She seemed content with his response.

But when Robert broached the subject of calling off his marriage to Lady Montgomery, his mother's demeanor changed. Under no circumstances would she entertain such a notion. Lady Montgomery claimed it had been Donald's dying wish that she and Robert marry. The discussion was closed, in his mother's opinion, and he had been dismissed.

Winfield intercepted him at the base of the staircase with a nod and a furrowed brow. "The rooms you requested have been prepared. How went your meeting with the Duchess, Your Grace?"

"Well enough. There is no need to show me the way. Could you have a tray of food brought to my rooms? The gingerbread biscuits my mother provided were delicious, but I would appreciate something more substantial from the kitchen, if that is possible. I am starving."

Winfield gave a slight bow. "Very good, Your Grace. I will also have hot water brought up for a bath."

Robert nodded his thanks and took the stairs two at a time, heading in the direction of the west wing. His rooms were located well past his father's. Wall sconces sputtered, giving off faint light along the dark hallway. He and his brothers knew the dark rooms and corridors by heart. This was where his father kept alive the history of their family, with portraits on the walls, and rooms that housed weapons and suits of armor.

He and his brothers had spent their youth in these corridors, dressed in armor, fighting imaginary dragons and enemy knights. Good memories. It was not his intent to occupy his father's rooms, but he longed to see them, nonetheless, to briefly evoke a few memories.

When he reached the double doors to his father's rooms, he hesitated. He could not bear to claim these rooms as his own just yet. But seeing them would help him feel closer to the man he wished had been here with his mother to welcome him home. Taking a deep breath, he opened the doors.

A fireplace glowed amber, giving the only light. His father's crossed swords were over the mantel, as always, and on a nearby wall hung the stuffed head of an elk. Robert remembered that, near the bed, his father had pistols placed within easy access. His father's fear of attack had bordered on obsession, after someone had once attempted to assassinate his brother. The duke's habit had been to have his pistols cleaned and then reloaded on a regular basis.

Whispered voices drew Robert's attention. On the far side of the room, the firelight briefly illuminated the silhouette of a man and woman locked in each other's arms. His first inclination was to leave them to their privacy. The second was irritation at their insensitivity and disrespect by choosing his father's rooms for their rendezvous, when the castle overflowed with other meeting places.

"Who goes there?" Robert heard the man say.

Robert froze in place, recognizing the voice. Lord Reginald Devonshire was as familiar to him as his brothers and sisters. Devonshire was his cousin, the only child of Robert's father's brother Henry. When Lord Henry committed suicide after his wife's death, Robert's father had taken his brother's seventeen-year-old son under his wing.

Devonshire emerged from the shadows holding a pistol in each hand. "Who goes there?" Devonshire's eyes widened, and then his mouth curled. "You made a grave error coming here." He aimed the pistol in his right hand toward Robert and cocked the hammer.

Chapter Six

Madeline and her mother had been shown to connecting rooms in the west wing and were assured that if they needed assistance they were to pull the bell cord. There was still the smell of fresh paint on the windowsills, and the mahogany furniture was polished to a high sheen. The walls were covered in paper hangings with images of rosebuds and hummingbirds, adding to the cheerful atmosphere.

They had been treated like Madeline envisioned those of royal blood were treated. There was a lot of bowing, and their clothes were unpacked and either hung in the wardrobe or taken to be washed. The whole experience was unsettling.

She and her mother were frauds and they did not deserve such luxurious surroundings. What would happen when the Duchess of Conclarton discovered their secret? Would they be sent to Newgate Prison? Or shipped to Australia as criminals?

"My stars," her mother said, pulling Madeline's hands down from her waist. "Stop fidgeting. What is wrong with you?"

Madeline pressed on the tight corset. "How do women breathe in this contraption? Please help me remove it."

Her mother, still slender at forty-and-three, used the bell cord on the wall to ring for assistance. "Remember that we are wealthy ladies from America who need help dressing. We must play our parts, even when we believe no one is watching. And ladies do not breathe deeply in England. Gentlemen value a slim waist over a woman who speaks her own mind."

"Censuring our opinions will be difficult for us both."

Her mother gave a short laugh. "Difficult but not impossible. Those were my mother's words, and she was the wisest woman I ever met."

"You speak of her often. I wish I had met her."

Her mother tucked the pistol she had brought from America into the top drawer of the desk. After the incident in Boston, her mother had insisted that they carry protection. "I did not appreciate my mother when I was a girl younger than you, or what she had to endure. I suppose that is the way of most relationships between mother and daughter. What I never doubted was that she loved me beyond measure. Over time, I came to realize she was a survivor, a trait she passed down to us."

"I hope you are right. But I worry about this plan of ours. How did you talk me into this scheme? It was doomed from the beginning. We will never pull this off. Besides, I do not want to marry. Marriage is little more than servitude. I want my independence. Like you, I want to own my own business and live life on my terms."

Her mother lit a cheroot. The flame at the tip matched the shades of red in her mother's hair that matched her own. "Fancy words," her mother said, "and spoken by women of means, or women with little sense of how the world turns. You want a business like mine, then? All glitter on the outside, and tarnish and ruin on the inside?"

"No," Madeline said and looked away toward the embers of coal burning in the fireplace box. "I have other ideas."

Her mother sat beside a table by an open window and took a drag on her cheroot. "Until those ideas become reality, we will continue with my plan."

A woman screamed, followed by the sound of a gunshot.

Madeline yanked open the drawer where her mother had placed the pistol, grabbed the gun and raced out, down the hallway in the direction from whence she had heard the sound.

Chapter Seven

"Bugger! You shot me!"

Robert pressed his hand to his shoulder, fighting to stay conscious. Blood seeped through his fingers as he staggered back. He felt numb in body and soul. He had been wounded in battle enough times to recognize the signs—his vision was blurring and his muscles weakening. He was losing too much blood and would soon lose consciousness.

A faint smile lifted the corners of his mouth. Ironic that he had survived the battlefield, infections, broken bones, gunshot wounds, poor rations, and nights sleeping on the ground in the pouring rain and the freezing cold, only to return home and be shot in his own home.

In his father's rooms.

Adding to the irony, if he were correct, he had been shot by one of his father's dueling pistols. He recognized the woman in Devonshire's arms from the miniature his mother had given his father's solicitor. She was the Lady Montgomery, Donald's fiancée, and the woman his mother insisted he marry.

He swayed again and sank into a chair that rocked back and forth precariously until settling into place. He could rush Devonshire, yank the pistol from his grasp, and shoot him. He doubted that he'd be charged. This was his home. He was the Duke of Conclarton and he had surprised his brother's fiancée in the arms of his cousin. It was a crime of passion, for bloody sake.

He weighed his chances of overpowering the bugger who was pointing his father's pistol with one hand and gesturing to the Lady Montgomery with the other. Impeccably dressed in black tails and breeches, silver waistcoat, and elaborately arranged cravat pinned in place by diamond pins, his attire seemed more suited for an audience with Queen Charlotte than a tryst. But then, Devonshire had always flaunted his wealth and handsome appearance to his advantage, a trait that had earned him the fickle attention of the *ton*.

Devonshire and Lady Montgomery were locked in an argument of some sort. Robert could not tell if she wanted Devonshire to finish him off or drop the weapon.

Robert had disarmed men before, in barroom brawls and on the battlefield. He wagered his chances of yanking the pistol from Devonshire as better than average odds. His cousin was more bark than bite and had never been reliable in a fight. Devonshire was a coward, more prone to run than stay and finish what he had started.

A surge of anger at the betrayal of Donald's memory had coursed through Robert's veins at sight of Lady Montgomery in the arms of his cousin, but that had now cooled, replaced by a dark hole of despair. Energy drained from his body, and his arms and legs were numb.

He had not known Lady Montgomery other than from the likeness in the miniature his mother had sent to the solicitor. His mother had claimed it was a love match between his elder brother and Lady Montgomery. Seeing the lady with Devonshire belied that theory. Or was a woman's love that fleeting? A fine debate on the merits of each tumbled around in his head like pebbles caught in a windstorm.

Did he want revenge, then? And what would that look like? More death. More lives destroyed.

Leaning forward in the chair, he supported his head in his hands. His mind was in a fog. He no longer knew what he wanted. Yes, he did. He wanted to lie down and close his eyes. He was so tired. Weary of battle. Tired of the knowledge that those you loved could die before their time.

He watched dispassionately as Lady Montgomery pulled the bell cord, and he heard Devonshire shout some obscenity. The sound seemed to come from a great distance away.

A ridiculous thought sprang from his memory. He remembered when the bell cords had been installed in the castle. They worked via a series of copper wires, springs, and pulleys to pass the vibration from pulling the cord to the bells in the servants' quarters. Ingenious. Extravagant. A device designed so that the privileged did not have to wait for their every whim to be fulfilled.

The pain in his shoulder throbbed, banishing the memory. Devonshire had shot him, and from his feral expression meant to finish the job. Did Robert care? He was not certain.

The door banged open. A woman, with hair that cascaded down her back in crimson waves, burst through the door, holding a pistol. She had removed her dark green traveling coat and wore a high-waisted, ice-blue frock that flowed over her curves like silk. His breath quickened. He recognized her instantly. She was the lady from the carriage—the Lady in Green and more lovely than he had remembered.

The room stopped spinning as he drank in her

beauty.

She glanced toward him as though in slow motion, her eyes widening in recognition. Then she looked toward Devonshire and Lady Montgomery as though assessing the situation.

She seemed to have made a decision, and instead of lowering her weapon she kept it focused on Devonshire. "Drop your weapon." Her voice was steady and her grip on the pistol confident.

"Who are you to order me about?" Devonshire said, with an arrogant lift of his chin.

"I am a person who never misses," she said, her voice as cold as steel. "That is who I am."

Robert saw the determination in his cousin's expression falter. But war had taught Robert a valuable lesson. When an enemy was cornered, they were unpredictable. Devonshire would shoot the lady who Robert now regarded as his rescuer, then turn his weapon on Robert to finish the job. Devonshire was a viscount. His power and position would protect him, and with both the lady and Robert dead, no one would dispute the story, as there was no certainty of being able to rely on Lady Montgomery.

A sudden surge of protectiveness for his rescuer gave him renewed strength. Robert pushed to a standing position and moved between the Lady in Green and his cousin. He did not doubt her capable of pulling the trigger, but even the most seasoned soldier might hesitate, and Robert did not want to take a chance that she would be caught in the crossfire.

"Stay where you are," Devonshire shouted toward Robert as he gripped the pistol with both hands to steady it, then addressed the lady who held the weapon. "This thief entered my room with the intention of robbing me." His voice quivered as he widened his stance. "I was defending myself and the Lady Montgomery."

"Are you a thief?" She said to Robert suddenly with the lilt of a smile in her voice.

He applauded the lady's calm demeanor. He would wager this was not the first time she had held a pistol or encountered danger. Not only was she kind to strangers, she was fearless and brave. Intrigued by the combination of the lady's virtues, he shook his head to indicate that he was most certainly not a thief.

"I would know your name, brave lady," Robert said, weaving as though he were as drunk as a wheelbarrow.

She chuckled, shaking her head. "You are a strange one. You were shot, you are bleeding out on the carpet and moments away from being rendered unconscious. And oh, yes, your assailant is holding a pistol pointed at your head." She paused to widen her smile. "Remarkable. You are either the most fearless man I have ever met or the most foolish. Do you really want to know my name?"

"It is of the utmost importance to me."

She laughed outright. "My name is Madeline. Miss Mercer. And yours?"

The oddity of them asking for each other's names, for all the reasons she mentioned, caused him to smile at their circumstances. He tossed her name into his thoughts. He had never paid a mind to names one way or another, but at this moment he decided that he very much liked the sound of hers.

But before he could respond, Winfield entered, without knocking, in a great show of concern. He was holding a candle and accompanied by a footman who carried a pail of water in each hand. "Lord Devonshire," Winfield said, his normally placid expression creased with worry lines. "Begging your pardon, milord, but I was unaware you had arrived. Derby and I were bringing His Grace water for a bath when we received word that someone in the Old Duke's rooms had pulled the bell cord. Then we heard gunfire."

The footman set the pails of water on the floor as his gaze found Robert's and Miss Mercer's. His bushy eyebrows seemed to disappear into his hairline as he leaned over and whispered to Winfield.

Winfield held his candlestick higher to better view the room. He swore and sucked in a breath. "Your Grace. I did not see you in the shadows. You have been shot."

"It would seem so," Robert said, as Winfield and the footman rushed to his side.

"Your Grace." Devonshire's expression crumbled into panic as he looked between Robert and Lady Montgomery. The gun rolled from Devonshire's hand to the carpet as he bowed. "Forgive me, Your Grace. We were told… That is to say… I did not know it was you. The Lady Montgomery and I…" He straightened. "It is not how it looks.

Robert bit back a spasm of pain. "It looked as though you and Lady Montgomery were on the verge of rutting like rabbits."

Chapter Eight

The woman who had been referred to as Lady Montgomery screamed and crumpled to the floor, while Devonshire raged that he hadn't recognized the Duke of Conclarton.

Madeline knelt beside the duke to check his wound, shaking her head in disbelief. Was she the only one to notice that the duke had lost consciousness? She was surrounded by chaos, which was the only way to describe it. Lady Montgomery's scream seemed to have led to a flurry of activity.

Winfield tried to calm Devonshire while instructing the footman to remove the unconscious Lady Montgomery to her quarters. A trio of women servants carrying food trays, ostensibly on their way to the duke's rooms, ducked in to investigate, then shrieked, dropping their trays. Pottery shattered, metal utensils clattered, and tureens of steaming soup and a pot of tea drenched the carpet.

Ignoring the noise and confusion, Madeline tore a strip off the hem of her dress and pressed the fabric over the duke's wound. "I have to stop the bleeding," she said to him in as calm a voice as she could manage. In her peripheral vision, Devonshire left as the women who had brought the trays of food fussed like hens at mealtime to clean up the mess. She wanted to scream at all of them. No one paid any mind to the fact that the duke had been shot. "What is wrong with these people!"

The duke chuckled as he opened his eyes. "I have been asking that myself for as long as I can remember."

Madeline sighed in relief. He was still conscious. That had to be a good sign. But she couldn't stop the bleeding. She ripped off more fabric from her hem. "I apologize. I did not mean to say that out loud. You must think me…"

He covered her hand with his. "I think you are my personal angel."

She blinked to clear her vision, surprised at how his words had touched her. She'd been called many things. Too outspoken for a woman. Rebellious. Opinionated. Never an angel.

"This bullet must be removed if I am to have a chance to stop the bleeding," she said, trying to keep the rising panic from her voice. She glanced in the direction of the bed. When she first entered the room, the bed hadn't seemed that far away. Now it looked the distance of a city block. The duke was broad shouldered, and at least a head and a half taller than she was. Although slender, the way he had controlled his horse when he chased down her carriage suggested he was solidly built. Lifting him without help would be impossible.

"Do you think you can walk, Your Grace?"

Winfield joined Madeline at the duke's side. "It is under control, Your Grace. Devonshire assures me it was an accident, and someone is tending to Lady Montgomery. She looked very upset. Oh, and the servants are cleaning the mess they made and will bring more food. How are you feeling?"

Madeline turned on the passive-faced butler, clenching her hands on the blood-soaked fabric she'd used trying to stop the bleeding. "Are you deranged, blind, or mad? Or all three? The duke is not doing well. Not well at all. He is bleeding to death, and I'm quite sure he doesn't give a flying fig about food stains on the carpet. Help me lift him to bed. He weighs more than a pack of wet dogs. I need to remove the bullet."

"Pack of wet dogs?" the duke said under his breath. "Curious comparison."

Winfield cast an inscrutable look the duke's way, then gave a quick nod and positioned himself on one side of the duke while Madeline chose the other.

"Please lean on me, and try not to bleed," she said with a curve of her lips.

"Your attempt at humor suggests I look as bad as I feel. And I feel fagged to death."

"Save your strength," Madeline said, using an authoritative tone she'd learned from her mother. She hoped it gave the impression that she meant for him to survive and would not argue the point. "You are not feeling well," she continued. "I heard you were in the military. Have you seen combat?"

"His Grace has seen more than his fair share of battles and has been decorated with medals for saving lives and advanced to the position of captain."

"You both are attempting to distract me from the reality of my condition and my likely chance of survival," the duke said. "You need not bother. I know the odds. Although I have a shoulder wound, and the bullet seems to have missed my heart and lungs, I know that I am not out of danger. I could die from infection."

"If you weren't injured already, Your Grace," Madeline said. "I would shoot you myself for being so annoyingly calm."

His eyebrows drew together. "Interesting. I would have thought you would appreciate a patient who was in control of his emotions."

"Emotions are a light into the soul."

He nodded. "Beautiful sentiment, but I am not sure how it applies in my situation."

"Winfield, can you bring more linens to dress His Grace's wounds?" Surprisingly, Winfield left without questioning her. He must be more rattled than he looked to leave her alone with the duke. She counted her blessings.

When Winfield had left, Madeline leaned close to the duke. "Yes, it is true that a hysterical patient is not helpful. But you are behaving too calmly, and I have seen this type of reaction before in men and women who have given up on their will to live." Unexplained tears gathered in her eyes again, and as before, she blinked them away. "Tell me that you want to live." She clutched the bedcovers. "Promise me."

His gaze locked with hers and held for the span of a few breaths. "I promise."

****

There were only a few instances in Robert's life, and he could count them on one hand, where he had been surprised. He prided himself on anticipating situations and acting accordingly. An invaluable trait on the battlefield.

His father's and brother's deaths, although a shock, had not been a surprise. Men of their wealth and status were a target. The only questions were *why* and *who*? Even his mother's demands that Robert marry Donald's fiancée had been predictable when he learned the circumstances.

No, he'd only been surprised, truly surprised, five times. The first was a surprise tenth birthday party. The second was when his mother told his father to give up his mistress or she would leave him. The third was when his father complied, and then begged forgiveness. The fourth was when the solicitor said Conclarton was in a financial crisis.

Winfield returned with the linens and Robert observed the lovely Miss Mercer whispering to him in an agitated tone. He heard only snippets but enough to surmise that Winfield wanted to wait until the leech arrived, while Robert's lovely rescuer rightly argued that time was of the essence. The bullet should be removed post haste, she had said, with a lift of her chin and a nod of her head.

The fifth surprise was when Miss Mercer had demanded his promise to her that he would live.

Miss Mercer turned from her conversation with Winfield, and her pleased expression told him she had won the argument.

"The bullet must be removed," she announced as she placed a cool hand on his shoulder. "I am very sorry. I fear it will hurt like blazes." She turned those hazel eyes toward Winfield. "Perhaps some whiskey for the duke? It might dull the pain."

"Pain and I are well acquainted. But what are you doing? It is not proper for you to see me unclothed."

"I just told you. I must remove your shirt. The bullet must be removed, and the wound sewn shut if we have any hope of stopping the bleeding."

"A maid should not see a man without clothes."

A smile teased her full lips. "I promise I won't look."

Winfield clicked his tongue on the roof of his mouth. "His Grace is correct. This is most improper, but I do not see a way around it. Please turn your back while I remove His Grace's shirt."

Miss Mercer did as Winfield instructed, affording Robert a view of her long mane of hair. He mused that he liked how it cascaded past her waist like bolts of silk. He never understood the fashion for women to pile their hair on top of their heads and adorn it with all manner of trinkets and whatnots. He preferred a woman's hair loose and accessible for a man's touch.

He dragged his gaze from Miss Madeline and the gentle curve of her waist down to her hips. "Good Lord. You are a vision."

"Robert, did you say something?" Winfield said.

He groaned in pain and swore under his breath as Winfield tried to remove his arm from his sleeve. He must be in worse shape than he had thought, to voice his opinion out in the open. Well, what was done, was done. "Please ask if the lady is married," Robert said.

"You may talk to me directly, Your Grace," she said with a sparkle in her beautiful eyes. "I am unmarried."

"I'm pleased to hear it," he said closing his eyes for a moment as a spasm of pain shook him.

Miss Mercer approached the bed. "The blood from your gunshot wound is drying on your sleeve and has adhered your shirt to your skin. If Winfield pulls too hard, it will make your wound worse. Let me help. Winfield, I'll need clean water, and the buckets you brought for the duke's bath were spilled in all the commotion."

"Propriety," Winfield managed. "It would not be proper if I left you alone with His Grace. Again. I do not know what came over me the first time. I was quite taken back by His Grace's condition, I suppose."

She folded her arms on her chest and stepped back. "Well, then, yank away. But be aware that His Grace has already lost a lot of blood. If he bleeds to death, it will be on your hands."

"I will be right back," Winfield said. "Your Grace, do I have your word as a gentleman that you will not...I mean..."

"Winfield, you have my word that I will not ravish the lady."

"I am not worried," Miss Mercer said. "He is too weak to do any ravishing. Besides, I am not his type."

Winfield gave a slight bow and hurried from the room, leaving the doors opened wide.

Robert's eyebrows knitted together as he frowned. "Although I am a gentleman and would not take advantage of a lady, I feel you have questioned my manhood when you said I lacked the strength to ravish you."

Miss Mercer rolled her eyes. "Men."

"What is that comment supposed to mean?" He pretended to pull a frown. He knew very well what she had meant in both the roll of her eyes and her tight smile, but he discovered he enjoyed sparring with her. She had a nimble mind and a quick wit, which he very much enjoyed. Not to mention that she was exceedingly brave. "And another thing. Why don't you think you are my type?"

"I overheard that Lady Montgomery is your fiancée. She is as slender as blades of grass and probably eats nothing more substantial than a few crumbs of bread, whereas I love to eat. She has that white-blonde hair, and the light complexion of women who spend their days either inside or under an umbrella. Again, nothing like me."

He met her gaze. "She was my brother's choice, his fiancée. I prefer your appearance to hers."

Chapter Nine

The fire had been built higher to warm the chilled room, and candles lit to chase away the gloom. But they did little to ease Madeline's concern. When Winfield returned, he had brought along her mother, who had learned of the incident and offered her help. Madeline and her mother had removed the bullet and bandaged the duke's wound.

Madeline accepted another blanket from Winfield to cover the man sleeping on the bed. She did not argue. She knew it was Winfield's way of trying to be useful. She had learned he was the butler, with the family since before the duke was born, and his concern was clear despite his delay in recognizing the seriousness of the duke's wound.

Her mother was folding unused linens and reacting as though everything was normal. Madeline wasn't deceived. Reacting with a calm demeaner was her mother's way of dealing with adversity. The calmer her mother appeared, the more worried she was.

To top things off, Madeline had learned that the man to whom she had tossed coins on the road was a duke. A duke, of all things! From her mother's descriptions, she had visualized that all Englishmen with titles behaved as though the world owed them everything.

She watched the sleeping man as his chest rose and fell. He did not seem like that to her.

"Mother," Madeline whispered. "Do you think the duke will be all right?"

"I am uncertain. He has lost a lot of blood."

Madeline had wished for a simple yes, but her mother was honest and did not believe in sugar-coating life. It had not been the first time she had helped her mother remove a bullet. Running a brothel had its share of brawls and gunfights. Physicians were not always available—or sober enough for the steady hands it took to remove a bullet.

Madeline was not sorry they had taken a respite from that life. If not for the judge's threats, they might still be in Boston. Her mother had said that as soon as Madeline was engaged, she would return to America. Madeline hoped for another outcome. Her mother's wealth was secure, and she often bragged that her resources revived some of the oldest families in England. She had made wise investments in property and gold mines out west. Madeline planned to write to Liam to ask advice on how to persuade her mother to sell Feathers.

Liam was not just her mother's most trusted bodyguard at Feathers but someone who had been with her mother for the past ten or eleven years. If he was amenable to Madeline's suggestion, perhaps he would know the best course of action. It was a risk, of course. Madeline did not know Liam's financial situation. He might not want her mother to sell.

You look pale," her mother said. Sensing Madeline's anxiety, she set the linens aside and glanced over her shoulder at the sleeping man on the bed. "Please try not to concern yourself. We have done what we can. He is a strong man and that is in his favor."

Madeline perched on the edge of the bed and took

his hand in hers. It was no longer cold to the touch. She marked that as a welcome sign. "There are so many scars on his chest and arms," Madeline said with a catch in her voice.

"War is brutal. That he survived means he is strong of mind and body." Her mother rested her hand on Madeline's shoulder. "But he also experienced a blow when he witnessed his brother's fiancée with another man, a woman who had promised his mother to be his own bride. From all accounts they did not know each other, and therefore it wasn't his heart injured. But the betrayal to both him and his brother was nonetheless severe. Emotional wounds do not heal as quickly."

"I do not understand. Why would his mother compel him to marry his deceased brother's fiancée?"

"The old families of England are not like us. They hold on to their traditions with an iron fist. It would be easier to move a mountain than for them to change. Change is a word they abhor. They believe that to change would mean the end to their comfortable, orderly way of life. But England is not alone in this belief."

A loud commotion in the hallway shattered the quiet, and Winfield crossed the room to open the door. A half dozen women marched into the room. Except for the woman dressed in black at its head, they looked like a living rainbow in shades of red, green, blue, yellow, and purple.

"Mother," Madeline said under her breath in a strangled whisper. "The woman in red. That is the woman the duke caught kissing another man. I cannot believe she has the nerve to show her face."

"She is certainly dressed the part of a strumpet."

"Mother, need I remind you that red is *your* favorite

color."

Her mother chuckled. "My point exactly."

"Give way," barked the woman in black, leading the entourage. "Where is my son?" She addressed Winfield. "I demand to see the duke at once. Does he live?" Her voice broke on the last word. Not waiting for an answer, she marched over to the bed, then reached for the bedpost for support. She clasped her hand over her mouth to muffle a cry. "Winfield…"

"He lives," Winfield said as he rushed to the duchess's side to give help if she needed it.

Madeline and her mother moved aside as the duchess released a sigh and placed her hand on the arm Winfield offered. "I thought for a moment…" She took another breath and allowed Winfield to guide her to where her son lay prone on the bed.

Winfield bowed to the duchess. "His Grace is doing as well as can be expected. He was shot, but the bullet has been removed and the wound cleaned and stitched, thanks to the tender care and attention of Mrs. Roseline Mercer and her daughter, Miss Madeline Mercer."

The duchess gave a slight nod to Madeline's mother, Roseline. "Mrs. Mercer, I was not informed you had arrived." There was a slight tremor in her voice as her eyes misted. "I am so grateful you are here and that you helped my boy. I am in your debt." She then reached for Madeline's hands and gave them a slight squeeze before releasing them. "I was informed of your bravery. A rare quality, to put a stranger's welfare above your own. Thank you as well. Winfield, make sure everything these ladies desire is theirs."

"It is not necessary," Madeline and Roseline said at once, receiving a robust laugh from the duchess.

"Well done, the both of you, to deny my offer. But it is necessary, I assure you, and would please me greatly. You must allow me this indulgence. We will begin with new dresses and go on from there." The duchess turned toward her entourage, who whispered behind her like buzzing bees. "All except for Lady Montgomery, wait for me outside."

The disappointment in the women's expressions was palatable. They looked reluctant to leave, but they did as the duchess commanded and flounced from the room with a flurry of disappointed muttering and fluttering from their fans. Madeline drew her mother aside while the duchess and Lady Montgomery approached the sleeping duke.

Madeline stiffened. Every muscle in her body felt ready to spring. "It doesn't seem as though the duchess is aware that her son caught Lady Montgomery kissing another man."

"Do not be fooled by the duchess's cool detached demeanor. Ladies of her stature are taught from birth the necessity of hiding their true feelings. I'll wager she knew of Lady Montgomery's involvement before she stepped into this room. Perhaps not about the kiss, but it will be only a matter of time before she learns of that as well. For now, she has her own reasons for keeping her silence."

"You sound as though you know the duchess."

"When is the physician expected?" the duchess asked.

Winfield slid a glance toward Madeline. "I believe the Viscount Devonshire was sent to fetch him."

The duchess huffed out her impatience. "What is taking so long? Did the viscount travel to London to *fetch* a physician, when we have capable doctors in the village?" She sucked in a breath. "Never mind. Thank the good Lord we were fortunate enough to have Mrs. Mercer and her capable daughter here. When this physician of Devonshire's arrives, I would speak with him without delay."

Winfield bowed. "As you wish, Your Grace."

The duchess cast the briefest of glances toward Roseline, then bid Lady Montgomery leave. When she had slipped from the room, the duchess ordered that another blanket be added to her son's bed. "The Lady Montgomery," the duchess said at last, "informs me that what happened to my son was an accident. She knew my son only from a family portrait and thus relied on Devonshire's opinion. Robert was much changed since he left for the war. It is plausible that the viscount did not recognize him and thus believed Robert a burglar."

The duchess turned to speak with Winfield, saying something nonsensical about whether or not the duke would feel better if he were bathed. Nonsense, in Madeline's opinion, since the man was sleeping peacefully, and if they bathed him, they would have to wake him when he should be allowed to rest.

Madeline had heard the expression "my blood boiled," but until now she had never understood its meaning. She was seething mad. How could the duchess believe Lady Montgomery's tall tale? Okay, so the duke looked like a beggar on the street. Madeline had made that assumption as well. But from what she had surmised when she arrived on the scene, the duke had not made an aggressive move. Which meant that he had entered, seen his brother's fiancée in the arms of another man, and Devonshire had shot him. Even if Devonshire had not recognized the duke, it did not seem plausible that the duke wouldn't have announced who he was.

Her mother put a restraining hand on Madeline's arm and whispered, "What has come over you? You look like you are ready to explode and attack someone. Do not worry. The duchess knows."

"How can you…"

Her mother just shook her head and put her finger to her mouth, indicating that they should remain quiet.

Madeline trusted her mother's instincts. She had less trust in other people. Well, done. She returned to one of her other worries. Why did Lady Montgomery have such an elaborate show of concern for the Duke? Was she sincere? Or was it an act, like Madeline suspected? Lady Montgomery must know that once the duke regained consciousness, more would be revealed and likely he would break off their engagement.

The duchess sniffled, glancing at her son again. "We should leave and let the duke rest."

"I will stay," Madeline announced in a louder voice than she had intended.

"What a kind offer, Miss Mercer. There is no need. Winfield will arrange for someone to stay with the duke. You and your mother have done quite enough already. Besides, it would not be proper for a single young lady to stay alone with my son unchaperoned."

"The duke is unconscious and poses no danger."

The duchess's mouth twitched in a smile. "A very good point."

"If the duke awakens, I could easily outrun him in his present condition."

The duchess nodded, as though considering Madeline's justification for remaining with the duke.

"And there is a bell cord in this room. I could summon help if the duke awakens."

The duchess shook her head, laughing, as she addressed Roseline. "Your daughter offers a salient defense that is difficult to refute. Can I assume you rarely win an argument with her?"

"Not since she was seven."

Chapter Eleven

In the end, the duchess agreed that Madeline could watch over the duke, but only after he had been bathed and provided with a change of clothes. Madeline paced before the fire in the room she shared with her mother. She estimated that an hour had passed, and with each passing minute her anxiety grew. Had his wound reopened? Had he contracted a fever? And what was to be done with Devonshire? She conceded that perhaps the duchess was correct and Lady Montgomery really hadn't recognized the duke.

She felt like a kettle boiling over on the hearth. A horrible thought struck her. "Do you think the duke will forgive Lady Montgomery for kissing Devonshire?"

Her mother lit a cheroot. "It is possible. There is more at stake than honor with these families. I overheard that the Conclartons are in financial difficulty and that is the reason for inviting wealthy heiresses to the estate during the Christmas season. The duchess needs her sons to marry into wealth. Her eldest son died before he could marry Lady Montgomery, whose family owns a number of estates and a townhouse in London. There was talk that his dying wish was for Lady Montgomery to marry Robert if he did not survive the hunting incident, or William, if Robert died in battle. But even if he hadn't asked for her pledge, I believe the duchess would have insisted on the match."

"How did you learn so much? We only arrived this evening. And why didn't you come after me when you heard the gunshot?"

"I did, but when I saw you and the duke had things well in hand, I kept in the shadows and met a few of the servants in the aftermath. They love to gossip, especially when they recognize a kindred spirit. Now we must get you changed. The hem of your dress is in tatters and the rest wrinkled. You must always look your best. It is not uncommon for a lady to change her gown three or four times during the day."

Her mother used the bell cord on the wall to ring for assistance.

"I worry about this plan of ours," Madeline said. "How did you talk me into this scheme? It was doomed from the beginning. We will never pull this off. Besides, I do not want to marry."

"Of course you want to marry. What a silly comment. That is the reason we have come to this dreary country."

"Marriage is little more than servitude. I want my independence. I want to own my own business."

Roseline's cheroot went out and she relit it. There was a sprinkling of gray in her hair that instead of tarnishing the red tresses gave them silver highlights that caught the candlelight. "Fancy words, said by women of means, or women with little sense on how the world turns. You want a business like mine, then?" The question was asked in an even tone. "All glitter on the outside, and tarnish and broken promises on the inside?"

"No," Madeline said and looked away toward the embers of coal burning in the fireplace box. "I have other ideas. I want to open an art gallery."

Her mother settled herself beside a table at the open window and took a drag on her cheroot, nodding slowly. "A grand idea. I approve, but for the lofty goal, connections are more valuable than a rich purse. A titled husband will help in this regard. More reason to continue our plan. And, must I remind you, we didn't have a choice. The judge launched a spirited campaign against me. The charges, although false, will take time and money to dispute. We also have that professor to contend with, who threatened to reveal you as the daughter of the owner of a brothel. He and the judge will be dealt with, but it will take time." She took another puff from her cheroot, leaned back in the chair, and glanced toward the window.

"I wish you would not smoke."

"Leave me to my small vices. The doctor said it would improve my health."

"There is nothing wrong with your health. I do, however, doubt your judgment if you think I can draw the attention of a nobleman who will ask me to marry him. A small waist I can manage. Keeping my opinions to myself will take more concentration."

Her mother flicked ash from the cheroot into an empty teacup. "I understand all too well. You are your mother's daughter. But please do your best."

"Even so, why would one of the titled men here choose a nobody like me over ladies with breeding who can trace their ancestors back into the golden age of the Tudors and beyond?"

Her mother took a long pull on her cheroot, then exhaled, enveloping where she sat in a cloud of cobweb-thin smoke. "Trust me. The size of a lady's purse will catch more attention in these times than her pedigree."

"Mother, before we left Boston, you were the owner of one of the most successful brothels in the city. Regardless of your wealth, I doubt these high-born nobles would approve of how you earned your money."

"It is *our* money, dearest, not just mine alone. You might not have been one of my working girls, but you had skill with numbers and kept my ledgers in order. And your skill with a pistol kept the men in line and respectful before we hired Liam. These noble families, with their lazy, do-nothing sons and daughters who believe working is beneath them, have run out of money to support their estates and expensive habits. They look to the wealthy heirs and heiresses of England's former colonies for husbands and wives for their children, and we will oblige them. We are here to secure you a marriage and a title."

Madeline cringed. "Must you put it that way?"

"I want you to have a better life than I had."

There was a soft knock on the door, followed by a woman servant's request for permission to enter.

Roseline stabbed out her cheroot. "Perfect timing. The woman will be here to help you change your dress."

Madeline closed her eyes in frustration. "Why is it that I must keep reminding everyone of this simple reality—The. Duke. Is. Asleep. He won't know I'm there. And if he does wake up, he was shot and will be so groggy he won't notice what I'm wearing or how I look."

Her mother gave a soft, husky laugh. "He is a man, and I've seen how he looks at you. Believe me, daughter, the duke will notice."

Chapter Ten

A short time later, Winfield knocked on Madeline's bedroom door. When she opened it, he had remarked on the beauty of her long-sleeved sunflower-yellow dress as being just the thing to brighten the duke's spirits. She convinced her mother to join her to help change the duke's bandages, since Her mother had more experience tending wounds than Madeline did.

As they arrived in the duke's rooms, Winfield assured them the duke was wearing breeches and a shirt. For some reason, those details were important. Her mother, however, insisted it was impossible to tend to the duke's bullet wound if he were wearing a shirt. Winfield had gone pale but agreed.

With the Duke's bullet wound cleaned, and new bandages applied, Madeline pulled a wooden chair beside the bed. Cleaning the wound had revealed the bleeding was stopped and there was no evidence of infecting, relieving some of Madeline's concerns. Winfield, a man of his word, had employed Mrs. Kenworthy as chaperone, in the eventuality that Madeline's mother might leave Madeline alone with the duke.

A round and cheerful middle-aged woman, her salt-and-pepper hair tucked snugly inside her cap, Mrs. Kenworthy had brought her needlework and the promise to help where needed. At the moment, after draining her tea, she had fallen asleep on a leather-bound chair and was snoring as loud as thunder clouds.

Madeline double-checked that the pistol was secure in the bedside table's drawer. Satisfied, she sat in the chair near the bed. She wasn't expecting trouble, but the whole matter of Devonshire shooting the duke had left her unsettled. There was something in Devonshire's eyes that reminded her of a caged animal.

"I do not intend to leave the duke and am not tired. I believe I will stay here for a while longer. I discovered a book on the shelf and plan to read to him."

Roseline folded the unused linens and set them aside at the foot of the bed. "You have grown quite attached to this the duke in a short time. You've always been one to bring home strays, but be warned, this is different. You must not become attached. This is a man, and many fall in and out of love with no more regret than the women here have for a discarded dress or bonnet. This is no ordinary man. His position and power make him dangerous to a woman's gentle heart."

Madeline let her mother's words hang in the air. She knew the bite of the words came from a hole in her mother's heart that might never heal. Her mother never had admitted it, but Madeline sensed that she had loved Madeline's father deeply and did not want her daughter to suffer the same fate.

"I am not attached to the duke," Madeline said, opening the book. "I am well aware that romantic attachments with men are dangerous and I have proven myself immune to their charms."

Roseline kissed Madeline on the forehead. "Whatever you say, dear. Whatever you say. I will ask Winfield to send you tea and biscuits, as Mrs. Kenworthy has devoured every crumb. In the morning, a little bone broth for the duke, in the eventuality he awakens, will suit nicely. It will give him strength. If he is restless or contracts a fever, pull the cord on the wall and have a servant summon me."

"I think Winfield is sweet on you. I noticed how his eyes sparkled when you were around."

"He is amiable enough, but we are here to ensure a match for you. I am well past the time for such frivolities of the heart. Please stop the matchmaking. You know it annoys me."

"That is not true. You loved it when I successfully matched some of the girls with good men. It's when I try to match you that you object. But isn't that what you are trying to do to me?"

Roseline tucked a strand of hair behind Madeline's ear. "Matchmaking implies a love match. I do not want a love match for you and certainly not for myself. I believe I have made that clear. Love fades. I want you to have security with a man who will treat you well. That is different. We must concentrate on our plan."

Madeline looked over at the duke. Although he slept, he did not look at peace. His forehead was furrowed as though his dreams were troubled. "When he recovers, he might reject Lady Montgomery due to her actions, which could mean that he would be looking for a wife."

"We have spoken of this before." Roseline put her hand on Madeline's shoulder. "You must not fall in love with him. For one, he is a duke. I do not want you to aspire so high. As I mentioned, the duke's relationship with Lady Montgomery is a contract between powerful families. It is not a love match."

"What you are discussing sounds more like a business decision than love."

"Precisely." Her mother set the folded linens beside the pitcher of water and basin near the bed. "Even in a marriage involving love, each person must weigh the advantages and disadvantages."

"You make marriage sound cold and distant."

"That is marriage in Regency England. Guard your heart. There is no future with the duke. It is likely that your kind heart took pity on a soldier returning from war and romanticized your feelings toward him. Then the two of you were thrust together once again, this time to face danger. But what do you really know about the duke?"

Madeline gazed at the sleeping man. His full beard and unruly hair disguised his appearance. She knew he had been in the military. She knew he was the second son, that both his elder brother and his father had died in a hunting accident, and that his name was Robert Oswyn, the Duke of Conclarton. His younger brother's name was William. The duke also had twin sisters, named Sophia and Lydia, who were still very young. All surface information. Her mother was correct. Madeline knew very little about the duke.

But beyond the surface, she knew he was brave. Injured, he had stood between her and Devonshire as though he would risk another bullet to protect her. Was his act of bravery the reason she felt this pull of attraction and the need to protect him in return?

The duke mumbled something in his sleep, shrugging off the covers. His arms free, he thrashed about as though he were fending off an attack. Madeline reached over and pulled his arms down and tucked the covers over his shoulders again. "He looks like a man who is haunted by his dreams."

Roseline nodded. "Men endure unspeakable horrors at war and return changed. Sometimes they cannot shake the experiences they survived or the demons that haunt their dreams. In addition, he is the Duke of Conclarton only because his father and brother are dead." She put her hand on her lower back and stretched. "I feel my age and need a good night's sleep. I promise that I will return before the sun rises so that you may have a few moments of rest before the dress fittings in the morning."

"You make it sound exhausting."

"It is," Roseline said with a smile. "It is also a lot of fun."

Madeline smoothed the blanket in place over the duke's shoulders. "What about Mrs. Kenworthy snoring on the chair?"

"Let her sleep. Servants on these estates rarely have a chance to rest. She will thank you for the small kindness." Roseline kissed her daughter on the forehead and bid her goodnight.

Madeline opened the book she had chosen, *A Midsummer Night's Dream* by William Shakespeare, and began to read aloud. Madeline was acquainted with Shakespeare's plays. Her favorites were *The Merchant of Venice* and *The Taming of the Shrew*. She was not fond of *Romeo and Juliet*. In her opinion, a love story did not end with the lovers dying. But she had never had the pleasure of reading *A Midsummer Night's Dream*.

With a smile on her face, she settled against the chair and turned the page to Act I, at the Palace of Theseus.

" 'Now, fair Hippolyta, our nuptial hour draws on apace.' "

Chapter Eleven

Madeline woke with a start. She had fallen asleep in the chair, and the book had dropped to the floor. Mrs. Kenworthy was still asleep and snoring. The disturbance that had awakened Madeline, however, was not snoring but the sounds of a muffled struggle.

On the far side of the bed, a tall man loomed over the duke and pressed a pillow over his face. The duke had regained consciousness and was fighting back. But it was clear that he would lose the battle. He was weak from the gunshot wound and loss of blood.

"Stop!" she shouted.

But the man ignored her as though she were no more important than an annoying insect. The duke had stopped fighting, and Madeline feared the worst.

Looking around for where she had left her pistol, she remembered she had secured it in the bedside table drawer.

She yanked open the drawer.

Empty.

"Looking for your weapon, miss?" The tall man waved the pistol as he moved toward her.

Heart pounding, Madeline slid a glance toward the bell cord. Even if she could reach it, would someone arrive in time? But she had to at least try. She backed toward the wall, lunged, and pulled.

The tall man yanked her free of the bell cord and

pushed her to the ground. She scrambled away from him in the direction of the window. Gray threads of dawn spread over the horizon. Would anyone be awake at this hour? If she screamed for help would anyone hear?

He towered over her, his eyes darting toward the window as though guessing her plan, then narrowing in anger. "No one is coming to save you."

"Why are you doing this?"

"Money. 'Tis always about…"

He stopped mid-sentence. A confused expression clouded his face. Eyes wide, the pistol slid from his grasp as he held his belly with both hands. A dark stain blossomed over his jacket. Blood seeped through his fingers as his eyes rose to hers in panic and pain.

His mouth opened and he babbled incoherently as he staggered away from her in the direction of the bedroom's double doors. He only made it a few steps before collapsing to the floor face down. His body went still.

The duke stood nearby, holding a sword dripping with blood. "Why is everyone trying to kill me?"

He swayed on his feet as the sword slid to the carpet.

She pushed to her feet and lunged toward him in an attempt to prevent him from falling, but her rush toward him as he pitched forward took them both to the floor.

Pinned under the duke, Madeline struggled to move out from under him. He was unconscious, with his head nestled against hers. She pushed against him, to no avail. He did not budge.

She had thought the man who attacked her was tall, but Lord Robert had towered over him. That was the least of it. She felt as though a wardrobe had fallen on her, not a flesh-and-blood man.

In the far corner of the room slept Mrs. Kenworthy, unaware that they had been in mortal danger. How had the woman slept through everything? She sucked in a breath, ready to scream for help, and then paused.

A scandalous thought pierced through her thoughts. How would Mrs. Kenworthy react? The duke lay on top of her. True, the man wore breeches, but his chest, except for the bandages around his shoulder, was bare.

From the moment Madeline had stepped on English soil, her mother had schooled her on the rules that governed a woman's actions and behavior. The number one rule was that a single woman must not ever be alone with a man, much less pinned under him.

She would be ruined and sent packing. And all because she was trying to protect the duke from attack.

What was she supposed to have done? Let the tall man kill the duke? If she hadn't awoken when she had, the tall man would have smothered the duke in his sleep and most likely killed both her and the snoring Mrs. Kenworthy to assure there weren't any witnesses. So, because she had prevented the duke's death, her reputation would be in tatters.

Frustrated and angry, she pushed against him again. "Get off me."

He mumbled, heaved a sigh, and started to snore.

She heard a sound over the snoring.

"Did you hear something?" Madeline paused. "Footsteps! Blazes... Someone is coming!" Trying to move him had not worked. She did the only other thing she could think of doing.

Madeline grabbed hold of his hair and yanked as hard as she could.

"Ow!" He lifted his head, then paused, focusing on

her lips, and gave her a wicked grin. "I like you under me."

"Men," she ground out. "I just saved your life and that's all you can say?"

He winked. "I think it was I who saved you, fair maiden."

"People are coming. You must get off me." Mindful of his chest wound, she seized her opportunity and shoved him the rest of the way off. She scrambled to her feet. Taking a deep breath to compose herself, she smoothed her dress, tucked strands of hair behind her ear, and—side-stepping around the tall man's body—ran to open the door.

It opened just as she reached for the handle. Winfield entered. It took only seconds for him to ascertain that Madeline and the duke had been attacked…again.

Chapter Twelve

Robert awoke to the rumble of conversation as each voice blended into the next. He had a vague impression it was daytime, although the thick curtains were drawn and candles and a rolling fire were the only source of light in the room.

He remembered another voice. The voice of a woman reading to him while he slipped in and out of consciousness. Her voice had been distinct in its crisp American accent and its way of laughing when she found a phrase humorous.

He recognized the story, one of his mother's favorites—Shakespeare's *A Midsummer Night's Dream*. He had asked his mother why that story and not *Romeo and Juliet* or *Taming of the Shrew*, and his mother's response had been curious. She had said she enjoyed the story because in it the people removed their masks of proper decorum and doing what others thought correct behavior and gave in to their inner desires and dreams.

The story gave him respite from the reality that he had been shot in the shoulder. It felt as though someone had stuck a red-hot poker into his flesh. Then someone had tried to smother him with a pillow.

A woman had intervened to save his life, not once but twice. He remembered her name was Miss Madeline Mercer, the same woman he had dubbed the Lady in Green and who had read to him.

When he first met her, on the day he had chased down her carriage, he had thought her lovely. Her eyes were expressive and changed color from forest green to sapphire blue. But it was her kindness and courage that brought out her unique beauty, the type of beauty that lasted a lifetime.

Had she been harmed in the attack? No. He had used his father's sword and run the bugger through. Why were people trying to kill him?

He had been shot and attacked before, but what was different this time was the quiet. He tried to pull himself higher on the bed and a sharp pain chased through his shoulder, a reminder that he was still healing.

Robert had tried to concentrate on the threads of conversation he had overheard since he had been shot, but it was to no avail. He kept losing focus. At one point he overheard his mother's voice as well as Lady Montgomery's, overlaid with others in the room, as he drifted in and out of consciousness.

He remembered a conversation between Miss Mercer and her mother. Miss Mercer was here to marry a man with a title, and her mother encouraged her to set her cap for his brother, William. The announcement had unsettled him, and he did not understand the cause.

The door to his room opened and a fresh wave of people entered, sending the buzz of conversation higher until it rang in his ears.

Miss Mercer approached his bed, a vision in meadow green with snow-white lace gracing the high neckline and the cuffs on her sleeves. "Your color has returned."

"I feel better." And he did. Seeing her was like a breath of spring.

"You are awake," she said with a gentle smile that warmed his heart and soul.

"Apparently."

"How do you feel?"

"Like someone shot me."

She laughed, the sound like chimes teased by a summer breeze. "You have a sense of humor. That is a good sign. Are you hungry?"

"Your name is Miss Mercer. Madeline."

"You remembered," she said, smiling. "And you are the Duke of Conclarton."

"Robert. You saved my life."

"I cannot call you Robert, Your Grace. You are the Duke of Conclarton."

He wanted to object. She was right, of course, but he longed to hear his name on her lips.

He liked her smile. It was natural, as though she liked to smile and did it on a regular basis. The women he was acquainted with had smiles that looked as though they had been painted on with a brush.

"I always remember the people who save my life."

Her blush brought a rosy glow to her cheeks. "You saved mine. So, we are even."

He waited for a beat, drinking in her beauty. "Not even close."

She tucked a curl behind her ear as though flustered, which pleased him for some reason.

"Thank you," she said at last. "But in the incident with the pistol, I'm sure Viscount Devonshire wouldn't have fired again."

There was a quality in her voice he recognized, particularly when she said the viscount's name. She did not like him. Well, that made two of them. Robert had overheard enough of the conversation between his mother and Lady Montgomery to surmise that the consensus had been reached that Devonshire had not recognized the duke. That conclusion was blatantly false.

Robert remembered identifying himself to Devonshire. Robert also remembered the look on the man's face. It was not a warning shot. His cousin had aimed to kill. It was fortunate for Robert that Devonshire was a poor shot. But why did he want Robert dead?

"It is a good sign you're hungry," Miss Mercer said, interrupting his thoughts. "I will let Winfield know. He has been very concerned. I do not think he has slept well since you were injured." She drew the covers over his shoulders, a gesture that seemed familiar.

"How long have I been asleep?"

"The time is measured in days, not hours."

He raised an eyebrow.

"When Scully tried to smother you in your sleep, you fought back, and your effort to fight him off opened up your bullet wound." Her voice faltered as though reliving the trauma.

"It is over," he said. "What has become of this Scully?"

"He is dead. You had a fever." Her lips thinned and she turned away for a moment before continuing. "My mother and I rebandaged you. Are you aware that you talk in your sleep?"

He wanted to reach over and take her hand to comfort her. Propriety held him back. The servants in the room would spread the word that the Duke of Conclarton held the hands of a single lady who was not his fiancée, and a scandal would brew in a matter of minutes. He would not subject his lovely rescuer to such talk. A gentleman did not take the hand of a lady unless they were wed, or at the least an offer of marriage had been made.

"I am sorry. Did I say anything in my sleep that was not for a lady's delicate sensibilities?"

Miss Mercer blushed. Then she laughed. "My mother said it was the sort of talk men said when he thought a lady was not listening."

He grimaced. "That does not bode well. My sincere apologies. But you have me at a disadvantage, for I am unclear as to what I am apologizing for. You have me curious."

Her blush deepened, but so did the dimples on her cheeks when her smile broadened. "And curious you will remain. It is my opinion that a man should apologize often and well."

Robert's laughter exploded. "Well said and true."

"What is true?" Jeremy asked, bursting into the room, out of breath, his hat in his hand.

"Lord Dumont is here to see you, Your Grace," Winfield announced, chasing after Jeremy. "My apologies. He was most insistent I show him in at once."

Miss Mercer gave an awkward bow in Robert's direction. "I should leave." She turned to go and then paused. "I am glad you are feeling better."

Jeremy bowed to Miss Mercer as she left then rushed over toward Robert. "Damn, Robert," Jeremy said, going around Winfield. "I just received news this morning that you were shot. I leave you alone for a few days and bloody hell rains down. I heard you were winged and that someone tried to finish the job. Are you really on the mend?"

Robert pulled himself to a sitting position on the bed

and winced. "Better than I deserve."

"You look like the devil, but was that our Lady in Green I saw leaving?"

"The same."

Jeremy laughed as he drew a chair beside the bed and sat down. "Well, well, I know you fancied her, but getting yourself shot is a bit extreme even for you."

"Pardon for the interruption, Your Grace and Lord Dumont. I will see to that meal Miss Mercer requested for you, and a plate for Lord Dumont as well. The cook made a lovely venison stew, fresh baked bread, and an apple pie."

"Yes, thank you, Winfield."

Robert scratched his beard as Winfield left, settling in to talk to his friend. "Yes, the Lady in Green is Miss Madeline Mercer. She saved my life. Never seen the like."

"I overheard that Lady Montgomery was with your mother for hours, crying and begging forgiveness. Might work, too. It is rumored that the Montgomeries have more blunt than the queen, and Lady Montgomery wears jewels to prove the theory. Your mother is in a state. After her conversation with Lady Montgomery, she locked herself in her rooms. Everyone fears she will cancel the Christmas Ball."

"Cancelling the ball is not an option. She invited heiresses from America and the continent in the hopes of my brother finding a rich bride."

"In the meantime, I'll offer to host a ball at my estate. That will give the *ton* a chance to find another scandal to gossip about. Since I returned, all Molly talks about is hosting a grand squeeze. She will be thrilled, and it will give your mother time to recover."

"You are a true friend, and a fortunate man to have a wife like Molly. I do not know what to think when it comes to Lady Montgomery. She seemed innocent, and perhaps the tryst with Devonshire was an unfortunate accident, as the lady claims."

Jeremy swept his hair from his forehead. "I have heard enough regarding Lady Montgomery to last a fortnight. Miss Mercer is what interests me. She sounds as though she is intelligent and brave. I like her."

"And kind. But we both know emotions have no place in choosing a bride. At least for my brother and me."

"You found Lady Montgomery in the arms of Devonshire. It is possible their relationship has been going on for some time and that it was consummated. Could you live with not knowing whether or not the child she carried was yours or if it belonged to someone she had a brush with once?"

"Bollocks. You come straight to the point of it."

"Tell me you haven't thought the exact same thing?"

"That is all I can think about."

Chapter Thirteen

A week had passed since she had seen the duke, and Madeline longed to check on his progress. From her mother's sources, she had learned that the duke's wound had reopened after his confrontation with Scully. The duchess assured Madeline that all was well, as she had procured a doctor from the nearby village. She had turned away the physician Devonshire had procured, saying she wanted someone she trusted to care for her son.

After Lord Dumont's visit, the doctor had declared that the duke was no longer to have visitors. The doctor had said it would over tax His Grace. Madeline had been denied access with the excuse that it would cause him too much excitement. There had also been a comment about it being improper. She had begun to hate that word.

Poppycock!

The distraction would do the duke some good, she reasoned, but this time her comments were ignored. She couldn't imagine how an active man was tolerating inactivity. He must be going mad. What she was most worried about, however, was the attempt made on his life. Unlike the incident where the duke's cousin had shot him, the man named Scully's attempt had been deliberate. Scully had been dismissed for stealing, and the authorities declared the two cases unrelated. They advised the Conclarton family to treat it as such.

Apparently, they had, and they went on as though the world had turned right side up again.

Madeline had not grown up as a member of the crème de la crème of English society, and therefore she did not understand their penchant to accept an explanation if it meant they could continue their lives unencumbered by worry. She could not reconcile the author's account of why Scully had attacked the duke. If the man had been dismissed, how had he been able to gain access to the upstairs rooms of the castle? Had there been a lack of security, as the authorities suggested, or had Scully had help?

Madeline sat at a small table beside the window and sipped her cold tea and broke off a corner of a stale biscuit. She grimaced, setting the biscuit aside, and tried to rid her mind of these questions and concerns.

She had wanted black coffee, eggs, and slabs of bacon, ham, and a steak; rare. The look on the cook's face when she requested the meal, combined with the duchess's lecture that it was not proper for a lady to partake of such a robust meal, caused Madeline to rescind her order. As a result, she was hungry, which added to her irritation. If she was correct and Scully had not acted alone, that meant the duke was still in danger.

A winter sun peeked out from behind the clouds and filtered through the windows, capturing Madeline's attention. Its light transformed the pale pink and yellow, creating new shades and shadows. She usually didn't draw indoor scenes, but there was something about the play of light on the room that intrigued her.

She retrieved her drawing pencils and sketchbook from the chair and arranged them on the table and began to sketch. Her mother had suggested she learn needlework, as all the fashionable young ladies of the *ton* were proficient in the artform. Madeline gave her mother a polite "no" in response.

The duke's twin sisters, in matching blue dresses and blonde ringlets, chased each other into the sitting room. Their faces and mannerisms were so identical it was difficult to tell them apart. Following close behind was a woman around Madeline's age, wearing a high-waisted butter-yellow dress with puffed short sleeves.

"Sophia. Lydia. Please slow down. Your mother does not approve of you running through the house in such an unladylike manner. The two of you are making cakes of yourselves. In a few short years you will be of eligible age for your first season. Gentlemen of the *ton* want a suitable bride, not a chit."

"La, Miss O'Brian," Sophia, the taller of the twins said. "Lydia and I have not decided if we will marry if it means we would be separated from each other."

Miss O'Brian let out what sounded like a longsuffering sigh. "Yes, you have made that comment frequently, but I assure you, when you are older you will change your mind. It is every woman's dream to have her own family."

Lydia jutted out her chin. "We will not. We have made a blood oath." She thrust out her hand, proudly displaying a small cut in the center of her hand. When she did so, Sophia held out her hand as well, showing a similar scar.

"Oh, my!" Miss O'Brian said. "What will your mother say, and where did you get such a notion? Blood oaths? I have never heard of such a thing."

"We read about blood oaths in one of father's history books of the Anglo-Saxons," Sophia said.

Sophia's comment silenced the governess, as Madeline suspected it was meant to do. How could a mere governess criticize the girls for reading a book in the old duke's library? Madeline admired the twin's ingenuity, smothering a smile.

The governess cleared her throat. "We will discuss the matter at another time. For now, let us resume our geography lessons." She nodded for the twins to follow her to a table near the fireplace.

"May I join you?" A blond gentleman wearing a dark blue waistcoat with gilt buttons and light-colored breeches, bowed his greeting. The man was Lord William Oswyn, the duke's younger brother. She had met him at dinner last night and they had gotten on amiably. He wanted to know all about the wilds of America and if she had ever seen a buffalo or witnessed a gunfight. She had said yes to both questions and then had to describe both events in great detail.

She nodded her consent and motioned toward the chair opposite hers. "Have you heard how your brother fares?"

"He is well. His fever has not recurred. But the doctor feared it might and wants him confined to his room for another day. On a related topic, the authorities assured me that Scully was acting on his own. A grudge against the family, or some such."

Madeline doubted that seriously.

She went through the motions of adding sugar to her tea to keep busy, lest she say something out of order. The family clearly wanted the matter settled and forgotten.

Sophia and Lydia spied their brother, yelped with joy, and rushed toward him.

Sophia jumped on his lap and looked over at

Madeline. "You are the lady who saved our brother Robby."

"Sophia," Mr. Oswyn said. "Remember your manners. I must introduce you to Miss Mercer first. Then you may speak."

Madeline laughed and gave Sophia a wink. "I am not fond of manners or rules. My mother says that when I was your age, I loved to climb trees and play games of all sorts." She smiled at the twins. "Your brother also saved me. He is a very brave man."

"I like her," Lydia said. "She called Robby brave."

"I like her too," Sophia said, nodding until her curls danced around her face.

Lydia drew nearer to Mr. Oswyn, resting her head on his shoulder and looked over at Madeline's drawing. "That is a picture of our dog, Toby."

"Let me see," Sophia said. "You drew Toby wearing a red bow." She frowned. "He never wears a red bow."

Madeline laughed. "He wears one in my imagination." She tore two pieces of paper from her sketchbook and handed one to each of the girls. "Would you like to draw a picture for your brother? I wager that will cheer him up."

Both girls nodded and scooted onto chairs as Madeline set them up with paper and drawing pencils.

Lydia heaved an exaggerated sigh and added a pout. "Mother said that Robby is sleeping, and we are forbidden to visit."

Mr. Oswyn frowned. "I am not allowed either," he said in hushed tones.

Madeline lowered her voice to a conspiratorial whisper. "Well," she said exaggerating the word. "When we show your mother these wonderful pictures that we have drawn for your brother, I think she will have to approve our visit."

The girls giggled and set to work.

Lydia paused and glanced toward the window. "Will you help us build a snowman?"

Madeline smiled at the rapid change of topic. She loved that about children. They were so spontaneous.

Mr. Oswyn chuckled, kissing each of his sisters in turn on the check. "My darling sisters, it is not snowing."

"But you must promise that you will help us when it *does* snow," Sophia said.

He laughed and glanced in the direction of the governess. "I promise. When snow does fall, we will ask your governess, Miss O'Brian, to help us build the grandest snowman in the area. Now back to work on your drawings for Robby."

"I am in your debt, Miss Mercer," Mr. Oswyn said. "My brother is very dear to me. I say, would you like a tour of the castle and its grounds?"

She shook her head. "I think I will stay here. My mother mentioned a fitting for the Christmas Ball. And it seems there might be more than one."

"I fear so. My mother is insistent her sons find wives before the New Year. I had a respite after my elder brother's engagement to Lady Montgomery, but now she has resumed her campaign. She is more insistent than ever that I find a bride." He cast a glance toward Miss O'Brian, and then dragged his gaze back toward Madeline, but not before Madeline noticed the longing in his gaze when he looked at the governess. "The prospect of a lifetime in a loveless marriage is a bitter pill to swallow."

The sky darkened as a light snowfall drifted against

the windowpanes. "Interesting. I never looked at that from a man's point of view. Women, me included, long for love, and to be loved in return. But it is more a young woman's dream, and thus we count our blessings if a marriage brings us security and a kind husband."

"A sad commentary that we are content to settle." He glanced over his shoulder as though worried that they might be overheard.

"It is snowing," Sophia squealed, jumping to the window. "Now can we build a snowman?"

Chapter Fourteen

Madeline enjoyed the snowfall. It reminded her of the winters in Boston. The weather continued to cooperate, dumping snow in the morning, then pausing long enough to allow a break where the sun could peek out from the clouds. It was at this moment that William declared it was the perfect time to build snowmen.

In the grand hallway of Conclarton Castle, Madeline stuffed into her pockets the treats she had secured from the kitchen. The treats weren't for her but for the girls, of course. She then buttoned her long coat and tied her bonnet in place while she and Mr. Oswyn waited for Miss O'Brian to help Sophia and Lydia with their coats and gloves. Sophia and Lydia declared that there was enough snow to build a family of snowmen, women, and children, and the adults could not refuse.

Madeline's mother would not have approved of her inviting the governess on the tour of the castle with Mr. Oswyn. Madeline's goal was to secure Mr. Oswyn's affection, not encourage complications. She could hear her mother say that she had squandered the perfect opportunity to spend time with Mr. Oswyn alone.

Her retort to her mother's disapproval was easily explained. A single, unwed lady, when accompanied by a gentleman, must be chaperoned. Miss O'Brian accomplished that requirement.

Of course, that was not the only reason.

It was apparent that Mr. Oswyn and Miss O'Brian were smitten with each other, which changed how Madeline felt about her prospects with Mr. Oswyn. She now considered him off limits. She had witnessed the breakup of relationships when a third party thrust themselves into the mix. It was cruel and selfish. She would never be that person. Mr. Oswyn and Miss O'Brian were not engaged or married, but if Madeline's instincts were correct, their hearts were committed to each other, and that was the same thing for Madeline.

The impact of what she had done struck home. Mr. Oswyn's mother would never approve of a match between her son and a commoner. Aside from the reality that Miss O'Brian was a governess, and thus beneath their station, she was penniless. The duchess would never approve their marriage. Madeline had made things worse.

"What have I done?"

"Miss Mercer," Mr. Oswyn said. "You look unwell. Are you all, right?"

"I am well," she lied. "A little tired."

"We could postpone…"

Madeline shook her head. "The fresh air will do me good. Look, Miss O'Brian has arrived with the children."

Mr. Oswyn brightened when Miss O'Brian emerged from the hallway that led to the servant's quarters. "My, Miss O'Brian, I very much like your bonnet."

Miss O'Brian ducked her head to hide a smile, but not fast enough to hide a blush as Sophia and Lydia dashed past the adults and outside.

"Shall we go then?" Mr. Oswyn said, holding out his left arm to Madeline and his right to Miss O'Brian. "What a lucky man I am. I am escorting not one but two lovely ladies. We shall oversee the building of the snow family, then tour the grounds. Out there is the best place to view the castle. Tread carefully, however. The rains created deep holes and the snow may have camouflaged the danger."

Mr. Oswyn had not exaggerated regarding the condition of the gardens. But it was not the mud but the neglect that stood out. Weeds choked out the cultivated plants. Rose bushes and berry vines spread over hedges and across pathways. Madeline estimated years had passed since they had been tended.

"Over here," Mr. Oswyn announced with spread arms. "The perfect location for our snow village."

His location universally applauded as perfect, Madeline led the way, with the children and the governess in her wake. Madeline helped Sophia gather snow and form a ball on the ground as Miss O'Brian and Mr. Oswyn helped Lydia do the same. The base for two snow people completed, they bent to the task of creating more.

"When my grandmother was alive," Mr. Oswyn said, placing the middle section on one of the snow bases, "these rose bushes were her pride and joy. Robby and I would come out here before lessons and help her tend the garden." Mr. Oswyn pointed in the direction of the coast, where a section of towers lay in ruins, then began work on another snowman section as he explained, "Conclarton Castle began as a square keep, a military outpost protecting England from attack from Spain and France. Each generation made improvements, such as towers added, and spacious living quarters, with larger, more decorative fireplaces that had chimneys to draw the smoke out. Robert drew plans on how to repair and expand one of the wings, but Father said it was a waste of time and money. In the end, it was not attack from neighboring countries that caused the most destruction to our castle, and others across England, it was our own civil war, between the Cavaliers and the Roundheads."

"You know your family's history," Madeline said, packing snow to form another base. "Now I am the one who is impressed."

"Mr. Oswyn excels in many subjects," Miss O'Brian said as she kept an eye on the children. "Sophia, drop that snowball. You will not throw it at your sister. We are building snow people, not planning a snowball fight."

Sophia stuck out her tongue but complied, bending to work on a small snow person she and her sister were building.

Miss O'Brian regained her composure and continued as she rolled a snow base next to the one Mr. Oswyn was building. "Mr. Oswyn often visits the nursery and tells stories of this castle or the history of England."

"It is a passion of mine," Mr. Oswyn said, stepping back to examine the snowman he had created. "This snowman needs more to make him stand out," Mr. Oswyn said, rubbing his chin as though in deep thought.

"You mentioned the Duke drawing plans on how he envisioned expanding and repairing the castle," Madeline said, lifting a snowball-shaped head on top of one of the bases Sophia and Lydia had built. "Are any of his drawings in the castle?"

Mr. Throne shrugged. "Yes, and no. At first, he drew landscapes, but he said that was boring. He claimed they were not as good as the work of well-known artists.

I disagreed, of course. I did and still do look up to him in all things. We were but two years apart, he and I. Our elder brother, Donald, was four years Robert's senior. When we were all children, we played together, fighting imaginary dragons and rescuing fair maidens." The reminiscences brought a faraway look of pleasure to his eyes. "As we grew older, father insisted that Donald concentrate on more serious ventures. He was, after all, destined to become the Duke of Conclarton." Mr. Oswyn grew silent once again and tossed the snowball he had created a short distance away.

Miss O'Brian, sensitive to Mr. Oswyn's moods, glanced toward him. She reached to touch his arm, but pulled back, aware of the inappropriateness of the gesture. "Will...Mr. Oswyn."

Madeline looked from Mr. Oswyn to Miss O'Brian and then back again. She had rarely seen two people more hopelessly besotted. It felt like a scene out of Shakespeare's *Romeo and Juliet*. No wonder she detested that play. She liked stories to end happily.

"I am well, Miss O'Brian. Momentary lapse is all. Where was I? Oh, yes, Robert. What interested him most was this castle. His drawings involved the improvements he wanted to make, but as usual Father said there was not the money to spend on such foolishness. His argument bordered on the superstitious, remarking that the castle had stood for generations and change might cause its destruction."

"Robert's drawings are like those of an architect I met once," Madeline said. "How wonderful."

"Very much so. In fact, he studied architecture at university. He had grand plans for Conclarton Castle and believed he could convince our father of the need for change. He wanted to reinstate it as a working estate, improve farming and cattle-raising methods. Along with architecture he also studied farming. In fact, his excitement was contagious, and I majored in classes on animal husbandry. We wanted to bring back the jobs to this area."

"What happened?"

He shrugged. "Father set us all down and gave us a grand lecture. He said it was time to marry and breed heirs. That the castle and lands had supported the Conclarton family for centuries without change or improvements. It was unseemly for men of our titles and heritage to subject ourselves to labor of any sort. We were gentlemen."

"Oh, dear."

"Indeed." He pursed his lips and stepped back to view the snow village they had created. "We have built quite a menagerie of snow people, but they are lacking something."

"They don't have any clothes," Sophia said.

"Or eyes," Lydia added. "Or a nose or mouth."

Madeline nodded in an exaggerated seriousness. "This is a critical time. I wonder what we are to do. I have an idea."

She pulled the bag of treats she had gathered from the kitchen earlier and set the bundle on the ground. Sophia and Lydia gathered around as Madeline opened the bundle. Inside were walnuts, carrots, hazelnuts, raisins and cranberries.

"Faces!" Lydia shouted. "Look, Miss O'Brian. We can make faces!"

Sophia and Lydia jumped for joy and leapt into Madeline's arms, toppling her over. Laughing, Madeline regained her balance, and dusted snow from her coat as the two girls gathered handfuls of the assorted items and ran to decorate the snow people.

Mr. Oswyn helped Madeline to her feet. "Brilliant."

"Yes, Miss Mercer," Miss O'Brian said. "You have made the girls so happy."

A snowball whooshed past Madeline.

Sophia and Lydia giggled and threw another snowball toward Madeline, then threw snowballs toward Mr. Oswyn, and Miss. O'Brian.

The adults ducked, but not fast enough. Soon they were covered in snow.

Madeline laughed and scooped up snow and packed it, then threw it over the children's heads. She did not want to hit the girls. The snowball landed against a window on one of the castle's upper floors.

Sophia grew very still. "Now you are in trouble."

"Why am I in trouble?" Madeline said. "Those windows are leaded glass, made with thick glass and reinforced with lead. They won't break."

Mr. Oswyn came up beside her, nodding. "Those are the duke's quarters. The noise might wake my brother."

Madeline nodded, staring up at the windows. "Children, are you thinking what I'm thinking?"

Lydia gazed up at the window, tilting her head back so far her bonnet slid off. She grabbed it, setting it back in place as a smile exposed her dimples. "I think my brother needs to wake up."

****

Robert heard something thumping against his window.

It was a muffled sound like a bird would make when it flew into a window. As a boy, the plight of those birds had bothered him, and as a result he had requested his windows always be left open when he slept, even in the winter months. The air in his room now smelled stale and sour, which meant the windows had been closed tight. Had he really been gone so long that this longstanding command had been forgotten? For as long as he could remember he'd wished the windows in his rooms to remain open and allow in the fresh air. Or were his wishes ignored?

He rose to investigate and winced as his feet hit the cold floor. He felt groggy and disoriented, and his shoulder where he had been shot hurt like the devil. No doubt about it, he had been in bed too long.

Robert opened the window, inhaling the fresh, crisp air, grateful snowballs had hit the windowpanes and not a bird.

Below, in the gardens, three adults and two children were engaged in a snowball fight. He recognized his brother right away, and his sisters. His brother was off to the side with a woman Robert presumed was his sisters' governess. It saddened him how much Sophia and Lydia had grown while he was away. He had missed so much of their young lives.

Feeling unsteady on his feet, he leaned against the windowsill as snow fell gently over the frozen ground and the people chased each other below. Flakes, each one delicate and unique, drifted in a gentle breeze and swirled around him like a promise.

In the thick of the snowball fight with his sisters were two women, one with blonde hair and the other with fire-light red hair. He recognized Miss Mercer immediately, not only from the color of her hair but the curve of her face and the way she tilted her head when she smiled. Even from this distance he noted the fire in her eyes. She had spirit. She had not been a dream. She was real. And he was attracted to her.

He drew nearer to the sill, hoping to hear her laugh. He smiled, imagining the sound, both musical and magical, would help him forget the guilt of the past, if only for a moment. His sisters chased her, throwing snowballs in her direction. Laughing, she waved her arms, and staggered back, pretending to fall so they could catch her. His heart warmed at the sight of his sisters rushing over to give her hugs. She knew how to play with children and appeared to enjoy their company and their games.

Suddenly interrupting his thoughts, a voice he recognized said, "Glad you are on your feet, old friend. Long past time to be out and about."

"Hello, Jeremy." Robert didn't turn, his gaze still following the play outside as his sisters took off running to a nearby snowbank. "I need to leave this room or I will go mad."

"Are you well enough?"

"Have you forgotten? This it is not first time I have ridden a horse with a bullet in my shoulder. Thank goodness Devonshire is a poor shot. The bugger was aiming for my heart. Where is he?"

"I heard he headed back to London. Good thing, too. Your brother threatened to challenge him to a duel."

"Good man. Now, as soon as I dress and eat something more substantial than the watered-down porridge the doctor prescribed, we will go for that ride. Or join my sisters for a snowball fight."

He chuckled, watching as his sisters rejoined Miss Mercer, carrying armfuls of snowballs they had made.

Miss Mercer had made an impressive lot herself.

"I have brought someone with me," Jeremy said in a flat tone. "She awaits outside your door. Before you react, promise me you will listen to what the Lady Montgomery has to say."

Chapter Fifteen

The next morning, Madeline slapped a slice of ham on her plate. Next, she heaped a generous portion of eggs and potatoes from the buffet table in the dining room onto her plate. She did not care that proper English ladies had the appetite of hummingbirds. She was hungry.

She was not agitated, and certainly not jealous. The duke was free to speak with anyone he pleased. He was certainly free to speak with that brazen, loathsome, cheating, fiancée of his. When she and his brother and sisters had thrown snowballs at his window, he was alone, smiling at them. Her heart had fluttered, and her face had warmed under his steady gaze.

A short time later, she and the others had gone inside for hot cocoa and biscuits, and she had learned that when Jeremy and the duke had gone for a ride, Lady Montgomery had joined them.

She was such a fool. Madeline plunked a slice of bread onto her plate and looked for the best place to sit down.

She had spent a late night, drawing, and was the last to arrive for the meal. The duke's sisters had already dined and were with their governess. Her mother had asked for a tray to be brought to her room. A few lords and ladies conversed in groups, drinking their tea and stealing glances her way. Unwittingly, she had drawn attention and knew that she was viewed as a curiosity.

Comments ranged from the innocent to the absurd when news spread that she had prevented another attack on the duke's life. Were all American women as brave as Madeline? She wanted to tell them that yes, American woman were brave, but not all were foolish enough to fall in love at first sight. In her defense, when she'd seen him galloping toward her carriage, she thought he didn't have as much as two farthings to rub together. She should have heeded her mother's advice and erected a giant wall around her heart the moment she learned the infuriating man was a duke.

Surprisingly, no one knew that Lady Montgomery had been involved, or at least it hadn't been mentioned.

She heard the duke's voice, deep and unguarded, conversing with Lord Dumont. A gaggle of ladies swarmed around them, blocking the duke and his friend from entering.

But a glance from him was all she had needed to freeze her blood.

The duke had shaved, combed his hair back, and wore a midnight-blue jacket, tan breeches, and Hessian boots. He looked magnificent, unapproachable, and epitomized rank and privilege. She preferred the disheveled, bearded version. She found she was less attracted to this version.

Liar.

Madeline had lost her appetite. She abandoned her plate of food and fled. She found the library, her personal sanctuary, and snatched one of the books from the shelf. A fire had been lit and roared out warmth and a cheery welcome. Ignoring the fire, she headed toward the window seat. She was not interested in the amber glow of the flames. She needed natural light.

Sketching would help ease her racing heart. She had allowed herself to dream the impossible. Learning that the duke spent time with Lady Montgomery and seeing him dressed formally brought her back down to earth. He was a duke, and she was the daughter of a woman who owned and operated a brothel. Their lives couldn't be further apart.

She settled on the cushioned bench seat and drew out the blank sheets of paper she had brought from America, as well as a drawing in progress. She had a few sheets of paper remaining and would ask Winfield how she could purchase more. She was stuck in this castle for the foreseeable future.

She had heard that some painters sketched in the margins of books when paper was scarce. She would not draw in any of the books in the library. They did not belong to her. The duchess valued reading as an acceptable accomplishment for young women—if done in moderation, of course. If Madeline could persuade someone to take her into town and purchase a few books, that would solve her problem.

Madeline scooted closer to the window. The book she had taken from the shelf slid to the floor.

"*The Mysteries of Udolpho*, by Ann Radcliffe," the duke said, retrieving the book and handing it to Madeline. "It is my mother's favorite."

The duke's voice, strong and deep, vibrated through her, confusing her in both mind and body. "I find that surprising," she said without turning to hide the warm blush that his presence produced. "Your mother said she did not like reading."

"That is what she wishes people to believe. Reading is one of her passions."

"You shaved your beard and combed your hair." The words sounded like an accusation in her ears, and she meant them as such. She did not recognize this man. He dressed formally, his cravat tied to perfection, his long coat and tan breeches immaculate. This man did not ride a horse in wild abandon. This man rode in carriages, ordered servants about, and expected women to swoon. She tucked the sketchbook closer, waiting for his response.

She decided she did not like this version of the Duke of Conclarton.

He rubbed his smooth face. "My friend Jeremy suggested I join the land of the living."

She could only nod.

He looked confused at her nonverbal response and plunged forward. "Regarding my mother, there are a lot of surprising things about her that I am still learning. Your likeness of my sisters is quite good. I find that surprising."

She followed his gaze and realized he was staring at her drawing of Sophia and Lydia building their snow people. She remembered the list of acceptable and unacceptable traits men desired in a bride. An unacceptable trait was a woman who aspired to perfecting a skill as a painter. But she hadn't set her cap for the duke, so what did it matter what he thought?

"Why is that surprising, Your Grace? She said it with a deliberate edge to her voice. "Have you never met a woman who painted?"

He seemed taken aback by her terse response. "My father purchased several portraits from women painters, but I have not seen them."

"You haven't seen them? Is that because they are of

such poor quality, being painted by women, that they are hidden away? And before you ask, I attended Bradford College in Massachusetts, and my mother hired private art tutors. Which means I can discern a gifted painter from an amateur."

"A school that accepts females," he said evenly. "How extraordinary."

"Is there something that you wanted, Your Grace?"

His eyebrows drew together. "Have I done something to offend you? I came down to break my fast, knowing you were in the dining area. Yet you left without finishing your meal, and I know you saw me enter. Are you avoiding me? I thought we were friends."

"We are friends. Just friends. Thank you, Your Grace, for the reminder. If you will excuse me, I must see to my mother."

****

Madeline stormed into her mother's room and slammed the door shut. Her mother sat at the desk by the window reading a missive. When she glanced up toward her daughter, she folded it and tucked it into a drawer.

Frustration and anger twisted a knot in Madeline's stomach at her response to the duke. The man was infuriating. Mentally, she knew the duke was the same man without a beard as he was with. But her heart screamed a different tale. She was pulled to the bearded man. He was approachable, flawed, vulnerable. The clean-shaven duke exuded confidence, privilege, and caution. Everything she was not. And worst of the worst, she had heard that he had been talking with Lady Montgomery.

Her mother glanced up and poured tea into her cup. "What did the duke do this time?"

Madeline paced a path in front of the fireplace. "Why do you assume this has something to do with the duke?"

Her mother arched an eyebrow.

"Very well. As you must know, I was in the dining room planning to break my fast. I heard him laughing and talking to his friend, Lord Dumont. When he entered the room, he looked different. Mother, he wore a formal jacket and breeches—and he had shaved his beard."

"I am confused."

Madeline drew in an exasperated breath. "He looked like a duke."

"He *is* a duke."

"I know. But today he *looked* like one. I could not face him, so I ran away and hid in the library. You know what he did next?"

Her mother added milk to her tea and stirred. "I cannot imagine. Enlighten me."

"He *followed me*."

Her mother's mouth twitched at the corners as she sipped her tea. "Did he ravish you? Compromise you? I am told that here in England that if a man is caught taking liberties with a woman, that woman can force the man to marry him. If he did compromise you, our problems are solved."

Madeline rolled her eyes. "Mother, please. The duke was a perfect gentleman. He did not take advantage of me. We had a fight."

Her mother closed her eyes and sighed. "That is what I love about English men. They have perfected the art of foreplay and hold all that lovely sexual tension in check." She opened her eyes and winked. "Once it is released..." She sighed again.

"Mother. It wasn't like that. He said we were friends."

"Dear one, I warned you…" Well, you must forget about the duke and set your cap on someone else. Mr. Oswyn, for example."

"He is in love with the governess."

"What a muddle. Well, regardless of how you feel toward the duke and he you, I have learned through my informants that he and Lady Montgomery have announced a date for their wedding."

"Then it is over."

"It is never over until a couple pledges to love, honor and obey."

Madeline paused by the fire to stare into the flames. "You should have seen him. He looked out of my reach. I could never compete with someone like Lady Montgomery."

Her mother rose to join her by the fire. "It is for the best, then."

"You make it sound easy."

"Nothing is easy, but neither is it impossible. I have it on good authority that the duke hired a dance instructor for the ball that will take place at Lord Dumont's estate. There will be many eligible, titled gentlemen in attendance."

"Lady Montgomery and the duke are not in love."

"True. But these people are not like us. Love is not their main concern. Women might dream about finding a love match, or at the least learn to care for their husbands. Most are forced to reconcile to an amiable existence, content with children and a secure future. Their main concern is duty. Now you must hurry. The dance instructor is scheduled to arrive within the hour."

"I do not know why learning to dance is so important."

"The art of the dance in England is another form of sexual foreplay. Flirting is acceptable—in fact, it is encouraged. An innocent brush of the skin takes on new meaning. A look or a smile holds longing and romantic possibilities. It is not uncommon for a man to make an offer of marriage to a woman simply because he enjoyed dancing with her."

"A lifetime together because your partner danced well. That is frightening."

"Or very romantic," her mother said.

Chapter Sixteen

Waiting for the dance master to arrive, Madeline warmed her hands by the fire in what she had learned had been the great hall in the castle before it had been repurposed as the assembly room, where people gathered for balls, to see and be seen. The high ceilings, with carved wood beams and hunting murals, retained the look and feel of medieval times. Floor-to-ceiling windows and doors led to terraces, while sterling silver chandeliers, polished to a high gloss, dropped down on golden cords.

She loved it all.

Her favorite stories, as a child, had been about knights and their ladies, romantic tales of true love, dragons, and good conquering evil. That was one of the reasons she had warmed to England. She loved the history of the place and that this castle was hundreds of years old. She had spent half a day exploring the hallways and rooms, viewing portraits that spanned generations. She wondered about the sober-looking people and what their lives must have been like. Had they married for love? Had their lives been adventurous or dull? She made up stories about them and longed to ask Robert the history of his ancestors.

Madeline also wanted to ask the duke if he felt the same sense of awe that she did, or did he take it all for granted? But that was foolish, and her mother was right.

Madeline shouldn't spend more time with him. She should find ways to avoid him. She should explore the gardens and woods on her own. She didn't mind the weather. Truth be told, she enjoyed the cooler climate and how the snow transformed the trees into a magical forest. The only negative she had was that they needed more Christmas decorations, but she did not know how to approach the subject without sounding as though she were being critical.

Her mother had insisted that she change into another new dress, arguing that the right gown might make a man fall in love faster. The one her mother had chosen was a lighter green than Madeline usually wore, and the neckline deeper. Her mother said it brought out the color of Madeline's eyes. Madeline believed her mother had officially lost her mind. But, to be honest, she felt like a fairy princess in the gown, with its beaded bodice and Belgian lace trimming at the sleeves and hemline.

Madeline nodded as people drifted into the room. She had started to recognize the guests and their moods—or peculiarities as her mother called them. Mrs. Carmicle and her daughter, Veronica, were the first to arrive, and when Veronica was nervous, she fidgeted with the hem on her sleeve. They came from Texas oil money and were friendly and open. The next duo was Mrs. Abernathy, a banking widow, and her daughter Sarah. They kept to themselves, but Madeline noticed that Sarah paid particular attention to the duke's brother, William.

The flood gates seemed to open and three more sets of mothers with their well-dressed daughters arrived, followed by a half dozen English-born bachelors.

Madeline liked everyone she had met very much.

Her mother had given Madeline the names of the numerous guests staying in the castle, as well as their backgrounds and, in some cases, scandals. What passed as a scandal amused Madeline. One young lady's scandal resulted when she forgot to wear gloves to a ball, and another when a lady refused to dance when asked. Madeline commented to her mother that the scandals were silly but in awe of her mother that she had gained so much information in a short period of time.

Her mother countered that if there was a juicy scandal waiting for discovery, her mother would find it. People with wealth considered their servants invisible and of little consequence. As a result, they spoke openly around them. Servants loved to gossip, and Madeline's mother was friendly and easy to talk to, a perfect combination.

Madeline heard the chattering sound of voices as a group of three young women entered the room. These were dark-haired beauties, wearing the latest fashion, each in a slightly different color, and matching pearl necklaces. From her mother's description, these were the MacAfee sisters, whose father was a wealthy land baron. Their father had been accused of cheating on his partner, but the charges had never been proven. The sisters were here to marry a man with a title, with the belief that an English title would repair their family's tarnished reputation.

More entered. There was a tall, slender woman with chestnut brown hair, accompanied by her small elderly mother. Her father, an import-export merchant, was too busy to make the journey to England. Another woman, similarly companioned, could boast a father who owned a large fabric distribution business in South Carolina. A dog yipped, and Madeline knew the cute animal belonged to the Texas heiress whose family was in the oil business. Men also started to arrive. They were of various sizes, shapes, and ages. According to her mother, they were here to find a rich American wife.

Madeline had remarked to her mother that she had not expected so much competition. Her mother dismissed Madeline's concerns, spinning a classic saying to illustrate her point. "Cream rises," she had said. "And you are the cream, my child."

Madeline drew back from the fire, at odds with where to stand as she viewed the crowd, searching for the duke. As of yet, he had not arrived. He had mentioned he would attend. Had he forgotten? Or had he been pulled away on a business matter—or worse, changed his mind? Or perhaps he was with Lady Montgomery… This last thought dampened her mood. She must remember they were only friends, and that was all they would ever be.

She refocused.

Despite her mother's encouraging words, Madeline was at a disadvantage. English men expected a prospective bride to be proficient at certain things. They cared less for the mind and more for appearances. At the top of the list was the ability to dance, and Madeline lacked that skill.

On the journey by ship from New York to England, her mother's intention had been to hire a dance instructor. Unfortunately, there was only one lesson. The winter storms and bouts of seasickness kept people inside their cabins.

Their dance instructor on the ship had spent the first lesson going over proper ballroom etiquette. He stressed that a lady could not refuse to dance with a gentleman unless already engaged for that dance. A lady had to wait for a gentleman to ask her to dance. If a lady did not know the gentleman, she would have to wait for an introduction before accepting his invitation to dance. The list went on, with stricter rules for the gentlemen. Their instructor ended with the promise that in subsequent lessons he would teach English country dances, waltzes, quadrilles, and the traditional end of the night dance: the Boulanger.

But that never happened. The ocean had been too stormy and rocky, rendering most of the people, including the dance instructor, too seasick to consider anything except keeping to their beds.

The duchess entered the assembly room with an entourage in tow—a portly man with red cheeks and hair that stood up on his head like winter wheat, and whose waistcoat looked so tight the buttons threatened to pop, and his opposite, a reed-thin man with pinched lips and thinning hair.

"May I present to you, the Master of the Dance, Mr. Higgins."

The portly man stepped forward and bowed, waiting for the duchess to make the next introduction.

"And this is his accompanist, Mr. Wallaby. These gentlemen are well-versed in the current dance steps and etiquette. I leave you all in their capable care."

Mr. Wallaby followed Mr. Higgins' example and bowed as well.

Mr. Higgins bowed again. "Thank you, Your Grace, for your generous recommendation. Will you join us?"

"My days of dancing are long past, and I have other matters that need my attention."

When the duchess had gone to her various duties, Mr. Higgins clapped his hands. "Let us begin. Please form two rows. Women on one side and the men on the other. Be quick about it. We do not have all day!"

Mr. Wallaby removed sheets of music from his leather satchel and positioned it on the pianoforte and began playing.

Chapter Seventeen

The telltale sounds of the pianoforte intermixed with the shouted orders of Dance Master Higgins brought back memories as Robert headed toward the assembly room. He did not need lessons, but—God help him—he knew Madeline would be in attendance and he wanted the excuse to spend time with her. He caught himself up short and revised his assessment for attending the lessons. As the Duke of Conclarton, it was his obligation to ensure all his guests were comfortable. And if he found himself enjoying her company, what was the harm? They shared the same belief that romantic love was reserved for novels. In life, it did not exist.

As he drew closer, he heard Mr. Higgins' commanding voice shouting out orders.

"Hop, step-step and jump. No. No. No! Not step, jump, step! You are doing it all wrong! Let us begin again. Mr. Wallaby, from the beginning, if you please."

Robert grinned. Time had not softened the dance master's demeanor. Robert had chafed at the need to learn to dance. He had preferred hunting and learning to fence and box. His appeal to his father had been countermanded by his mother's intervention. "A gentleman must learn to dance," she had said, ending the matter.

His mother's will prevailed, as it had in most areas, and a portion of Robert's days were devoted to learning the minuet, quadrille, cotillion, country dances, and the waltz, some with such nonsensical dance names as the Porcupine, Bloom of the Pea, and Merry Cobblers. As he grew older, he preferred the waltz. It gained him the opportunity to hold a woman in his arms, a heady experience for a young man on the verge of manhood.

With his hand on the doorknob of the assembly room, he encountered Lady Montgomery as she rushed to block his path. "A moment of your time, Your Grace."

The sight of Lady Montgomery brought back the scene of her in the arms of Devonshire. She had told him during their ride with Jeremy that she had an explanation, and she had asked him to be patient, as all would be revealed as soon as it was possible. The problem was that he was not a patient man. He had agreed with his mother that he would honor his brother's dying wish that he marry Lady Montgomery, even going so far as to set a date for their wedding.

He was having second thoughts, however, and he knew it was due to his growing affection toward Miss Mercer. As a gentleman he would not back out of his agreement with Lady Montgomery. But after seeing her with his cousin, he wondered if perhaps she was reluctant to marry Robert, if her affections lay elsewhere and she felt as trapped as he did.

She fidgeted with a lock of hair that had fallen from a carefully constructed hairstyle that included silk flowers and diamond hairpins. "You are most kind to agree to these few moments. More kind than I deserve. But it is urgent that I speak with you."

Something in the tone of her voice drew his interest. Had he detected sadness, despair, panic? Or a combination of all three?

His reply was measured. "I am also pleased we will have a private opportunity to speak to one another. My father's study is not far. Please follow me."

As he led the way down a hallway, he realized his father's study now belonged to him. In such cases, when a father died, the heir would redecorate the study, obliterating traces of its original owner. Robert had no intention of following that trend. He had fond memories of his father and wished to keep his memory alive, not bury it.

He had always found his father's study a quiet place for reflection and contemplation. It might prove to be the perfect setting to broach the subject of calling off their engagement.

He opened the door and allowed Lady Montgomery to enter.

"I was only in this room once," she said, taking the chair in front of the desk as Robert offered.

"I am surprised you were here at all," Robert said, moving toward the seat behind the desk. "What business did you have with my father?"

"You are direct. Very like your father. However, it was not your father whom I met but your brother Donald. We believed your father's study was the most secure place in the castle. As you know, this old castle has many hidden corridors behind the walls, where servants can listen in on conversations and then relay gossip to the highest bidder. Your father made sure the ones behind these walls were boarded up."

Her lips quivered. "You must know the whole of it." Lady Montgomery retrieved a letter from her reticule and handed it to Robert. "Donald had learned that Devonshire was deeply in debt. Although not unusual these days, what was unusual were the rumors that Devonshire bragged that he was well positioned to inherit the Conclarton title. Perhaps he thought of it as a way to keep his creditors at bay. When I met Donald here, he did not tell me the whole of his findings, however. According to the letter you hold in your hands, the Crown had their concerns as well but regarding another matter. They suspected Devonshire of stealing jewels while attending last year's society events. I discovered this letter from the Crown, and Donald's notes regarding Devonshire, after Donald died. It is my belief that your father's and brother's deaths were not accidents."

Feeling drained, Robert sat down in the chair behind the desk. It was one thing to suspect that his father and brother had not died accidentally, but another matter to have that suspicion confirmed. He had witnessed evil on the battlefield, and part of him had not wanted to believe it existed so close to home. Devonshire had planned to wipe out all the male heirs of Conclarton. If Robert hadn't returned, likely William would have been next.

"Their deaths were not accidents," he said more to himself, to confirm his darkest thoughts, than to Elizabeth.

"Your brother was an accomplished hunter and equestrian," she said. "When he died, I decided to find proof against Devonshire myself. I contacted the Queen and persuaded her to grant me an audience on the pretext of discussing my forthcoming nuptials with you, the now Duke of Conclarton. It was an easy ruse. Your father and brother were well respected, and all were devastated when they heard of their deaths. I confess I fabricated that your brother's dying wish was for us to wed, but that helped in securing an audience with the Queen. She found it very touching. I will, of course, have to confess to her of its falsehood. Once secluded with the Queen, I shared my concerns about Devonshire and offered to find proof of his guilt."

"But why were you secure in Devonshire's affections to the degree that he might bring you into his confidence?"

"He is a man deep in debt, and when your brother died, he visited me with both an offer to console me and an offer of marriage. I wanted neither and, in a panic, I told him the story I had told the queen regarding your brother's dying wish that I marry you. I believe that is the reason your cousin tried to kill you. You must believe me that I did not know it was you who burst into your father's rooms that day. In fact, I had gone to your father's rooms to find a book your mother had mentioned she believed she had misplaced. Devonshire surprised me. I was trying to fight him off when you appeared."

"If Devonshire discovered your treachery, he would not seek your ruin but would want you killed also. You risk much, and I apologize for misjudging you."

"Women are always underestimated. I know that I ask much of you to continue this ruse. I have seen how you look at Miss Mercer."

"We are friends." He winced at the word choice he had used, realizing he wished it was not so. He took a calming breath. "I do this for the memory of my brother and father. I would be honored to help you bring Devonshire to justice."

"You must promise me that you will tell no one about our arrangement. I do not want to place more people in danger."

"You have my word as a gentleman. The world will believe we are engaged to be married. When Devonshire is behind bars, you are free to break off our engagement. If I can do anything to help you find a suitable husband, please let me know."

"Her Majesty promised to grant me a man of my choosing when this is concluded, but I have no intention of accepting her gift. She would essentially be forcing a man to marry me against his will. That is the sort of experience women feel when they are placed on the marriage market each season. It is dreadful and demeaning. We are judged by our appearance and the size of our dowry. I will marry for love or not at all. Besides, I have little interest in remaining in England. I will travel to the Americas. If Miss Mercer and her mother are an example of the people who live there, I know I will love it very much."

Robert unlocked a drawer to his desk and withdrew a velvet-covered box with a gold clasp. He opened the box and presented it to Lady Montgomery. "This ring belonged to my grandmother, and my father requested that I give it to the bride of my choosing. If we are to convince the *ton* that we are indeed an engaged couple, your wearing of this ring will go far in proving our intent."

She gazed toward the box, shaking her head. "I cannot accept it. It is too precious a gift and holds great meaning, as it will be passed down to each generation. It is a ring you will hand down to one of your sons and he to his sons. You must give it to the woman you intend to marry and who will bear your children." She slipped a gold chain from around her neck and removed a ring with a cabochon ruby. "This belonged to my mother and has brought me luck," she said slipping it on her finger. "We will tell everyone that it was a gift from you to me."

There was a knock on the door.

Robert stepped from around the desk and reached for Lady Montgomery's hand. "That will be Winfield, inquiring, no doubt, about castle business or the ball Lord Dumont and his wife have planned. We will attend and show the *ton* that we are pleased with our arrangement.

"Then the masquerade begins," she said.

"Indeed. Enter, Winfield."

Chapter Eighteen

Preparation for the night of the ball at Lord Dumont's estate had been a whirlwind. Madeline entered the ballroom as the orchestra began to play. Her mother had surprised her with a gown fit for a princess, in ice-blue silk with seed pearls and crystal beads. In comparison, all the ladies in the ballroom were dressed like jewels in a crown, and their escorts were in formal attire.

Ready for the dancing to begin, the men and women faced each other in the same manner as they had under the tutelage of the music instructor, polite smiles frozen in place and the hum of conversation blending with the notes of music. The dance commenced, each step perfection.

At the bottom of the staircase, a woman in a rose-pink gown approached Madeline with a man she recognized as Lord Dumont. His jacket matched the woman's gown.

"You must be Lady Madeline," the woman said. "This handsome man is my husband, Lord Dumont, the Duke of Conclarton's friend. Please call me Molly. I detest titles. I am told you need a husband."

"Wife," Lord Dumont said, frowning. "Why would you be so bold? You just met Miss Mercer!"

"Because it is the truth."

"But perhaps she already has a suitor."

Molly threaded her arm through Madeline's. "Do you? Have a suitor, that is?"

"Sadly, no."

Molly patted Madeline's arm and gave a satisfied glance toward her husband. "As usual, dear husband, I am right. Madeline, why don't you and I have a chat, and you can tell me the type of man you would like, and I will find him for you."

"Molly," Lord Dumont said. "Choosing a husband is not like choosing a dress for a ball."

"I beg to differ. In all the ways that matter, it is the same. You need to find a husband that fits. He must complement you. If a man, like a dress, is too rigid, you will not be able to breathe and will feel unable to move freely. And so it goes. Off with you, husband."

He gave a slight bow. "I will take my leave, my love."

The moment Lord Dumont had left, Molly drew Madeline into an alcove. "You are the woman who saved the duke's life. Am I correct?"

"I am given too much credit. His Grace had things well in hand."

"You are modest. Another of your many good qualities, I am told. That is not how I heard the tale. Is it also true that the woman with Devonshire was the duke's fiancée, none other than the Lady Montgomery?"

"I shouldn't say…"

Molly smiled. "Never mind. I should not have questioned you. The truth wiggles out sooner or later. Let us find you a husband. Have you considered the duke?"

Madeline held her breath. "I… That is, he is betrothed to Lady Montgomery. And even if he were not, he has made it clear that we are only friends."

Molly tapped a finger to her chin. "Interesting. But you admire him, do you not?"

"Who could not?"

"So not the duke, but a man like him. Let us get to the details. Do you care for men with light hair or dark? Blue, green, or brown eyes, or shades in between? Tall or your height? Is a good frame important? How about temperament? Do you desire a man who is well read and in possession of a quick wit and an intelligent mind, or are these attributes not important? How important is his title? I understand that you and your mother are wealthy, so a yearly income is not of importance. Or am I mistaken in that assessment?"

"Oh, my!" Madeline smiled. "Your questions really do suggest that choosing a man is like choosing a dress. Was this how you chose Lord Dumont?"

Molly glanced over at her husband talking with a group of men by the refreshment table. At that same moment, Lord Dumont looked toward Molly and raised his glass to her. She blushed a rosy pink. "I considered none of those things when I met Jeremy. He smiled and I fell in love at first sight." She lowered her voice. "Was that how it was with you and the duke?"

"Molly, I told you…"

"I know what you said. But I also know how your voice sounds when you say his name. Do not worry, though. Your secret is safe with me."

"It does not matter how I feel. The duke would never choose me. Please, can we talk of something else?"

Molly nodded. "I will not say another word on the matter. The important thing is to find you a suitable match, and I may have a number of candidates in mind."

"More than one?"

"Yes, more than one. It is important to have many suitors. The more suitors, the better. Men like a competition. If they believe someone desires you, they will rush to the chase. Come. I spy Lord Hastings with my husband. He is a good place to start. Hastings is a viscount, and his lands border the duke's. He has made it known that he is in need of a wife. He began looking last spring but found none of the ladies to his liking. He will like you, however."

"How can you be so sure?"

"Because your reputation precedes you. Times are changing, and men are searching for a woman who is more than a decoration on their arm, although many might not admit to this conclusion. They are seeking a woman with more substance. And that, my new friend, is you."

****

Robert retreated into the shadows to avoid the obligation of dancing with the single, husband-hunting ladies, and downed his whiskey in one gulp. In the past two hours, mothers had produced their single daughters to him for inspection. The ladies blended together in a glittering assortment of silk, satin, and lace.

This was a problem. As an engaged man, he should have been crossed off their list of eligible bachelors. On the surface, the *ton* believed that he and Lady Montgomery were engaged, but like a hound who smells the blood of the chase, the *ton* suspected something was amiss. Was it that Lady Montgomery's attention at present was focused on Devonshire that had their tongues wagging?

Much hung in the balance. If he and Lady Montgomery succeeded in bringing proof against

Devonshire, all would be well. If they failed, Lady Montgomery had the most to lose. Devonshire could defame her character in retaliation—or worse. Robert was sincere in his commitment to marry and protect her. Lady Montgomery had loved his brother and was loyal to the Crown. He would not forsake her.

But he had to do something. He could not sit idly by.

His gaze drifted toward the dance floor. To add to his distress, Miss Mercer had no lack of suitors. It should not bother him. She had made it clear that she needed a husband, and he was, simply put, off the market. It should please him. He should desire her happiness. But every time another man bowed and led her to the dance floor, his blood simmered.

She floated on the dance floor, laughing and conversing with fluid ease. A few men, mesmerized by her beauty and charm, boldly touched her waist, or brushed their hands against hers. It took all the strength he possessed to stand in place and not strike the men down.

"You look in ill sorts, old man," Jeremy said. "Does the shoulder bother you?"

A servant swept close by, and Robert set his glass down on the tray and ordered another. "I am bothered by your wife. She has introduced every bachelor in this room to Miss Mercer."

"Miss Mercer came to England searching for a husband, and until you decide your fate with Lady Montgomery, what choice does she have?"

"You talk madness. Miss Mercer and I do not suit. She has made that clear."

"What choice did you give her? You insist on honoring your engagement to Lady Montgomery. As for suitability…"

"I merely worry for her," Robert interrupted. "These men are more interested in her wealth than in the lady herself. I wonder if she felt the need to travel across an ocean to find a husband. Aren't there suitable men in America?"

"Quite a number, I am told. Perhaps her reason for arriving on our shores in search of a match is the same reason as the other women from America. We have what the men in America lack. We have a title."

"Miss Mercer does not appear that superficial," he said absently, watching her swirl around the room in the arms of one of his neighbors. Charles was the Marquess of Wentworth. An amiable sort, good equestrian, in possession of an estate in Sussex and a townhouse in London. He detested the man.

"Indeed, she does not," Jeremy said. "A puzzle, then. You should ask the lady what she truly desires. If you dare."

Robert thanked the servant when he returned with a whiskey. "What is your meaning?" he said to Jeremy.

"You always place the needs of others before yourself. You are ruled by duty. Duty to your family. Duty to your country. When you choose a bride, you will choose the person your family recommends, without thinking of what you want. In your case, you accepted the bride your brother chose for you. Lady Montgomery is well mannered, even tempered, fashionable, and attractive. She is also wealthy. The perfect match for a man in need of a wife who could restore the depleted treasury, a depletion caused by his father's gambling debts."

"I believe your wife approaches," Robert said

evenly.

"Right you are, and I recognize her expression. She desires a dance. Before I married, I was a fool. I believed I understood women. I believed there was little more in their pretty heads than the desire to arrange shopping excursions for ribbons and lace or trapping a man into marriage. If you are fortunate enough to marry a woman such as Molly, you will learn of their depth of caring and desire to protect all whom they hold dear." Jeremy clapped Robert on the shoulder. "I only wish the same for you, old friend."

Molly joined Jeremy with a broad smile that shone in her eyes. "The most handsome men in the room are hiding away like hermits. Shame on you both. I intend to dance with my husband, and the duke, since Lady Montgomery is dancing with Devonshire, should choose an unattached single lady. Might I suggest Miss Mercer?"

Chapter Nineteen

The next day, Madeline roamed aimlessly through the castle. Her thoughts were clouded and confused, and her emotions flying in a hundred different directions. According to Molly, Madeline's first ball had been a success. Madeline danced every dance. A few men had asked to dance with her twice, which meant they were interested.

Her mother was thrilled.

But the only person Madeline had wanted to dance with was the duke.

She rounded a corner and headed down a back staircase. She was lost, but she didn't care. This obsession with how a person looked and the number of dances a person danced was new to her. In America, she had a purpose. In England, she was bored out of her mind.

When living in America, she had attended school and, when she was home, helped her mother with the ledgers and with overseeing the wellbeing of the women in her mother's employ as well as those who came asking for charity.

She was starving. Agitation and frustration had that effect on her.

Madeline had roamed aimlessly through the castle and been lost a few times, but the smell of baking bread was like a beacon, so she knew she was going in the right direction. Along the way to the kitchen, she passed separate rooms, each dedicated to storing fish, poultry, or game meats. In addition, there were larders that stored fruits, vegetables, spices, and flour. She had stopped for directions and was told the castle had its own dairy larder and smokehouse, also. She had never seen so much food in her life. They had enough to feed an army.

She passed the scullery, where servants were chatting to each other while hard at work washing dishes. Across the room, others prepared and cleaned vegetables and fruits on clean counters or in sinks.

The kitchen was a few doors down and buzzed with activity. Laughter and conversation combined with the smells of baking bread and the fragrance of spices. Bread and pies were removed from brick ovens, while additional bread and pastries were being prepared. At a door that led outside, one of the cooks handed a woman and small child a small basket of bread and cheese.

When the cook closed the door and turned, she noticed Madeline. Startled, she curtsied. "Miss Mercer. Can I be of assistance?"

All conversation ceased.

The half dozen cooks in the room all turned toward Madeline at the same time, all curtseying. Too late, Madeline realized her presence would be viewed as an intrusion. England was more formal than America, with a separation between servants and nobles that felt at times as wide as the Atlantic.

"I apologize. I did not mean to intrude. I was lost," she stammered out the last, truly sorry she had bothered them.

"Name's Mary," the cook who had been the first to notice Madeline said. "Would you like something to eat?

We pulled hot cross buns from the oven, and they are a good batch, if I say so myself. The ones from the oven are too warm to frost, but I have a few remaining from the ones we made this morning."

Madeline shook her head. "I am not hungry," she said, even as her stomach betrayed her and grumbled.

"You don't say." Mary's eyes twinkled in a face full of smile lines. She tucked wisps of salt-and-pepper hair into her cap and reached into a cupboard for a plate rimmed with delicate blue flowers. "Back to work," she ordered the other cooks as she set the plate on a table by the window. "Sit, Miss Mercer, if you please. The duchess does not abide her guests going hungry. Servants as well, if, truth be told. Not like the old lord who believed hunger was a good motivator. The old nipcheese was as stingy with a coin as a pinchpenny."

Her last comment drew a collective gasp which Mary ignored.

Madeline settled down in front of a frosted hot cross bun, which smelled of cinnamon and nutmeg. Her mouth watered. "Thank you. Can you join me?" Madeline said to Mary.

Mary folded her arms across her waist. "Would not be proper, Miss Mercer."

"Please, can you call me Madeline? If it's only just you and me. All this formality is, well, annoying, if you must know."

"The duchess said we'd like you, didn't she, gals?"

The other cooks giggled and nodded, then resumed chatting as they had before they had noticed Madeline.

"This does look delicious," Madeline said, breaking off a corner and popping it into her mouth. She closed her eyes and moaned. "This is wonderful!"

Mary beamed. "Would you like another?"

"This will be fine. I do have a question, however. I saw you talking to a mother and her child when I entered. Were they from the village?"

The chattering in the kitchen ceased again.

Mary tightened her grip on her hands. "Ruth Hoffman and her child are from the village. Her husband died when he fell off a roof he was fixing and broke his neck. They were poor when he was alive, but now..." Her lips pinched together. "We have our Poor Laws to help such as Ruth, and the parish does the best it can. But when winter comes, there are too many mouths to feed. Ruth and her child were turned away from the parish, as she was not a member of their church, and I fear she is bound for the workhouses. Not many survive those conditions. When Ruth stops by, we do what we can."

"You mentioned that the duchess does not like people going hungry, and the rooms I walked past to find the kitchen were overflowing with food. We could load up a wagonload and..."

Mary exchanged glances with the other cooks. "Here is the thing. The duchess says we must tread lightly when it comes to giving to charity. The old lord was against it, saying the Poor Laws levied taxes against the wealthy to pay for the poor. He shared some of his peers' views that poverty was caused by bad habits and laziness."

"I still do not understand. The old lord has passed, and the duchess in now in charge."

"But she is not, not really. The duke has the final say on everything, and he made it clear that he did not want to change the policies of his father."

Madeline wiped her hands and mouth on the linen

napkin and stood. "Oh, he did, did he? We will see about that." She nodded to Mary. "Where do you think I might find Mr. High and Mighty?"

'Who?"

"The duke. Where do you think he is this time of day?"

"Most likely in his father's study, going over the ledgers and the like."

Madeline nodded, headed toward the door, then paused. "Where is the study?"

Chapter Twenty

In the end, Mary led Madeline to the duke's study. Aside from directional comments, Mary had remained silent. Madeline understood all too well. What she was about to propose to the duke might cause trouble as a result of the servants educating Madeline on the plight of the people in the estate's village. She planned to be careful.

When they arrived at the study, Madeline turned toward Mary.

"Thank you. I promise that I will not inform the duke of how I found out about Sarah or the others in the village."

"That is kind of you. You are a good one, Miss Mercer."

Madeline hesitated long enough for Mary to disappear down the hall, then knocked on the door of the study. When she did not receive a response, she knocked louder.

"Winfield," she heard the duke say from the other side of the door, "I told you. I am not to be disturbed."

"It is Miss Mercer. May I come in?"

There was the sound of shuffling papers and a chair scraping over a wood floor. "I am not presentable."

"Are you wearing clothes, Your Grace?"

"What a preposterous question."

That was not exactly an invitation to enter, but close

enough.

The duke rose as Madeline entered. He looked disheveled and out of sorts. That seemed the only way to describe his appearance. He had not shaved, his hair needed a comb, and his cravat was askew. He claimed he was not presentable, and she would agree that the *ton* would find his appearance unacceptable. She, on the other hand, thought he looked adorable.

It struck her that the inside of the study reminded her of a dungeon, guarded by a trusty knight. The heavy emerald-green velvet drapes were drawn, and the wood paneling was so dark with age it looked like polished ebony. The only thing remotely cheery was the fire in the stone hearth, and the candles on the desk, but even they seemed to glow more blood red than amber.

"Why are you here?" Dark circles dragged at his eyes and his voice had lost its luster. 'You made it clear that you do not approve of me or my opinions."

It was not anger she heard in his voice but pain and confusion. It was possible that he had not understood why he had offended her when he had remarked that he considered it extraordinary that a school in America accepted female students. His condescending tone had vexed her, and she had stormed out of the room.

Instead of leaving, she should have stayed and explained why his remarks bothered her so, but she knew it took time and patience for change, and she sensed that he was not quite ready. Besides, there was a more important issue at stake than their differences. She needed to set her personal feelings aside and push forward before she lost her nerve. She must help the villagers.

"I am here to ask for your help in an urgent matter."

"That sounds like it will cost me money," he said sarcastically, and yet his expression had softened and spoke of other emotions that caused her pulse to quicken.

The impulse to run felt overwhelming, but it overshadowed the urge to comb her fingers through his hair, sooth his troubled brow, and ask him why he looked so troubled. She strengthened her resolve. She was here on a matter of great concern. Allowing her unexplainable attraction to the infuriating man to distract her was unthinkable. Her mother had taught her that there was nothing more dangerous than a handsome man.

"Are you aware that there are people in the village who do not have enough to eat?" She blurted it out before she could change her mind.

His expression turned from troubled to confused as he resumed studying the papers on his desk. "You have been misinformed. They are taken care of through the parish charities. My father assured me before I went off to war that my mother's concerns were unfounded. The villagers thrive, and those few who do not, can choose to apply for aid at the local parish or enter a workhouse."

"Are you sure, sir?"

His eyebrows knitted together. "Quite sure. Why are you so troubled by people you do not know?"

She longed to explain that she supposed her soft heart toward those in need was the result of watching her mother react in a similar manner. To do so, however, would contradict the story they had told regarding the source of their wealth.

Her mother never turned anyone away. Her mother had said it was because when she needed help, friends and strangers alike helped her, and she had vowed that she would do the same. If Madeline shared this explanation, however, the secret her mother had wanted hidden would tumble out. She decided on another path.

"We are taught to care for those less fortunate." Madeline said simply. "I helped you. Remember?"

He sat back against his chair. "Yes, you did. That was a different matter. You saw plainly that Jeremy was a gentleman because of the clothes he wore, and that I was a soldier of high rank. Both of us were worthy of your charity. I will concede that even given those circumstances, not everyone would have been as generous as you were."

She edged closer, her temper rising. "Worthy? Are you mad? I was not thinking of whether or not you and your friend were worthy of charity. Such a ridiculous statement. I was grateful that I had the means to help men who appeared down on their luck." She gritted her teeth. "You English would describe your behavior as being 'high in the instep.' You are not high in the instep. You are an ignorant fool."

"Careful with your comments, Miss Mercer. You go too far."

She perched her hands on her hips. "I am not one of your servants that you can order me about. Nor am I an Englishwoman. I am an American citizen. You cannot throw me in the Tower of London for speaking my mind."

"More's the pity." He stood slowly, placing the palms of his hands on the desk. "Which is precisely why we consider the colonies to be comprised of hoodlums and uneducated barbarians."

She cocked a smile. "And yet we succeeded in beating your English bluebloods—and not once but twice."

He growled out an oath. "We stray from the point. My father's advice on charity was clear. We are charged a levy that is paid to the parish, which manages the distribution of clothes, fuel, and bread to those who prove that they belong to the parish and therefore have a right to its support. If a person is not a member of a parish, there are workhouses."

"Workhouses? That is your solution if a parish cannot provide? Have you ever seen a workhouse?"

He rubbed his stubble of beard. "Lord Dumont and I had occasion to pass several workhouses on our return from the war. The conditions of these places and the people who live there was not an easy sight to behold. In the end, we decided that it was better than starving."

"Did you bother to ask those people that question?" Madeline folded her arms across her chest. Waited. When he did not respond, she continued, "You speak with the insensitivity of someone who knows that he will never have to experience the horror of a workhouse. You grew up privileged, attended prestigious schools, knew that when you wished to marry you would have no end to women clamoring to gain your favor." Feeling her temperature rise with frustration, she paused for breath. "Your every wish was granted. Servants cared for all your needs. Did I leave anything out?"

The duke folded his arms in the same manner as Madeline's. "You criticize me, but how was your life any different than mine?"

It was her turn to remain still.

He straightened. "Your silence adds to your mystery. You were raised in privilege, and yet you sympathize with those less fortunate. I have long wondered why some of us feel more empathy toward those less fortunate than ourselves, but as yet I have not found the answer. When I told my parents my intentions of fighting for King and Country, they were perplexed. I still have not discovered the reason I felt compelled. It would have been easier to stay home." He paused. "My mother claims I have changed."

Madeline leaned forward. "In what ways?"

"I learned that there are no winners in war, only losers and the dead."

"Well, that is something. You are not hopeless. Are you interested in the plan?"

"Concerning…"

"Feeding the poor in your village, of course."

"We discussed that the poor are cared for through parish charities."

"A chant you keep repeating." Madeline shook her head. "You decided and I disagreed. The parish needs your support and persuasion to help all people who ask for their help, not only those who belong to the parish. The winter will be harder for those who must pay for not only food but wood to keep their homes warm. You have rooms filled to the ceiling with food. I propose we load up wagons and take the food to the parish. They can distribute what is donated to those in need."

"You are not giving up."

"That goes against my nature."

"So I am learning." He sat back in his chair. "I feel as though you are my conscience. But we do not have an endless supply of food. The food in our storage rooms goes to feeding not only my family but our servants and their families through the long winter months. What you propose will deplete our stores and put many in jeopardy."

"You raise a good point."

He steepled his hands. "Finally, a compliment. I am not as hard and unfeeling as you make me out to be. We have limited resources. I could spare some of our food to do as you say, but it will not go far."

She slid into the chair that faced his desk. "I have an idea. Your mother talked about a Christmas Eve Ball for close family and friends. What if the ball were expanded to invite a wider guest list?"

"More guests means more food. I do not see how this solves your problem. A ball of the magnitude of which you speak will deplete our supplies. That means we will have less to give."

She scooted forward in her chair and folded her hands on his desk. "We would send out word about this elaborate ball on Christmas Eve. In order to attend the ball, people will have to buy tickets. We will say that the money earned will go to buy food for the poor in the village. This is Christmas, a time of giving and charity."

"It might work. I know that my mother would approve of the idea. Helping the poor in our village has been a longstanding goal of hers. She and my father had numerous arguments regarding the topic. There were times when she would defy him and take food into the village on her own. When she returned, he retaliated by cutting her clothing allowance."

"Let me guess—she told him to go to blazes," Madeline said with a smile.

The duke chuckled, coming from around the desk. "Yes, and she went a step further. They were invited to a ball at one of the neighboring estates and she wore an old, faded gown that was out of season. My father was furious and told her that her choice of gown would diminish her in the view of her friends. My mother was not known for her silence. She told everyone within earshot that she was married to a man who spent more on his hunting dogs than on his wife. His ploy to discredit my mother failed spectacularly. He was the one shunned that night, not her. That was the last time he cut her clothing allowance."

"I like your mother." Madeline stood. "Do I have your permission to inform the servants that they can load a wagon full of food? I will be happy to accompany the wagons to the parish and help with the distribution."

"If I said no, I have a feeling you would do it anyway. You are very much like my mother in that regard."

He had moved to stand close to her, and suddenly she had trouble breathing. "There now," she managed, "we are getting to know each other."

"Why don't we go together? My father believed people should help themselves. That the reason they are poor is that they are lazy."

"Is that what you believe?"

"Yes, and you will discover that I am right. The village is well cared for and the people content."

"One wagon or two?"

"I beg your pardon?" The duke said.

"Can I ask the servants to help me load one wagon full of food from your storage rooms, or two?"

"I was thinking more on the line of baskets. My father approved my mother bringing baskets to select families at this time of year." He rubbed the back of his neck. "You have that look on your face."

She arched an eyebrow.

"The one that says you will not give up until you

have your way. Be content. I conceded. You have permission to load one wagon."

"Zounds!" she screamed. "Thank you," she said and rushed to give him a hug. His arms threaded around her. She pushed back. "I am so sorry." She stepped out of his embrace. "I was just…"

"Pleased that you had won the fight?" he offered.

"I should leave," she said, backing toward the door. "There is much to do." She fumbled with the door. "Why won't this open?"

"Let me help." Robert leaned over her, then opened the door and stepped aside.

"Thank you again. Tomorrow morning, then? I will have the wagons outside the kitchen?"

"Wagon. Singular. You should quit while you are ahead, Miss Mercer."

"I never quit. You should know that by now.'

Chapter Twenty-One

The next morning, the wagon loaded with supplies rumbled toward the village over a snow-packed road. Sunshine played, moving behind the clouds only to emerge moments later, like a child playing a game of hide and seek. Rays of the sun glistened over icicles hanging from branches or from the eaves of thatched-roof cottages they passed along the way.

Robert sat beside Madeline, holding the reins. She had fallen asleep and was leaning her head against his shoulder. He enjoyed the quiet intimacy of the moment. Having her beside him felt natural and right. He had overheard the servants mention that Madeline hadn't slept the night before. She'd spent the time collecting clothing from his sisters and mother and brother and making sure all was packaged well. When he had found out, he added clothes from his wardrobe to her growing collection. He was pleased at how positively his family had reacted and how generous they had been.

The food and clothing were lashed down with ropes and teetered precariously high. He had helped with the loading and packing of the wagon, reminding her that he had agreed on one wagon only. He smiled, remembering how he had challenged her, saying it would not all fit. But of course, it had.

Madeline shifted beside him and rubbed her eyes. "How long have I been asleep?"

"Not long."

She yawned and stretched her back. "Thank you."

"You are welcome. We are on the outskirts of the village. Do you want to go directly to the parish church?"

"Why do you ask?"

He directed the team of horses around a bend in the road. "I noticed you talking with my mother and Mary. I remember her mentioning servants who used to work for us and lived in the village. During the Christmas Season she would bring them baskets."

"Would you mind? I know we agreed on the wagon going to the parish for distribution. The duchess is most concerned about Jane and Ted Murphy."

He turned toward her. Her face shone in the gentle winter sun. There was a dreamy expression in her eyes as she rubbed them again. He wanted to reach out and kiss her eyelids, the tip of her nose, her full lips. Unwise, he cautioned.

He focused on the road. "I would not mind. If I know my mother, she prepared a special basket for Jane and Ted."

"Do you know where the Murphys live?" Madeline said.

"Mother would take me and my brother and sisters to their cottage after they left our employ. Jane had been a cook, and Ted tended the kitchen gardens. I remember they have a whitewashed cottage with a blue door."

"It sounds lovely. Your mother surprised me," Madeline said. "She is different from what I expected, and my mother and she get along well. They chatter like old friends."

"There is a change in my mother since yours has arrived." Robert took time to think over the revelation.

He was about to say she was happier. The idea that his mother had not been happy earlier troubled him. He supposed he was like most children and did not consider a parent's happiness, only his own.

"I am pleased your mother and mine are friends," Robert said, pulling onto a narrow road that led to a cottage with an overgrown garden and rusted gate. "We have arrived. The cottage is not as I remember, though. The last time I was here was a little over five years ago."

Robert jumped from the driver's seat to secure the horses, then went around to where Madeline sat and raised his arms to help her down.

"Do you think they are home?" she asked, her arms resting on his as he helped her from the wagon. "I do not see lights in the cottage."

"They might be at church service," he said, holding onto her waist a trifle longer than was proper.

If she noticed, she made no comment as she retrieved from the wagon the basket his mother had packed.

The door of the Murphys' home had been left ajar. The interior was cluttered with broken furniture and covered in cobwebs and debris that had blown in from the open windows.

Madeline set the basket on the only table in the room that was still in one piece. "The cottage looks deserted."

Someone knocked. "Looking for the Murphys?" an old woman with a plaid shawl inquired. "Purse-pinched, they were, and too old for most work. Only place for them was at the local workhouse, and there's where they died. Within days of each other, I'm told."

Robert steadied Madeline before she fell. She had turned pale as milk. With an unspoken agreement from

Madeline, he thanked the old woman and offered her the basket meant for the Murphys.

Back in the wagon, Robert slapped the reins and directed the team toward the village.

"How will I tell your mother?" Madeline said. "She mentioned that she had visited the Murphys last year." Tears trailed down her cheek. "Why does this bother me? I did not know the Murphys. You no doubt think me such a silly fool. Oh, and we must find Ruth."

Robert pulled her closer to him on the bench seat. Waves of emotion crashed over him, and none classified Madeline as silly. "You are a caring person. More kind than anyone I have ever met. The Murphys' deaths bother you because you realize how senseless it was. It concerns me as well. You mentioned the name Ruth…"

"Ruth Hoffman and her child stopped by the kitchen begging for food. They were also turned away from the local parish. Her husband died when he fell off a roof he was trying to repair."

"We will find her, I promise.'

"You could offer her a job in the kitchen," Madeline said, brightening.

"A wonderful idea. All this could have been prevented. The blame does not fall on my father alone for casting the Murphys out of our home and denying them any employment or support when they grew too old to work. I said nothing." His voice caught. "How many others will face the same fate as the Murphys or possibly Ruth?"

Madeline slipped her arm through Robert's and leaned her head against his shoulder, in the way she had when she had fallen asleep. "We can mourn them and then try to prevent something like this happening again.

We won't be able to help everyone."

Robert fought the impulse to give in and kiss her. It would be beyond inappropriate. "Thank you," he said instead.

She gazed up at him, her eyes brimming with tears. "I do not understand. Why did you thank me?"

"For not judging me. I told you everyone in the village was well cared for. You could have said, 'I told you so.' "

"My mother believes those words are mean and spiteful and not in the least helpful."

"I am grateful for your mother, then."

She snuggled closer to him. "As I remember, I yelled at you."

"You did not yell. You were forceful. I am glad I came with you."

"Me too."

He drove in silence into the village, heading in the direction of the parsonage. The village reminded him of his impression of the road leading to Conclarton Castle. Neglect hung over the village like a shroud as villagers wandered through the shops. He had the impression that the villagers were doing more looking than buying. Millinery and dressmakers' shops flanked one side, and a general store the other. There was a mill and bakery by the river that bordered the village and a one-room schoolhouse near the church in the center of town.

But in between were stores with boarded-up windows where Robert had remembered had once been a bookstore, and a bootmaker's shop. The establishment with the most activity was the Stuffed Pig Tavern. By the number of men dressed in the British redcoat uniform, it must be a popular military meeting place.

He reached the United Methodist Church as the service ended and parishioners were leaving. The clergyman, dressed somberly in a black cassock, noticed Robert and hurried to greet him.

"Your Grace," the man said, bowing toward Robert. "We are most grateful for your generosity. My name is Mr. Neverberry. My wife heard of your generosity last evening. Our little parish has struggled mightily in these challenging times." A woman dressed in a plain navy wool dress and matching bonnet joined the pastor, who introduced her as his wife.

"We are glad to help, but how did you hear about us so quickly?" Robert said.

"Mary sent her son to tell us the good news last night." She turned her smile in Madeline's direction. "You must be Miss Mercer. Mary spoke of you as well, in glowing words."

"We stopped by to see the Murphys," Madeline said.

"A tragedy," Mr. Neverberry said. "Very unfortunate. They were not part of our parish, and we had no recourse but to turn them away."

Robert felt his temper rise. "What are you…"

Madeline pressed her hand on his arms and interrupted. "We understand, and that is one of the topics we wish to discuss with you. Is that not correct, Your Grace?"

Her expression implored him to use reason and calm. He knew she was as angry as he was that the Murphys had been turned away for the simple reason that they were not members of this parish. It struck him that in such a short time she could discern his thoughts, and even more astounding, that she knew her touch would calm him.

She was correct in assuming that confronting Mr. Neverberry would accomplish nothing. He was a man who followed orders, not a man capable of independent thought.

Robert rested his hand over Madeline's, feeling the warmth of it penetrate through him. "Miss Mercer is correct. There are matters we wish to discuss. But first, could you direct us to where you would like the goods we are donating to the parish?"

"I will direct a servant at once."

Mrs. Neverberry tugged on her husband's arm. "Dear, we are forsaking our manners. Please invite His Grace and Miss Mercer in for tea. They must be chilled to the bone."

"My wife, as always, is wise beyond her gender. Would you like to join us for tea in the parsonage? Our cook has prepared a lovely lemon sponge cake."

"We would be delighted, Mr. and Mrs. Neverberry," Madeline said. "Wouldn't we, Your Grace?"

Robert nodded and bit down on the corner of his mouth to keep from smiling. Mr. and Mrs. Neverberry bobbed their excitement that he and Madeline had accepted their invitation for tea. No doubt they would brag to their parishioners that the Duke of Conclarton and Miss Mercer had partaken of tea and lemon sponge cake during their visit. What the clergyman and his wife missed was the edge to Madeline's voice. She wanted to strangle these people as much as he had for turning the Murphys away.

He leapt down from the wagon, and as he helped Madeline down also, he whispered, "You are, without a doubt, the most amazing woman I have ever met."

Chapter Twenty-Two

Madeline had been wandering aimlessly through the castle again since her return from bringing food to the village. She had been looking for her mother when she stumbled onto this room with its floor-to-ceiling windows. The windows were frosted and coated with snow now, but she envisioned that in the spring and summer months the view overlooking the gardens would be breathtaking.

The duchess sat in a pale shaft of light, her needlepoint in her lap and her cat, Mariah, at her feet.

"I apologize for intruding, but have you seen my mother?"

The cloud-white cat, with a tail that looked as though it had been dipped in ink, acknowledged Madeline's presence by opening one eye. The duchess, however, kept to her task. "Your mother mentioned that she had business in town. Will you join me for tea?"

"That is most generous, Your Grace. Thank you." Madeline's mother hadn't mentioned business in town and hadn't left a note. "What are you up to, Mother?" Madeline said under her breath.

"Did you say something, dear?"

Madeline shook her head. Too restless to sit, she strolled about the room. "You have a beautiful collection of art in this room."

"As with most objects we humans acquire, art has a

story to tell. It was the late Lord Conclarton's collection and was meant to vex me. He called this room the 'women's room.' He went on a grand tour of the continent and brought back works by women artists: Rosalba Carriera, Angelica Kauffmann, and Marie-Louise-Élisabeth Vigée-Legrun."

Madeline leaned forward. "Marie-Louise-Élisabeth painted portraits of Marie Antoinette. A painting by her must have cost a fortune."

"Impressive." The duchess returned to her needlework. "You know your art. The portrait of Marie Antoinette cost several fortunes, in fact."

"Was that the reason it vexed you so? The expense?"

The duchess set her needlework aside and lifted Mariah onto her lap. "The expense was not what vexed me. He bought the paintings not to show support of the women artists but as a cautionary tale. He did not believe women should aspire to roles more suited to men. In displaying these paintings, he would use the opportunity to instruct our daughters of the tragedies that befell most of these women artists. It was far better, he preached, for a woman to be content with marriage and children. Men rule the world of art and women are not allowed in the British Royal Academy. We are allowed our little expressions through sewing and needlework, or the occasional sketches, as long as we do not aspire higher. He forbade Sophia and Lydia to sketch."

"I draw," Madeline said in a flat voice.

The duchess stroked Mariah as she purred contentedly. "Yes, I am aware. Do you find it curious that, of all the places in England, your mother thought to find your titled husband in this dreary part of England?"

Madeline sat as silent as a stone. A series of

incidents, like the toppling of dominos, had brought her and her mother to England. But truth be told, she had never questioned why her mother had selected Conclarton Castle as their destination.

Madeline laced her hands in her lap to hide their trembling. "I assumed because you had invited an American heiress to your Christmas Ball."

"Happy coincidence." The duchess set Mariah gently on the ground and rose. "It is time for dinner. Did Robert tell you that his father and I met?"

"He did not."

"Well, well, a story for another time, then."

Madeline rose to examine a painting of a woman with dark hair, wearing a black cape over a cream-white dress, a pearl necklace, and pearls on her wrist. "I recognize these brush strokes and the technique of the artist." She looked closer. "This is a self-portrait of Michaelina Wautier?"

"Good eye. How do you know the artist?"

"My mother has one of her paintings. *Triumph of Bacchus*."

The duchess tilted her head. "I have heard of that portrait. Scandalous. And your mother displays it in her home?"

Madeline hesitated. Usually, women were scandalized when they learned her mother owned such a portrait.

But the amusement tucked around the corners of the duchess's eyes gave way to laughter. "That is so like your mother," she exclaimed.

Before Madeline could question the duchess's odd comment, the duke's sisters ran into the parlor, rosy cheeked and out of breath.

"Children," their mother said, rising to her feet, "what is the meaning of this, and where is your governess?"

Sophia skidded to a halt. "Miss O'Brian is packing for our journey."

"It is so exciting," Lydia added.

The duchess pressed her hand to her waist. "Packing? What nonsense. Have you lost your minds?"

Sophia plopped down next to Madeline on the sofa. "It is true. We were playing a game of hide-and-seek with Robby. He said he thought of it when he went into the village with Miss Mercer. Lydia and I mentioned that we are all so bored. And wouldn't it be nice to attend the Frost Fair in London?"

Lydia sat down on the other side of Madeline and nodded until her curls bounced. "Our brother remarked, "'Not this year,'" in that way he does when you know he is only half listening. Then I said we thought that Miss Mercer might like to go, since we were sure she hadn't been to one."

Sophia tugged on Madeline's sleeve. "Should we have asked you first? It all tumbled out before we thought, and the Frost Fair *is* magical. The River Thames freezes over and there is skating and sledding, and gingerbread."

"And hot apples, and puppet plays," Lydia said.

"The Frost Fair sounds wonderful. Yes, I would love to go. What did your brother say when you said you thought I might like to attend?"

Sophia giggled. "Robby said was that so? We all said it was indeed so. Then he told us to instruct Miss O'Brian to pack. Isn't that wonderful?"

Lydia squealed. "We leave at the end of the week."

"What is this?" the duke said, entering. "You have spoiled my surprise of agreeing to travel to the Frost Fair."

"And a grand surprise it was, my son. You are to be commended. To what do we owe the honor of your company? Your father said he never liked the women's room and would never visit me here. Is your presence meant to change that habit?"

The duke scanned the room, focusing on the painting by Angelica Kauffmann, *The Temptation of Eros*. Eros was depicted as a cupid, making people fall in love by shooting an arrow into their hearts. In the painting, Eros was whispering in the ear of a lovely maiden, dressed in sheer, silk-like fabric.

The duke frowned, venturing a glance toward Madeline as though to gauge her reaction. "My father believed these paintings too provocative for the gentle sensibilities of a woman and therefore disapproved of them creating such images. In order to do so, women would have to view the male and female form unclothed."

"And yet it is considered of no consequence for a man to hire nude models," Madeline said with a forced smile.

"Precisely," the duke said, missing the set of Madeline's jaw and the rising anger in Madeline's expression. "Men have the capacity to appreciate the naked form without giving in to the needs of the flesh."

Madeline curled her fingers into claws, with the intent of strangling the man. The duke stood with a stone-faced expression, attempting to convince her that women could not control their lustful thoughts while men had the fortitude of saints. Even if her mother had not owned a brothel, she hoped she would have had enough sense to realize the duke was delusional.

She took a step, but the duchess restrained her, casting her a conspiratorial smile. "Son, if it is improper for a woman to paint images such as the ones in my collection, what would you believe to be appropriate?"

"Why, the lovely sketches Madeline drew of my sisters. Or bowls of fruit, or landscapes and the like."

The duchess shook her head slowly. "I love you dearly and had hoped that venturing out into the world would have expanded your awareness. But you are quite the beef-head."

"You call me daft? I excelled at Cambridge."

The duchess glanced toward Madeline and rolled her eyes. "I apologize. His Grace is quite the jolterhead, is he not?"

Madeline smiled, releasing the tension she had been holding close. She had expected the duke to share the opinions of the rest of the *ton*. What had surprised her was that the duchess did not seem to share the same views. Even more surprising, the duchess had not sided with her son but with her. A perplexing conundrum.

She focused her attention on the duke. "I agree with your mother. Women should paint whatever subject they desire."

The duke glanced between his mother and Madeline. "I need a whiskey."

Chapter Twenty-Three

Madeline had misgivings regarding the Frost Fair. She and the duke would be forced to spend time together. Her encounter with the duke over the type of paintings women should draw, and the duchess's surprising comments, were confusing. The duchess had taken Madeline's side as though she wanted to match Madeline with the duke. That was preposterous. Her son was engaged to Lady Montgomery.

Her mother, however, was delighted at the prospect of Madeline attending the Frost Fair. Many of the eligible bachelors in the area were planning to join the Conclarton Carriage Caravan to London. After Madeline's success at the Dumont Ball, her mother felt this was the perfect opportunity to secure one of the gentlemen's attentions. Which was the reason for Madeline's misgivings. She found none of them attractive. There was only one man who held her interest, and unfortunately, he was engaged.

As of now, she sensed that he enjoyed her company. If he knew the truth about her and her mother, that would change. Still, she hated keeping the truth from him.

She spun a wool shawl around her shoulders and walked out on the wide expanse of the terrace. What was happening to her? She felt close to him in a way she had never felt before to any man. He was easy to talk to and she felt as though she had known him all her life.

What tugged at her and would not let go was that she had lied to him.

She was not the heiress of a wealthy railroad tycoon, with mansions in New York, Boston, and London. She was the illegitimate daughter of the owner of the most successful brothel in Boston, which her mother had named *Feathers*.

What would he do if he discovered the truth?

Madeline leaned against the stone railing and pulled her shawl around her. The voices of two men arguing drifted toward her. Below the terrace, the Viscount Devonshire and a footman were locked in a heated conversation.

She frowned, remembering the expression on the viscount's face when he had shot his cousin. She knew he denied recognizing the duke, but there had been a flash of recognition in the man's eyes which ran contrary to his comments. She did not trust Devonshire.

The footman she recognized as one of the twins who had flirted with her mother when they first arrived. He reminded her of a snake: thin, colorful, and deadly.

She did not know why they were out here in the cold and did not care. She turned to leave and then heard Devonshire mention the duke.

"Your cousin is a hard man to kill," the footman said. "It is foolhardy to try again."

"And yet I must. I have debts to pay. Meet me in two days at the Stuffed Pig Tavern in the village. I have another plan in mind."

Heart racing, Madeline slipped back inside. Despite her frustration with the duke, she had to find him and tell him what she had overheard.

Chapter Twenty-Four

The next day was a travel day. Although a light dusting of snow had fallen during the night, the morning sky was clear and crisp, and the roads were declared safe to travel.

The inhabitants of the castle were in a festive mood as Madeline adjusted her gloves, buttoned her long coat, and descended the stairs to the awaiting carriages. She wished she could have shared their enthusiasm.

She had found the duke the night before and informed him of the conversation she'd overheard between Lord Devonshire and the footman. He shared her concern and instructed her not to speak of Devonshire's conversation to anyone. It was as though he could not get rid of her fast enough.

She held out her hand and a footman helped her into the next carriage when it pulled up. Although similar to his brother in appearance, he was taller, and his hair slightly darker and longer than his twin's. This was not the same man she had overheard talking to Devonshire last night. Was he involved as well? Should she suggest that possibility to the duke? She looked over the guests boarding other carriages, but the duke was not amongst them.

"Will you mind company, Miss Mercer?" Lady Montgomery said from the interior of the carriage. Her long plum-colored coat was lined with fur and embroidered with green and gold swirls around the hem and sleeves. It matched her velvet high-waisted dress to perfection.

It occurred to Madeline that Lady Montgomery did not have a signature color. According to her mother, women in England liked to settle on a shade they felt suited both their coloring as well as the image they wished to project. If her mother was correct in her assessment, could that mean that Lady Montgomery was not as sure of herself as she seemed?

"Before you dismiss my offer," Lady Montgomery continued, "please know there are matters I would wish to discuss with you in private."

Madeline eyed Lady Elizabeth Montgomery. At a quick glance, her appearance looked confident and flawless. Closer examination revealed dark circles under her eyes and a pinched, worried expression. Madeline had not understood the duke's change of course regarding this woman. After he had discovered her in the arms of Devonshire, he had been hell bent to end the engagement. Or so she had thought.

Then, suddenly, he had changed his mind. She should have known. This was her reward for becoming attracted to a kind and good-looking man. At least with a rake you knew, or should know, that his intentions were always and forever selfish. She had told her mother she would not fall in love for that very reason, never expecting to meet someone wonderful.

"Miss Mercer? If you prefer, I can ride in one of the other carriages."

Startled back from her thoughts, Madeline nodded a welcome and tucked a wool blanket around her knees. She was the one who was selfish. Her mother had taught her better than to judge a person on appearances alone.

"I shall love the company,' she said, making conversation. The British were a polite culture. She painted on a smile, remembering the encounter she and the duke had had with the Methodist pastor, Mr. John Neverberry and his wife, Beatrix. They had denied the Murphys and, she suspected, Ruth and her child any food and shelter for the ridiculous reason that they had not belonged to the village parish. What was worse, they had not seen the hypocrisy. They continued to consider themselves righteous people. Madeline had wanted to strangle them, which would not have been a godly thing to do. Still…

She widened a smile she did not feel. "Yes, of course, please call me Madeline. Is it a long distance to London?"

"A day's ride in good weather, and you must call me Elizabeth." She spread a blanket over her legs as well. "I overheard His Grace mention that if the condition of the roads slowed our journey, we would spend the night at an inn along the way."

"Lady Montgomery?" The footman knocked on the side of the carriage lightly to gain her attention. "Would you like your valise with you or tied to the carriage's roof?"

"I would like it beside me, thank you. I packed diversions for our trip—cards, a few games, and whatnot. Would you fancy a game of whist?"

Madeline abhorred card games and had planned on sketching, but she smiled and said she would be delighted. After all, Elizabeth was trying to be friends, and it would not do well to appear the surly American.

When the door closed, Elizabeth leaned back against

her tuffet seat. "Truly? My instinct tells me that a game of whist is not to your liking, and I agree. As a matter of fact, playing games, of any sort, is tedious, and I sense you harbor the same judgment. I only said that because it is expected that women have nothing better to do." She chuckled as she turned her attention to the mayhem that had erupted in the courtyard. Something concerning a trunk of dresses from Paris not arriving.

The carriage lurched forward as the Conclarton Caravan commenced its journey to the Frost Fair.

Lady Montgomery laced her hands in her lap. "In a sense, men are correct. We do play games. But our games do not involve a deck of cards. If we play our games correctly, it will result in our own happily ever after. But I am babbling on and on. I should have begun with the sentiment that I hoped you did not wish to play cards, as I detest all manner of games and view them as a complete waste of time. Ladies are expected to love them, however, and doing what is expected is the easier path. Now that we are all settled, I have a story to tell. Am I correct in my calculations that you are attracted to the duke?"

Chapter Twenty-Five

With the cat, Mariah, fast on her heels, Roseline Mercer joined Duchess Dorothea Conclarton at the window as the carriages left for London and the Frost Fair. She knew her daughter had wanted her along, but Roseline had declined. She had wasted enough time already. She had received an unexpected missive with an invitation to join the author of the letter in town. Good sense cautioned her to refuse the request from the gentleman and let sleeping dogs lie. Good sense?

The notion caused the false smile she gave people when she spoke of such things. The smile passed quickly, allowing the sharp pain of regret. When had good sense ever ruled her life when it came to a man?

Dori chuckled at Mariah as she padded over to her and wove around her legs. "I see that Mariah has included you in her circle of approved friends. She is most particular in that regard. Her approval proves her good judgment."

"I have always been fond of animals."

"I remember." She sighed as she followed the path of the last of the carriages over the bridge. "Our children have made a mess of things, Rosy. I had hopes they would pull down their barriers and open their hearts to love."

"You were always the matchmaker. We tried, Dori, indeed we did. Our children are determined to ignore good judgment. We know they are right for one another, even if they cannot recognize the truth."

"They are much like us in that regard, I fear. You had the worst of it, however. I wish your life had not been so difficult." Her expression hardened. "I am a terrible matchmaker. If I had known that you were still alive…"

Roseline gave her friend's hand a squeeze. "I made my choices and did not want to burden you. I have my darling Madeline, and for that gift I wouldn't change a day."

"You have a forgiving nature. But the fault is mine. I should never have introduced you to that rake."

"It was well intentioned. How were you to know that the man you introduced me to wanted to marry a woman with a rich dowry and not the only daughter of an impoverished earl who had fallen from the *ton's* favor?"

"We were a pair, you and I. My parents were quite beside themselves in their attempts to control our behavior. You taught me to climb a tree, as I remember."

"Yes, it was you who reached the top branches before I did." Roseline nodded slowly. "Even after my father lost his money gambling, you pressed your parents to fund my education. I am forever grateful."

"And why would I not? Your father and mine were good friends. *There but for the grace of God go I* was a saying he lived by."

"I was a fool to participate in a Season," Rosaline said. "I should have set my cap for a clergyman. But I was young and did not understand the ways of the world. I fell in love with an earl and thought he felt the same."

Dori scooped up the cat and rubbed her face against its soft fur. "Your memory of the past is different from mine. I was barely seventeen and terrified when my parents decided to introduce me to society. You agreed to go with me. It was the first Season for us both. We were both so young and full of thoughts of love. I was a silly child, smitten with…oh, my, I have forgotten his name!"

"The Right Honorable Lord Hampton, a third son and destined for the clergy. Your father was horrified. He wanted you married to a duke or, at the very least, an earl."

"My father got his wish. I had no idea that someone would make an offer in my first Season. I am not sure I would have survived that first year, and the birth of Donald, if you had not been there with me. I cried throughout the entire wedding ceremony."

"Your husband proved to be a good man."

"He was a good man, and I grew to love him in my way. But I always wondered…"

A middle-aged servant, dressed in a dark blue uniform and starched white cap, entered and curtsied. "Your Grace," she said, "would you and Lady Mercer like tea and biscuits?"

"That would be lovely, Mary, thank you."

Mary bobbed another curtsey and left the room as silently as she had appeared.

"Do you believe Mary overheard us talking?" Roseline said when Mary had closed the doors behind her.

"Most likely," Dori said, setting the cat down on the ground. "But Mary already knows our connection. She is more than a servant. She has become a friend. She came into our employ shortly after you discovered you were carrying the earl's child. He should have done the right thing and married you."

Roseline rubbed her neck. "I fancied myself in love and believed that Harold would do the right thing and marry me when he realized we were having a child. I had not considered the depths of his parents' disapproval and influence over their eldest son." She fingered the jewel-encrusted feather pin she always wore. "If it weren't for my mother's jewelry, I don't know what would have happened to me and Madeline. I sold the majority of it to help us build a new life. The feather pin is all that remains and is a constant reminder of my mother and her love."

"Do you think you will ever tell Madeline the truth about her father, or of our connection?"

Roseline chose her words carefully. "To do so would entertain questions about her father and subject him to a bad light."

"He does not deserve your forgiveness, but I understand. Your daughter will never learn the truth from me."

"Your tea, Your Grace."

"Perfect timing, Mary. Please join us. I would like you to get to know my friend Rosy."

Mary's eyes widened like saucers as she set the tray on the table. "You are very kind, Your Grace, but I couldn't. Wouldn't be proper and the like."

"Mary, I grow weary of what is proper and what is not. In the spring, I intend to host a literary salon, a bluestocking gathering of likeminded intellectuals. You, and Rosy, are more well-read than most of the *ton*. My profound wish is that you should join us not only for tea today but when I host the Bluestocking Salon. Now, Mary, what gossip tidbits can you share with us today?"

Chapter Twenty-Six

Robert rode his horse beside Jeremy, with a close eye on the carriages as they wound their way along the road to London. The carriage Miss Mercer rode in was positioned in the middle of the caravan and was easily the most ornate, with its gold brass trim, and a team of four white horses. To his surprise, Elizabeth had wanted Miss Mercer to join her in her carriage. Elizabeth had assured him their conversation would revolve around the latest fashions and gossip. Robert hadn't believed a word.

He had hired outriders for protection and ordered them stationed at the head of the caravan, at intervals on either side, and behind the last carriage. Still, he did not like that his plan to capture Devonshire would begin with abandoning the caravan for a slightly different route.

If all went as proposed, however, he and Jeremy—if his best friend was willing—would leave the carriages with no one the wiser. He wanted Jeremy by his side, but he just had to find the right moment to break it to him that a member of the *ton* was a traitor.

There were many pitfalls and dangers along the way. Highwaymen were a constant worry, common thieves, anxious for an easy score. A show of force would deter the majority, but there were always the desperate and reckless sort to contend with.

Then there was always the unforeseen—weather

during this time of year, one or more of the horses going lame, or a carriage breaking down for any number of reasons, from a broken axle to a...

Jeremy spurred his horse alongside Robert's. "You carry more weight on your shoulders than normal, my friend. Why the worried expression? No one will attack. You hired enough outriders to assure the protection of a small village." He hesitated. "I know that expression. What are you planning?"

Robert chuckled. "You know me too well. What know you of Devonshire?"

"He is a man who gambles and doesn't pay his debts. More than that, you caught him in the arms of your brother's betrothed."

"There is more. Elizabeth believes he orchestrated the deaths of my brother and father," Robert said in an even tone. "Devonshire tried to murder me as well, but I am not as easy to kill."

Jeremy whistled low, and his horse twitched his ears. He soothed the animal with a stroke on his neck. "He means to wipe out the heirs and become the ninth Duke of Conclarton. Whatever your plan, know that I am with you."

"We leave the caravan at the next fork in the road, where there is less chance we will be seen leaving. We will double back to the village. Before we left the castle, I informed Winfield to alert a commander I can trust to gather his men at the Stuffed Pig Tavern. The local military often goes there, so it will not look suspicious. We head in the direction the Conclarton Caravan has taken and make it look as though we are riding away from the village, then double back. If all goes well, Devonshire and his co-conspirators will be in prison by nightfall."

"You mentioned that you learned this from Elizabeth. Can I assume, then, that her involvement with Devonshire was a ruse?"

"As is our engagement," Robert said. "When the time is right, Lady Montgomery has expressed her wish to end the engagement. Until then, our situation remains as it is currently." Robert watched as the caravan disappeared around the fork in the road. "Let us make haste. We need to reach the village before nightfall."

****

Robert and Jeremy rode in silence, each locked in their own thoughts, and reached the outskirts of the village ahead of schedule. The weather had held, but the frost in the air and the dark clouds that blanketed the late afternoon sky foretold a coming storm.

Ducking under a low hanging branch, Robert's own thoughts were troubled as the village came into view. He had related to Jeremy the information regarding his elder brother's spy work uncovering Devonshire's true nature. Even after Robert had had time to absorb what he had learned about Donald, he had difficulty reconciling the brother he thought he knew with the one who had existed.

The *ton* referred to his elder brother, Donald Oswyn, as either the Marquess of Richmond, or Lord Richmond, and he was recognized as his father's heir to the title Duke of Conclarton. Donald was impeccable in his dress and manners, attended the occasional fete, and never drank, gambled to excess, or appeared interested in politics. He blended into society, neither talking too much or talking too little, and as a result he would appear to Devonshire as a man of little consequence and therefore not a threat.

Robert gripped the reins of his horse tighter, sad in the realization that perhaps becoming invisible had been his brother's goal all along. Robert was sad because he realized that he had been too self-absorbed to take the time to get to know his brother as an adult. But neither had his brother trusted him enough to take him into his confidence.

How had he been so blind? The missed opportunities to become better acquainted with his brother consumed him with guilt. He wanted to believe he would have taken time to spend with his brother when he returned from the war. The truth was that he wasn't certain he would have, and the realization cut deeper than any wound.

Jaw clenched, Robert dismounted a short distance from the Stuffed Pig Tavern and secured his horse as Jeremy followed his lead. Boisterous laughter and a bawdy song about a dark-eyed woman with large bosoms drifted on the rum-soaked air from the tavern. Positioned in the shadows were men Robert recognized as belonging to his old regiment, with a few newcomers his commander had said were Americans who had arrived to help negotiate the peace treaty between the United States and England.

The men had shed their uniforms and wore working men's clothes—homespun breeches, cotton shirts, and faded short coats. Their disguise helped them blend in, much in the same way as Donald had when he perfected the persona of a rich man's son concerned only with how he dressed and the places he attended.

Patting his animal's neck to bring him back to the present, Robert turned toward Jeremy. "I have orders to wait until the commander gives the signal that Devonshire is in the tavern. We don't want to cause a ruckus if the traitor isn't even there." He paused. "You can change your mind. We don't know how many men are with Devonshire, and he won't go down without a fight."

Jeremy nodded slowly, glancing in the direction of the tavern. "I have been thinking about your brother, and there is something that bothers me. When we were younger, he was the one who led us into dark caves or was the first to dive off the cliffs beneath your castle, into the water."

"Or the first to reach the top of a tree or win a horserace," Robert said, wondering where the conversation was headed.

"He was fearless. He hated, as much as we all did, attending any sort of fete, ball, or gathering where we were forced to sit still and listen to a parade of eligible ladies sing off-key or play melancholy songs on the pianoforte. Then, right before you left for war, he changed. He became a dandy, a Bond Street Beau, who dressed in the height of fashion, accepted invitations to attend soirees, and frequented men's clubs in London. At the time, I thought he had decided it was time to assume his role as the next Duke of Conclarton and that life was part of it. Now, I'm not sure. What if he started working for the Queen as one of her spies before we left? What if he was spying on Devonshire all along?"

A shiver sped over Robert's skin as he remembered the gravesites of his brother and father. He had found it difficult to accept that they had died in a hunting accident. His mother's letter had given few details, but it had also been tearstained, and the handwriting shaky.

"They were both remarkable horsemen and hunters," Robert said in a flat tone. "Some say they were easily the best in Conclarton and the surrounding area."

Jeremy turned his back toward the village and lowered his voice. "I don't believe their deaths were accidents. Don't you find it strange that your brother was spying on Devonshire and then was conveniently killed in a hunting accident?"

"Very. Elizabeth doesn't believe Donald's death was an accident either," Robert said.

"She's a smart woman, and that would explain the lengths she has gone to in pursuit of exposing Devonshire."

Raised voices exploded from the tavern as the doors slammed open, and a dozen or more men rushed to the streets. The waiting men Robert had seen earlier now joined the fight.

"Devonshire is getting away!" a man shouted.

Robert and Jeremy exchanged glances. Then, hands balled into fists, they sprinted toward the melee.

Chapter Twenty-Seven

In late afternoon, the Frost Fair caravan of a half dozen carriages traveled single file over snow-packed roads as the sun dipped its weary face behind the winter-gray clouds. Inside the last carriage, Madeline retrieved her sketchpad as Elizabeth slept, then glanced out the carriage window toward the rolling countryside. Snow flurries swirled in the crisp air like bits of lace against the shadows of the approaching woods. Normally, a scene like the one she beheld provided endless inspiration. But the only image she wanted to sketch was the duke's.

She could not stop thinking of him. The way his eyes deepened in shade when he glanced in her direction. Or the breadth of his shoulders, or the strength of his hand when he held hers. She gasped, feeling her face warm, remembering when his body had fallen on hers when they fought the assailant in his room. The incident was brief, and an accident. At the time, she had pushed against him, and he had rolled away. What if she hadn't? Would he have touched her if she hadn't pushed him away? Kissed her?

She leaned out the window to cool her skin.

A few miles back, they had stopped for a light meal and to rest the horses. She had hoped to talk with the duke, but no one had seen him since the caravan left the castle. The consensus was that he and Lord Dumont were retrieving a packhorse that had run away.

Her disappointment was profound. She had regretted their conversation during their last encounter. She had meant to rebuke him over his misguided opinion of what was an acceptable subject for women to paint. Although she had not changed her mind regarding the rebuke, she conceded that her tone had been inappropriate.

Her mother had impressed upon her that Englishmen were creatures of tradition, the chief of which pertained to a woman's role in society. She should have used a gentler touch when expressing her views. But the thought of an apology rose like bile in her throat.

The carriage bumped over something in the road as they entered the winding forest road, jostling her and breaking her hold on her sketchpad.

"Bollocks," she said under her breath, reaching beyond Elizabeth for her fallen sketchpad. "I will not apologize to the insufferable man. This is no longer the Middle Ages. The duke should realize that women have a right to their own opinions."

Elizabeth yawned. "Did you say something? Have we arrived at the inn?"

Madeline helped Elizabeth replace the blanket covering her lap. "I was merely muttering to myself. We still have a distance to travel. Go back to sleep if you wish."

"A good idea," Elizabeth said, pulling the blanket over her shoulders.

Madeline watched the sleeping Elizabeth. Had she overheard Madeline's outburst? It did not appear so, but she must be more cautious. Elizabeth was not as she seemed, and although that pleased Madeline, it also meant the lady was skilled at ferreting out a person's secrets. Madeline had learned in her short stay at Conclarton Castle that if a woman was too bold, she entertained undue attention.

When Elizabeth mentioned she had a story to tell, Madeline never dreamed it involved intrigue and spies. Moreover, she had been delighted beyond measure that the lady's engagement to the duke was a ruse, created to fool Devonshire into thinking his plan to take control of Conclarton Castle remained secure.

Elizabeth believed Devonshire would fail. Madeline wasn't as sure and wished her mother was along to consult. Her mother had a gift for dividing difficult problems into manageable sections and sniffing out the truth as well as a solution. A skill her mother had said she had learned the hard way.

Madeline had witnessed her mother's gift in action, when they had learned that a man by the name of Hunter O'Shea planned to purchase a vacant building across the street from Feathers.

Her mother did not trust the smooth-talking Mr. O'Shea and had researched his background, learned the sort of rough clientele he attracted, and that he planned to build a rival brothel and saloon. Her mother purchased the property herself and turned it into a respectable hotel and restaurant, successfully derailing O'Shea's plans. The man had left town, but her mother had said he was like a bad penny and might return one day to even the score.

Elizabeth stretched. "Oh, my. I must have fallen asleep again. I fear I have been terrible company. You must have been bored to tears."

"Not at all. I have my drawings and the view of the countryside. You also gave me much to ponder."

Elizabeth folded the blanket and set it aside as she glanced out the window. "We have fallen behind the caravan. I cannot see the other carriages. I will ask the driver." She pounded on the ceiling of the carriage to get the driver's attention.

After a few minutes, the driver, a thickset man with a pockmarked face, leaned down from the driver's bench. "Yes, milady. Do you wish me to stop the carriage?"

"No, that will not be necessary. I would like to know why we lag behind the caravan. We can no longer see the other carriages."

"I was instructed to use another route, milady as there were complaints from one of the lords in the area that our caravan was destroying his roads. I was assured that this road leads to the inn where we plan to meet the others. But if you prefer, I can turn around."

"That will not be necessary and will delay our journey. The hour grows late, and I know I speak for Miss Mercer when I say we are anxious to arrive at our destination. Carry on."

The driver touched his hand to his hat in agreement and respect and resumed his position.

Elizabeth settled against the tufted seat. "What a bother. Oh, well. Cannot be helped, I suppose. I hope I haven't frightened you with all my chatter of spies and what not. Robert would be furious if he knew I told you about Devonshire. But I thought about it and knew it was the right thing to do. Because of how you bravely prevented Devonshire from carrying out his plan to kill Robert, you might be in danger. Forewarned is forearmed, as they say."

"An expression my mother also believes. Honestly,

I am glad you told me. Besides, the duke, who else knows about Devonshire?"

"In the beginning, the circle of knowledge was small, and I dare not reveal their identities. But be assured that thanks to the information you overheard between Devonshire and the footman, a plan has been devised to capture Devonshire. Jeremy and the duke have used the Frost Fair as a diversion. They join a contingency of the military in the castle's village, where they expect to capture Devonshire and his cohorts. That said, there are many hidey holes in the castle where the servants might listen in on conversations and potentially warn Devonshire. The duke and I did not want to believe that any of his servants might alert Devonshire, but nothing is certain. After all, one of the duke's own footmen was working with Devonshire."

Madeline nodded, bracing against the sides inside the carriage as it rumbled over a rut in the road. Elizabeth's words were a reminder. Had the servants also overheard conversations between her and her mother? The thought was unsettling. They must be more careful in the future.

"Hopefully, he is the only one who betrayed the duke. My mother is a firm believer that the greatest source of information is gleaned from befriending the servants in a household such as the one at Conclarton Castle. If you want to know a person's secrets, you ask a servant. She also believes that knowledge is the true measure of a person's worth. Perhaps we should find a way to question those at the castle without alerting them to our purpose. We might discover who else is working with Devonshire."

"An excellent idea. I will send word to someone I

trust at the castle. Your mother sounds like a truly amazing woman. Mine was a lot like yours and the duchess. My mother chafed at the rules that confined her and believed all women should have a voice in Parliament. There were a few incidents where women who were landowners were allowed to vote in government elections, but she worried that would be taken away. She told me she wanted a strong daughter, and she went against my father's wishes, naming me after the great Queen Elizabeth." She narrowed her gaze. "He wanted me named after his mother, Gertrude, a truly milk-toast of a woman."

Madeline laughed. "I am glad your mother prevailed. We were both fortunate. I would love to meet your mother."

Her brow deepened into a frown. "She died twenty-one years ago, giving birth to my brother, and I miss her still." Elizabeth leaned forward. "Enough of all that. What I long to learn is more about your country. Robert told me you attended university in America. How extraordinary."

"I am surprised he mentioned it," Madeline said, caught by surprise. "The duke seemed to disapprove."

Elizabeth smiled. "Robert fights a battle between two worlds. The world he was born into and the world he wishes to inhabit. Give him time!" She winked. "Tell me more of America."

Madeline's thoughts chased round and round. Was the duke more open to change than she had thought? And why did that idea please her so much?

"You are deep in thought," Elizabeth said. "Thinking of the duke?"

Madeline's breath quickened. Elizabeth was

uncanny, as though she could read her mind. "Collecting my thoughts, is all," she lied, turning back to Elizabeth's question. "In America, women are allowed more freedom and, in certain circumstances, encouraged to seek out their own endeavors. Because of her business, my mother was able to help women who were interested in seeking to educate themselves or better their lives."

Elizabeth eyed Madeline like a butterfly trapped under glass. "America sounds like a wondrous place of opportunity." She paused. "And new beginnings."

Madeline fidgeted with a loose thread on the cuff of her sleeve as she glanced out the window at the tranquil forest. Instead of offering peace, the quiet was unsettling. It was as though all the woodland creatures had fled when they witnessed the Frost Fair Caravan invading their forest. She breathed deeply, trying to dispel her own sense of foreboding. She wasn't as calm regarding the revelation of Devonshire as she had claimed.

"Yes, new beginnings are indeed something America aspires to as a goal for those who call it their home."

Elizabeth gazed out the window as Madeline had moments before. "I envy you your life in America. Men like my father would never have approved my attending university. He does not believe women have the intellect capable of grasping complex issues, beyond bearing children, doing needlework, and hosting parties."

"I am so sorry. I think my mother would have gone mad if she had been confined to those tasks with no other ways to occupy her time."

"Your mother was fortunate. Most women have little choice in how they live out their lives. Robert mentioned that she married a wealthy railroad tycoon, who died leaving her a wealthy widow. Few women in her position would feel the need to do more than garden or host parties. What is your mother's type of business?"

Madeline felt her blood run cold. Elizabeth had been easy to talk to and had taken Madeline into her confidence regarding Devonshire, adding that their mothers were both rebellious in their own ways as well as recognizing Madeline's growing attraction to the duke. Those revelations and confidences had lulled Madeline into a false sense of shared comradery. and she had let down her guard. Elizabeth was a product of her British culture, the daughter of an earl, and therefore would not approve of Madeline's deception nor her mother's occupation.

Madeline glanced out the window of the carriage to regain her composure as she slipped the mask of deception back into place. Trees, dusted with snow, slid past in shades of forest green and pristine white. "The carriage has slowed."

Elizabeth followed Madeline's gaze. "Understandable, given the state of the roads."

Elizabeth had also been gazing out the window but now brought her attention back to Madeline. "I notice you have not developed the art of deception. Some might question, let us say, that the disparities in your mother's story might invite unwanted scrutiny. There is a similarity between playing cards and the game of life. In each, a person must learn to keep hidden the value and secrets of their hand. Your expression gives you away, I fear. You and your mother are hiding something. It has been observed that your mother's mannerisms are more closely aligned to those of someone of noble breeding and birth than of a daughter of America as she claims."

Elizabeth reached over to take Madeline's hands in hers. "No, do not despair. We are friends. Please do not disagree, for I have declared it so. You are entitled to your secrets. My mother had hers. I have mine, and I believe the duchess has some as well. As women we must protect each other. I say this to you as a warning."

Elizabeth settled back against the seat. "Now for more interesting topics. Is it true that in America you are in constant danger of attack?"

Madeline cleared her throat, taking a shallow breath to calm her frayed nerves. She seized on the opportunity Elizabeth had provided to change the topic, relieved for a subject on safer ground.

She sat up straighter. "In America, lawlessness is common in the territories out west that have yet to join the union and become states. But my mother and I live in Boston, Massachusetts, and it is most civilized, not unlike your London."

"And the men—is it true they lack manners and are as handsome as sin?"

Elizabeth's remark caught Madeline off guard. When she recovered, she burst out laughing. "Handsome and dangerous. Your English rakes are like tamed domesticated animals in comparison."

Elizabeth clapped, her smile transforming her face into a very wicked glow. "I knew it. How do I get one of my own?"

A spark of light, followed by a gunshot, shattered the tranquility of the forest.

Chapter Twenty-Eight

The driver of the carriage screamed and fell, crashing into the underbrush. Frightened, the horses cried out in protest. Unfettered from the control the driver had held on the reins, the animals leapt forward, sending Madeline and Elizabeth careening against the inner walls of their carriage. The speed increased as each second passed, rocking the carriage precariously from side to side.

Madeline braced her hands on either side of the carriage, Elizabeth did the same, and the horses raced through the forest out of control as the sun set, deepening the shadows.

Tree branches scraped against the carriage as it rounded a sharp turn in the road, tilting dangerously to the side before righting itself.

"We are under attack! How could this have happened?" Elizabeth shouted, her face pale with fear. "Robert hired outriders to protect us against highwaymen."

Madeline had been thinking the same thing. When they started their journey this morning, she had noted the number of men the duke had hired to protect the caravan and believed it excessive. After all, she had mused, she had seen nothing of the dangers she had heard about from her fellow travelers on the ship she and her mother had taken from New York to London.

According to their accounts, she could well understand the necessity in parts of London for protection, but not in the serene countryside. In London, they had spoken of overcrowding and unsanitary conditions, areas where crime was uncontrolled and families lived on rat-infested streets. They talked about places like Covent Garden and St. Giles Rookeries as being the worst of the worst, where if a visitor, new to London, ventured in, they might never find their way out.

But not here. Not in the countryside of serene and protected estates owned by landed gentry. Here she had felt safe…until now.

"Wait," Madeline said as a chilling thought occurred to her. "When was the last time you remember seeing the outriders?"

Elizabeth's attention snapped toward Madeline. "When we stopped for a meal this afternoon. I did not think anything of it until now. I suppose I assumed they were behind us. And then when our driver told us he had taken another route…"

"You did not see them, did you?"

Elizabeth shook her head slowly. "I did not."

"Which means we are unprotected and in real danger. What could the men want who shot the driver?"

"To rob us…or worse." Elizabeth's eyes opened as wide as saucers. "We should jump."

Madeline stole a glance out the window to try and calm down before panic gained a foothold. She must think clearly. The forest sped past in a blur. A person consumed with fear lacked the ability to survive—another of her mother's many lessons. This was not the time to panic. This was the time for clear thinking.

"Jumping is a possibility," Madeline shouted back

over the constant clatter of the wheels as they churned over uneven ground. "But we're the last carriage and the others are too far away to know what happened to us. By the time they realize we are not behind them, it will be too late."

Elizabeth's chin trembled as she gave a quick nod, understanding their predicament. If they jumped, there were no guarantees they would survive the fall. If by some miracle they did survive and hadn't broken every bone in their body, they were alone. Alone in the woods, with it growing darker by the minute. The snow had increased and the temperature was dropping. Prime hunting time for four-legged animals or whoever had attacked their driver.

But they must gain control of the carriage.

Madeline saw that as their only chance. At the speed the carriage traveled, it would not take long for it to turn over or crash against a tree. None of which bode well for their survival.

They had only one option. They had to take control of the carriage.

"Please assist me out of my clothes." Madeline said, trying to reach the drawstrings on the back of her dress as she turned around. "If I can reach the driver's seat, and by some miracle the reins are there, I might be able to take control of the team of horses."

Voicing her plan out loud appeared to soften the fear-lines around Elizabeth's eyes. It had the opposite effect on Madeline.

The list of things that could go wrong was endless. Even if she managed to reach the driver's seat, and even if the reins were there, controlling a team of four frightened horses seemed daunting.

The carriage rocked back and forth as Elizabeth fumbled with the drawstrings on Madeline's dress. "You are mad. We should jump."

"Whoever killed the driver is still out there. I'd rather we take our chances and try to outrun him in this carriage than on foot. And if we jump, there is a high probability that either one of us could break our legs, and then where would we be?"

"At the mercy of the men responsible for killing our driver," Elizabeth said with a catch in her throat. She shuddered, her fingers pausing for a brief moment before resuming her task of loosening the ties on Madeline's dress. "Promise me you will be careful. Have you done this before?"

"I saw someone do it once."

"That is not the same thing."

"No, it is not," Madeline admitted with a flat tone. She refused to dwell on what would happen if she failed. It was true she had seen someone stop a runaway coach. But the coach hadn't been going as fast as theirs, and it was a team of two, not a team of four. Plus, the man was big, burly, and as strong as an ox.

Madeline shuddered, as Elizabeth had moments before. Cold air brushed against her skin as Elizabeth finished unlacing Madeline's dress and helped her remove it, rendering Madeline dressed only in her chemise. Her fingers trembled as she drew the back hem of the chemise between her legs and secured it in place with her ribbon belt.

Elizabeth was correct. Madeline was mad to attempt this.

"If I don't make it…"

Elizabeth pulled Madeline into a tight hug. "You

will make it."

Madeline nodded. "But if I do not," she repeated, "strap yourself to the seats in any manner possible. If the coach crashes, that might help you survive."

Madeline eased the door open. Icy wind and snow pushed inside the carriage as though trying to prevent her from leaving. Teeth chattering, she fought against the rising panic and cold and wrapped her arm around the open window's frame. She took a deep fortifying breath and prayed for courage.

With her free hand, she reached for one of the head irons that crisscrossed the side of the carriage. If she could reach the coach's step and pull herself up to the bench seat, she had a chance.

The carriage careered around a corner and hit a bump in the road. She lost her grip on the head iron as the door swung open, but she kept her hold on the window sash with one arm, her legs swinging free. Her body slammed against the side of the carriage. Pain exploded across her back as she grabbed the window frame with her other hand.

Elizabeth screamed and reached for Madeline, trying to pull her back into the carriage, but she was too far away to reach.

Hooves thundered over the road as a man raced toward her. Consumed by the shadows of the forest, his face was obscured under a tall hat pulled low over his forehead. The man's dark greatcoat billowed behind him like the wings of a predatory bird.

"Highwayman." The dreaded word tumbled over her lips. Fear spiked through her as she tried to retain her hold on the window frame.

The road narrowed and the highwayman was forced

to drop behind the coach.

Madeline did not want to consider what would happen if he overtook the carriage. It became imperative that she gain control. She gathered her waning strength and, with great effort, forced her cold hands to grip tighter on the window's frame. She struggled to find a foothold on the side of the carriage. After a number of failed attempts, she succeeded, and pulled herself onto the driver's bench.

Her fingers numb from the cold, she searched for the reins as the falling snow turned to icy rain. Between the rain and the lack of light, she had to resort to touch. She felt her way along the driver's bench and the floor to no avail. The reins must have dropped when the driver was killed. She fought her growing sense of dread.

The carriage buckled, tilted, and sent her sliding... Arms churning, she reached out and grabbed the seat iron and held on for dear life. Breathing heavily, she waited until the carriage righted itself, then pulled herself onto the floor of the driver's seat.

Pulse racing, she felt defeated. With the reins gone, she was at a loss what to do next. She had heard of men jumping onto the backs of a racing team of horses to grab the reins of the lead horse. Those stories had mixed results. Most of the riders were thrown, or trampled under the horse's hooves.

But she had to try. She took a deep breath and shook away her fear.

"Stay where you are," she heard a familiar man's voice shout.

Her heart soared even as she fought against false hope. The voice sounded like the duke's, but what if it wasn't? What if fear clouded her memory?

The road widened, and the man she had thought was a highwayman surged forward, racing past her toward the lead horse. His profile confirmed it was the duke. A sob of relief escaped. He had found her.

She pressed her hand against her lips to stifle another sob as a new fear clutched her heart. He might die trying to stop the runaway carriage.

Keeping pace with the team of horses, he leaned over and jumped onto the back of the lead horse, losing his hat in the process. He rode low over the horse's head as though speaking to the animal.

Moments dragged. Was it her imagination that the carriage had slowed?

A few more minutes passed, and the carriage rolled to a stop.

When the carriage was fully stopped, the duke jumped from the back of the lead horse, securing it to a tree with rope.

He rushed toward her. "What were you trying to do? Get yourself killed?"

The anger in his voice caught her off guard, evaporating the relief that this was the duke and not a highwayman. "Yes, as a matter of fact, that was exactly my purpose," she shot back.

His expression eased as the edges of his mouth curled, and he climbed onboard. "I would expect no less," he said gathering her in his arms.

Her limbs trembling, she leaned into the safety of his embrace. "I thought…I thought I would…"

"You are safe." He held her longer than he should, longer than was proper. She didn't care. She clung to him until the trembling ended and a new, unexpected sensation took its place. Desire. Passion.

He cupped her face in his hands and lowered his lips to hers. Warmly and tenderly he whispered, "You take my breath away."

She smiled against his lips. "Then you weren't really angry with me?"

"I was furious. Furious that you were in danger. Furious with myself that you were unprotected and that I was not here to save you."

"I am perfectly capable of saving myself, Your Grace."

He kissed her eyelids in turn, sending a surge of heat through her blood that threatened to ignite her in flames. She gasped, and as she did, he captured her mouth, deepened the kiss, and pulled her against him.

The world slipped away. Gone was her fear, vanquished by the touch of his hand on the small of her back and the way it moved to cup her breast. She gasped again. Her skin was on fire. She threaded her hands through his hair and pressed against him, wanting him closer.

He moaned, drew away, resting his forehead against hers. "We cannot," he said, his voice deep with passion. He opened his eyes, mirroring her own desire. They raked over her as his eyes grew wider.

"What are you wearing" he said, his breath labored as his expression heated. "My God! You are beauty itself."

She followed his gaze. Her chemise clung to her skin as transparent as the air she breathed. It molded against her body, leaving nothing to the imagination. It formed around her breasts as her nipples, pink and hard pressed against the fabric, as though aching for a man's touch.

He took in a ragged breath, removed his greatcoat, and spun it around her shoulders, pulling it around to cover her. "We must stop. Help me stop.

She lifted her gaze, drank in the desire reflected in his eyes that matched her own. He was correct. Her breathing, as ragged as his, took time to quiet. She nodded, took in a shallow breath of air and nodded again as her eyes misted. "I thought I was going to die, and then I saw you."

He wiped away a tear before it fell over her skin, and his lips parted as he kissed her forehead. "And yet you still bravely tried to avert the crash of a runaway carriage."

She held her hands laced in her lap, tearing her gaze from his lips and from the need to know how they would feel caressing her bare skin. "Someone killed our driver," she sniffled.

His expression darkened, glancing toward the forest as though searching for something or someone. "We cannot stay here. I heard the shot. I had gone to the caravan and heard that your carriage had taken another route. I was not sure I would reach you in time." He lifted her chin. "If something had happened to you…"

"It did not."

"But if it had? Madeline…"

A thumping sound came from inside the carriage.

He lifted his eyebrow. "Elizabeth?"

Madeline smiled with a nod. "She will not be pleased that we waited so long to free her."

He leaned down, brushing his lips against hers. "Elizabeth will have to wait a moment longer."

Chapter Twenty-Nine

Horses' hooves thundered over the snow-packed road, their riders emerging from the ink-black night like avenging angels.

Madeline shuddered, sinking deeper into his embrace. "Who…who is coming?"

Robert heard the fear in her voice and smoothed the hair from her forehead. "Jeremy," he said simply, and felt her take in a deep breath as she relaxed against him. He thought of her now as Madeline. Calling her Miss Mercer would not do. Too much had transpired between them. And yet, propriety dictated that he ask for her permission.

Pondering why he felt so conflicted, he kept her locked in his arms as Jeremy and a contingent of men surrounded the halted carriage.

As Jeremy approached, he cast a glance toward Robert, taking in that he held Madeline. For a brief moment, the shadow of a smile drifted over his mouth, evidence that he had indeed witnessed Robert and Madeline together.

He cleared his throat. "We found the body of the driver. I sent men to track down the shooter. We suspect Devonshire. Why would he kill the driver? He would know that would cause the carriage to run out of control, killing those inside."

"Revenge," Robert said simply, feeling Madeline

shiver again. "Have the men escort Madeline, er, Miss Mercer to the inn. I'll help you track down Devonshire."

"I am unharmed," Elizabeth said in an agitated tone. She stood framed in the carriage doorway. Her hair had come loose from its pins and cascaded past her shoulders in a wild display, as though tossed by the wind. Her dress and coat were torn and her face red with outrage. "Would someone help me down from this carriage from hell, or am I to manage it myself?"

"I will help you, milady," a man with an American accent said, as he jumped from his horse and strode toward her, holding out his hand.

"Who are you?"

"No one of consequence," he said with a broad grin.

"Elizabeth," Robert said as he jumped from the driver's bench and held out his arms to help Madeline. "You should thank me as well for saving your life."

Elizabeth huffed. "Madeline and I were doing just fine, thank you very much." She spared the American a glance, then pulling her torn coat around her, she marched toward Madeline. She looped her arm through Madeline's and drew her back toward the carriage. "Madeline had things well in hand. I am confident she would have been able to stop the horses. She is an extraordinary woman."

"Thank you, Elizabeth, but I feel as though the carriage would have crashed if not for the duke's help."

"Do not give the man so much credit. Look at him. Like so many of his gender, he is already puffed up with his own importance like a Christmas peacock, cooked and stuffed and ready for the table. If not for you and your clear thinking, we would have panicked and jumped, likely to our deaths. No, I credit you for saving our lives."

The American who had helped Elizabeth from the carriage touched his hat and gave a slight bow. "You do not have a high opinion of men, it seems."

"And why should I, when they have such a high opinion of themselves? If I added to the praise, their heads would be so large with pride, I daresay they could not carry such a weight."

Robert smiled inwardly at the exchange. Their argument held a light flirtatiousness about it. The American seemed smitten, and Elizabeth kept glancing in the man's direction as though assessing him from head to toe. He prayed his suspicions were correct. He wanted Elizabeth to find happiness.

"Surprisingly, the carriage is in working order," Robert said. "Do you know why the driver veered off the assigned route?"

Elizabeth shivered, blowing on her hands to warm them. "Our driver said that there were complaints from one of the lords in the area that our caravan was destroying his roads."

"A more likely scenario," Robert said, "was that the driver was working with Devonshire and Devonshire killed him to eliminate loose ends. I will act as your driver and my men will accompany us to the Rose and Thistle Inn."

Robert exchanged a glance toward Jeremy. Jeremy nodded, confirming that the men Robert had ordered were in place to track down Devonshire and guard the Rose and Thistle Inn. Devonshire was many things, but he was not a fool. Most likely, he was on the run.

Chapter Thirty

Later that evening, Madeline set her sketches on the carriage seat as the Rose and Thistle posting inn came into view. Elizabeth had accompanied Madeline but had dozed on and off during much of their journey, as had Madeline.

Lights shone from the windows of a stately, ivy-covered, four-story stone building that looked as wide as it was tall. The other carriages had arrived earlier, and from the sounds of laughter and music pouring from the inn, the merriment had started without them.

After the duke had stopped the runaway carriage and swept Madeline into a dream world of passion, Elizabeth had feigned outrage at seeing the duke and Madeline embracing, then laughed with the comment, "Well it is about time."

Elizabeth then ushered Madeline into the carriage and helped her change back into her traveling dress. As the duke drove them to the inn, Elizbeth showered Madeline with questions, the primary one being whether or not the duke had offered marriage.

Madeline had brushed the comment aside and changed the subject. But the question lingered to torment her. Why hadn't he offered marriage? And if he had, would she have said yes? It would please her mother if she were to marry the duke.

To distract her from her thoughts, she had sketched

the image of the driver who had been murdered. She knew it was possible that the man was working with Devonshire but perhaps the driver felt he didn't have a choice. She tried to capture the shock and fear in his eyes as he fell to the ground and disappeared from view as the carriage raced out of control.

Did the driver have loved ones who would mourn his passing? Did he have regrets? She wanted to honor his passing and had also sketched his likeness before he had been killed. She admitted she had not given the man much thought before. He was just someone who drove their carriage. She should have paid more attention to him, learned his name, and asked if he had a family. If he did, she planned to give them the sketch of him as he was in life.

Her mother had taken care to get to know everyone she met. Her mother said the servants in Conclarton Castle confided in her because they liked to gossip. That wasn't the reason. They confided in her because she took an interest in them and their families and they trusted her. Madeline examined the sketch she had started and vowed to be more like her mother. She would start with learning the man's name and if he had a family.

She glanced out the window as the carriage slowed, and her thoughts turned inevitably toward the duke.

There was little doubt she had feelings for the man. But marriage? Was that something she even wanted? Since arriving in England, she had been flooded with how a woman was ruled by the whims of her husband. He could dictate the parameters of her education, her activities, and approve or disapprove her friends. In America, she had experienced more freedom. Could she give that up?

She shook away the dark thoughts when Elizabeth nudged her, asking if something was wrong.

"A little tired is all. By any chance did you know the name of our driver?" When Elizabeth shook her head, Madeine replied, "No matter." She looked outside the carriage window again. "I wasn't expecting something this grand," Madeline said, remembering the one-story inns she and her mother had stayed in when they traveled from Boston to New York. The roofs in those inns had leaked and the walls looked as though they would collapse in a stiff wind.

"Robert assured me the Rose and Thistle is one of the finest posting inns along this route to London," Elizabeth said. "Speaking of the duke, here he is now."

The duke opened the carriage door and held out his hand. "The footmen are in short supply," he said while holding Madeline's gaze. "Might I be of assistance to you ladies?"

Elizabeth smothered a smile, speaking in a hushed tone. "I have never seen the duke this smitten before. It helps me believe in love again." With those parting words, she moved from her seat across from Madeline and reached for the duke's hand as he helped her from the carriage. Once settled on the ground, she turned toward Madeline with a wink. "I am off to choose a room and then join the others in the main room of the inn. I am famished. Madeline, it has been a pleasure." She inclined her head toward the duke. "Your Grace," she said, in parting.

The duke nodded farewell to Elizabeth and lifted his hand toward Madeline. "Would you do me the honor?"

In the torch lights of the inn, she noticed for the first time the state of his attire. His clothes were splattered with mud, his sleeve and jacket torn, and he had removed or lost his cravat. But his lack of attention to his appearance was not what concerned her. When he had raced to stop the carriage, and in the moments following, she had not noticed the state of his attire. She had not noticed blood on his clothes, but that did not mean he might not have sustained injuries.

"Were you injured when you stopped the carriage? If I had known, I would have tended your wounds."

"A few cuts and scrapes. If I had sustained serious injury, I would have happily welcomed your attention. These injuries were the result of my encounter with Devonshire, however. My cousin had more men with him than expected. He escaped, and we feared he might have headed in this direction. The attack on your carriage might have been related to Devonshire, but we cannot be sure. We sent soldiers in search of him. I regret we did not arrive before he killed poor Mr. Tinker. He was a good man and must have been forced to work for Devonshire."

The duke's comment confirmed what Madeline had thought about the driver. "You knew the driver's name," she said.

"I make it a point of knowing everyone in my employ, especially those who watch over those in my care." He paused. "You have not taken my hand."

So preoccupied with worry, she had forgotten she was still perched on the bench seat in the carriage. She glanced at his bare hand. He had also misplaced his gloves, and his knuckles were bloodied and bruised. "You fought with Devonshire."

"He and others."

She lifted her gaze. "How do the other men look?"

He laughed, a full-throated laugh that sounded like a blessed release. "Arrested and in a sorry state. Only Devonshire and a handful of his men escaped. Most women would comment on my inappropriate attire, not wonder at the state of the men I fought."

"I am not most women."

"Of that I am very aware. You still haven't taken my hand."

She cocked her head, reliving the feel of his arms and his kisses. The warmth of his embrace chased away fear and doubt and the near-death experience of her runaway carriage. She felt safe and secure with him and confident that he felt as deeply for her as she did for him. But then the doubts rolled back into her thoughts to torment her.

Were these doubts normal for a woman in love? Her mother had been betrayed by the man she loved, and had said she had been young and foolish and was certain Madeline would not make the same mistake. But the image of her mother as a single mother, alone with a child to raise, had been forever imprinted on her thoughts. She must not make the same mistake her mother had. She must guard her heart and her virtue with equal ferocity.

Was the reason he had not offered marriage because he considered her a plaything, a distraction? Was he like the others of his class, wanting both money and a title, and a woman he could control?

"May I be of assistance," the duke said, again offering his hand to help her from the carriage.

She nodded and fumbled to retrieve her sketches that had gotten scattered over the bench seat inside the carriage. A few of them fluttered to the ground as she stepped down.

The duke bent to pick them up. "These sketches are of the driver, Mr. Tinker. The ones of him before he was killed are a very good likeness. Those of him when he was shot, however, are a most inappropriate subject for a lady to draw."

She bristled, feeling the skin on the back of her neck prickle. She remembered the argument she had had with him at Conclarton Castle over a woman's right to paint the subjects she desired without a man's censure, and her blood heated. "And what would be deemed an acceptable subject for a woman? Your Grace." She said the last words with clenched teeth.

His eyebrows knitted together. "You must admit that women, by nature, are gentle creatures, and it is a man's charge to protect them from the cruelties life offers. It was unfortunate you were forced to witness Mr. Tinker's murder. But by painting his demise, you dwell on matters that can only cause you pain, and women are unsuited to deal with such things."

"What I admit is that I was mistaken about you." She snatched the sketches he had retrieved from the ground and marched toward the inn's entrance. Standing at the entrance was Lord Dumont, with a broad grin.

"Well, done," he said to Madeline as she approached. He offered her his arm. "You have done the impossible and rendered the duke speechless."

"That man vexes me like no other I have ever met."

"Robert is one of a kind and has that effect," Lord Dumont said as they entered the inn. "We are in luck. The Earl of Greyson has arrived and has saved us a table."

Madeline took in the Earl of Greyson. Her mother

would describe him as fashionable and well mannered. He stood as though at attention, waiting for her and Lord Dumont to join him. She did not know what his game was, but courting her was not the goal. She suspected that, like so many of the other men vying for her attention, it was the size of her dowry which drew pretty words and false smiles, not an affection for her. She was so very weary of this game. Once she married, she would be subject to her husband's whims, in return for security. Was security worth her freedom to choose her own path?

She had a possible glimpse of how that would look when the duke had expressed his disapproval of her sketches, and she did not like it one bit.

Music laced with the clatter of utensils and plates. The hum of conversation joined the smells of rich beef soups and baking bread. She inhaled, using the sight of a crowded inn with the inviting aromas to calm her breathing. Speaking with the duke was frustrating.

Lord Dumont patted the hand she had draped over his arm. "We must not lose sight of our goal to find you a husband. Two candidates, Lord Walford and Lord Kenmare, confided their interest in you and plan to join us at the Frost Fair. The duke's younger brother, William, has also joined us at the inn."

"Lord William Oswyn is not interested in me," Madeline said. "We are friends. He is in love with the governess, and she with him. I will not stand in their way."

"Commendable, but I doubt the duchess would approve of William marrying a commoner. I know when the old duke was alive he was vehement that all of his children marry people of impeccable lineage."

"Then changing her mind will be our goal."

Lord Dumont laughed. "First you arrange a romantic rendezvous between Winfield and your mother, although it came to naught. Next you set your sights on matchmaking William and the governess. I would suggest you help my poor brother, Trent, find his heart's desire. But you must take care that you do not forget your own happiness."

"My mother has often said much the same. But have you noticed there is less risk in helping others find their soulmates than in seeking our own?"

As Madeline and Lord Dumont approached, Lord Greyson rose from the table and gave a slight bow of greeting.

She acknowledged Lord Greyson with a smile. "It was kind of you to save a table for us."

"It was my pleasure," he said with another bow. "Might I fetch refreshments? A hot chocolate, perhaps?"

"That sounds wonderful," she said. "And welcome."

He hesitated a moment longer. "Would you do me the honor of the next set?"

She nodded a yes, as he smiled again and disappeared, presumably to procure hot chocolate.

"You have made a conquest, Miss Mercer. The duke approaches."

The duke bowed toward Madeline. "Miss Mercer. A private word. It is most urgent." He offered his hand as though she had no choice in the matter. "I would like a dance, to apologize."

"I thought you disapproved of dancing."

"You are mistaken. I disapprove of your dancing with anyone but myself."

He was trying to flirt with her, but she was in no mood for light banter. "You mentioned an apology."

He dropped his hand to his side and moved closer. "My words twist and turn in your presence and spill out in a jumble. I did not mean to offend when I commented on the subject you had chosen for your sketch. I merely offered a suggestion."

"You said my sketches were inappropriate for a woman."

"And so they are. You must agree that the sketch of the driver in the violent throes of death was a gruesome topic for a lady."

"But if a man had sketched or painted the driver, that would have been a different matter?"

"But of course."

She narrowed her gaze. "If you will excuse me, Lord Greyson has requested the next dance."

Chapter Thirty-One

Robert paced in front of the fire in the great hall of the inn as he watched Madeline dance with the peacock, Lord Greyson. The man was not worthy to breathe the same air as Miss Mercer. Yet she smiled at him as though he were a lord of the realm.

"Will you please stop pacing, Your Grace," Elizabeth said, sipping her hot chocolate. "You will wear a path in the floor."

"I am restless."

"You are jealous," she corrected. "You should ask Miss Mercer to dance."

"She refused me."

Elizabeth's eyes shone with merriment as she gazed at Robert over the rim of her cup. "Well done, Madeline. Perhaps she is angry with you."

He paused from watching Madeline. "Why would she be angry with me? I saved you both from death when I stopped the runaway carriage."

"Men. We do love you, but there are times when the word 'vexing' is not a strong enough description. You and Madeline were caught in a compromised position, yet you did not offer marriage. She brushed my question away when I asked if you had, but I could see the hurt in her eyes."

"The world believes you and I are engaged. It would not be seemly."

"You kissed her, sir, and she is aware our engagement is a ruse, nothing more." She raised an eyebrow. "And you kissed her. Under the circumstances, I am surprised she talked to you at all."

Robert shut his eyes, nodding slowly. "No wonder she wouldn't dance with me. I will apologize. I hold Miss Mercer in the highest regard. She is everything I could ever hope for in a woman. I intend to offer for her hand at the Frost Fair."

"Do not be surprised if she says no. You were most critical of her sketches. If I were in her place, I would look at that as an indication that you would be the sort of man who would dictate her every thought."

"But you cannot approve of her topic. She sketched the driver, a Mr. Tinker. The poor man met an untimely death at, we suspect, Devonshire's hand. It was a gruesome image and not appropriate for a lady to draw."

"Yet the sketch was well drawn. She has talent. Do you not agree?"

"Decidedly so. With that I agree. That is not my objection."

"Madeline is not an adornment on a man's arm, nor a person who needs guidance. She is a woman with strength of character and intellect who will help the lucky man she chooses build a meaningful and happy life. You must apologize…and often."

Robert felt as though the floor had disappeared beneath his feet. He glanced toward Miss Mercer. She was dancing with another gentleman who had joined the swarm of men vying for her attention. She laughed at something the gentleman had said, but when she turned in Robert's direction, her expression froze, and she looked away.

"I will apologize. What did you call me?"

"A dunderhead. You must do more than apologize, if you wish to gain her good wishes once again. A grand gesture is in order." She paused to gaze at him and then sighed. "I wish you luck, but I must leave you. I grow weary and long for a good night's sleep. I have hired a carriage and driver to take me to my estate, and with my persuasion that nice American will act as our guard. Do not give me that frown. I have also hired the driver's wife to act as chaperone, so it cannot be said that I traveled unchaperoned. Good night, Robert, and do not forget my advice."

Robert gave a nod of farewell toward Elizabeth and reached for a tankard of ale from the barkeep before venturing outside. The noise in the inn was deafening, and the constant laughter sounded shrill to his ears. Crowds usually did not concern him. Tonight was the exception. He did not delude himself on the root cause. He had been truthful when he told Miss Mercer that he could not abide seeing her dance with other men. It went beyond annoyance, however. He was jealous.

"There you are," Jeremy said, joining him. "It is warmer inside."

"Too crowded for my taste."

"Yes, Miss Mercer is surrounded by suitors. What do you plan to do about it?"

"Elizabeth asked me much the same question. I need to change the subject. What have you learned?"

Jeremy handed Robert a man's silk cravat. "We believe this belonged to Devonshire. It bares his initials. We found it at what we think was the ambush site. Elizabeth mentioned that she had seen a flash of light and then heard the gunshot. We searched the route the carriage had taken and that is where we saw the silk cravat snagged on a branch. There are tracks that lead away from the ambush site in the direction of London, but we lost them when Devonshire crossed a stream. It's hard to know if London really was his destination. But what could be gained by murdering Elizabeth and Miss Mercer?"

"Revenge," Robert offered. "Or perhaps he meant to rob Elizabeth when the carriage crashed. Elizabeth is known for carrying her jewels."

"Devonshire has had a head start," Jeremy said. "How will we find him?"

"He needs money to pay for his passage. He is a viscount and lives as though the trees on his estate produce gold crowns instead of fruit. According to Elizabeth, he is in debt and is believed to be a thief. At the ball you and Molly hosted at your castle, I overheard that one of the ladies lost a diamond bracelet."

"It could have been a coincidence. Molly complains that the clasps on her jewelry are not as secure as she would like."

"Perhaps. I do not think the missing bracelet and Devonshire's presence at the event were a coincidence."

Jeremy shook his head. "You suspect Devonshire is a thief."

"I do, and if I am correct, I know where he has fled. The Frost Fair is the perfect hunting ground for a man with an unscrupulous character."

Chapter Thirty-Two

Robert and Jeremy reached the outskirts of the Frost Fair as dawn spread ribbons of pale rose pink across the horizon. It had been a grueling ride, but they had wanted to reach London early in the hope of capturing Devonshire before he boarded a ship. Robert believed his focus on catching Devonshire would distract him from thoughts of Madeline. That was not the case.

Elizabeth had been correct. He had been the worst sort of fool for criticizing Madeline's sketches. He considered himself a modern man, and yet he had made remarks such as his father and grandfather might have made. Elizabeth suggested he make a grand gesture of apology. He had an idea but could only hope it would be enough.

Robert reined in his horse as Jeremy dismounted to stretch. They had questioned travelers along the way and were heartened when they described a man fitting Devonshire's description heading in the direction of the city.

The view along the Thames River resembled a few of the landscape paintings in his mother's gallery in her Women's Room. The scene before him was not one of reality but of fantasy. The dawn's muted light hid the imperfections of the Frost Fair's temporary town hugging the shoreline of the Thames River and spilling out onto the frozen water.

The previous night's excesses had been swept away in anticipation of the new day. Hastily erected wooden buildings and vendor's tents were covered with frost and looked like strings of pearls. Music drifted on an icy breeze from farther down the shore, a sign the Frost Fair was awakening. Soon entertainers would emerge and shops would open. He understood the attraction. The Frost Fair was open to everyone, not just members of the privileged *ton*. People would mingle and let down their guard.

A fertile hunting ground for a thief of Devonshire's skills.

Memories of his cousin rolled through his thoughts as he tried to reconcile the teenage boy who had lived with them for a time after his father's death. Even then, Devonshire had seemed distant, and easily sent into a temper, but Robert and his brothers believed it understandable. Devonshire had never had siblings or close family relations to ease the grief of losing first his mother and then his father.

Could Robert and his family have done more to help Devonshire adjust to his new life? The answer was that of course they could have. But looking back with regret never changed the past. It could, however, reconcile the present.

Yet Devonshire had killed, not in self-defense or defending his family or country but to satisfy his greed for power and wealth.

Robert vowed he would not let his own rage over Devonshire's murder of his brother and father cloud his actions for revenge. Devonshire must be captured and face judgment for his crimes.

"Be on the watch," Robert said as Jeremy mounted

his horse. "Devonshire might not be working alone."

Jeremy nodded toward a grove of trees a short distance away, from which they could hear music. People already gathered, dancing to the music of a three-piece band.

"The celebrations start early," Jeremy said.

"I believe this is a continuation from last night. Come. Perhaps someone has seen Devonshire."

The people in the small group had, indeed, been celebrating all night, and although they had not seen anyone fitting Devonshire's appearance join them in their merriment, someone from their group suggested a tavern known for gambling.

Robert and Jeremy missed Devonshire at the tavern, but upon interviewing the owner, they learned that a customer believed her necklace had been stolen by a man fitting Devonshire's description. The incident had been reported, but Devonshire had not been found.

"I am surprised Devonshire has not left yet," Jeremy said, as they drew near the establishment that had been suggested by the owner of the last tavern they had visited. "Surely, he has the money he needs by now to pay his passage. He risks being discovered."

"Perhaps," Robert said as he dismounted. "But I do not believe it is only about the money. You and I have witnessed members of the *ton* wager sums of money in our clubs we knew they could not afford. I saw the same when I was in the military. For some, and I believe Devonshire is in that category, gambling and thievery is an addictive vice that is not easily quenched."

Robert opened the door to the tavern, ducking when a metal platter was thrown in his direction. It clattered against the far wall.

A fight had broken out in the compact tavern. A chair was smashed over one man's head, tables were overturned. A bald-headed man with a thick mustache shouted for everyone to stop. His words were ignored as the fight continued.

"Thief!" someone yelled.

"Cheat!" shouted another.

Robert nodded to the corner of the room where the shouting came from. It looked as though a card game had been in progress. Cards, coins, and jewelry were scattered over the table and chairs overturned. The men who had shouted joined others as they attacked Devonshire. Devonshire looked as though he were fighting for his life. Two men had him pinned to the ground while others pummeled his face and upper body.

"It appears Devonshire's sins have caught up with him," Jeremy said. "They will kill him if we don't stop them."

Robert knew what Jeremy suggested was true, but Robert did not want revenge. He wanted justice. He withdrew his father's pistol, pointed it to the ceiling, cocked the hammer, and fired.

Silence dropped over the tavern as the sulfur smell of smoke from the pistol filled the air.

"Stand aside," Robert said. "I am the Duke of Conclarton and am here to take this man to the authorities."

Chapter Thirty-Three

It was late afternoon and Madeline was once again inside the carriage, jostling over an uneven road as the caravan made its way toward London Bridge and the River Thames. She had dressed in her green brocade travel dress and matching coat, hoping to see the duke, only to be informed that he had left in the middle of the night with his friend Lord Dumont. Lady Montgomery had also bid everyone farewell, announcing publicly that she had ended her engagement with the duke and wanted nothing more than to return to her own estates.

As a result, Madeline had a carriage all to herself. She had time to work on her sketches, but they lay in her lap untouched. Normally, she was comfortable with her own thoughts. Today was not one of those days, and she knew it had everything to do with the duke.

She was still troubled by her exchange with Lord Conclarton, but her fury had taken another form. How could she have fallen in love with a man who couldn't respect the type of drawings she wished to sketch? But was she being unreasonable? They were just sketches, after all. Or was this part of a larger concern? Would he expand his objections to the type of clothes she wore, the friends she kept, the books she read? She had overheard such things were possible once a woman was under the control of her husband.

Her mother said that a person's core values and

opinions were difficult to alter once they had reached their majority. Her opinion was that, although change was possible, it was more a gentle rounding of the corners than a changing of the mind. In Robert's case, Madeline surmised, she would need a hammer and chisel.

Madeline should have heeded her mother's advice and set her cap for a gentleman for whom she wasn't attracted. If that were the case, she would be less likely to acquiesce to her husband's wishes if they conflicted with her own. But was that a realistic option? If a man did not compromise before marriage, there was little to support a view that he would do so afterward.

What she did know was that, if she wasn't careful, she was in danger of following in her mother's footsteps and getting her heart broken. She could not envision a life with him that didn't end in heartache.

She glanced out the carriage window. A coal-burning winter fog hung over London in a gray haze, reflecting her mood. Buildings rose through the gloom like giants, casting their shadow and power over the city. There was a steely, unbending class structure in England. The titled and powerful ruled. But if one of them lost their wealth or reputation, the *ton* was swift in its judgment and shunned those out of favor. Was that what had driven Devonshire to such horrific extremes to retain his wealth and privilege?

She could not feel sorry for him. There were those, including her mother, who had lost the approval of the *ton*, yet not only survived but thrived.

But even amongst this elite group, this crème de la crème of society, allowances were made if the weight of a person's purse was impressive enough. What was unclear was if the fickle mood of the *ton* would tolerate a person's background. Madeline could not escape hers. If she wanted a future with the duke, he must never learn her true identity.

If he did, and still offered marriage, would he risk being shunned by the *ton*? She suspected that he would not care a fig if he was ever invited to another ball, but he would worry about the marriage prospects of his brother and sisters. His brother might escape the worst of it, but in a few short years Sophia and Lydia would enter the marriage market and, if disgraced because of the duke's relationship with the daughter of a brothel owner, they might be considered unsuitable matches for the sons of marriage-minded mamas. His sisters had become dear to her, and she could not risk their future.

She must tell him the truth and end their involvement before it went further. She leaned her head against the carriage. But how could she? When she had learned that his engagement to Elizabeth had been nothing more than a pretense, in order to force Devonshire's hand, she had begun to hope. And when he had come to her rescue and she felt his arms around her and the touch of his breath against her skin, and heard his words of endearment, her hope had turned to the possibility of a happily-ever-after ending to her quest for a suitable husband.

She dismissed her mother's words of warning, which echoed in her thoughts, to guard her heart. After all, it was her mother who had engineered this charade. If she kept the truth from the duke, all would be well and his sisters' and brother's future secure. But was that something she wanted, a future based on a lie? She was conflicted, battling a war between right and wrong, truth and lies.

The fog cleared as her carriage neared the shore of the River Thames, but not the confusion as she battled with her conscience. A marriage built on the foundation of a lie would crumble. Those hadn't been her mother's words but something she had read. Wise words. She pressed her hand against her chest to slow the erratic beat of her heart. But was it worth the risk, for a chance at happiness, no matter how fleeting?

The caravan slowed and headed to a clearing. Would the duke be here? Did she want to see him? She shook her thoughts of him free and concentrated on her surroundings. Vendor booths and tents lined the shore and spilled out onto the frozen river. She had expected a serene and quiet setting. Instead, the place was buzzing like a small city, with a steady stream of people pouring in from every direction to take part in all manner of entertainments and distractions.

In addition to the booths, there were bull-baiting activities in a corded-off area, and horse-and-coach races along the perimeter of the river's shoreline. She had never seen its like. Children joined their parents to cheer and ran across the frozen river. Trees, their branches frosted with ice and dripping with icicles, glistened like silver chandeliers in the glow of the afternoon's sun.

Couples danced along the shore; others skated on the ice. All variety of food and drink was laid out picnic-style on blankets spread over the frozen ground or on long wood tables. The whole scene reminded her of the Shakespeare play, *A Midsummer Night's Dream*, where anything was possible, and all dreams came true. But even in this play, there was a reckoning. What if the duke did not feel as she did? Even though they had shared a passionate kiss, he had not offered marriage.

The carriage jostled over a rut in the road, tipping her sketches from her lap and onto the floor. She gathered them and put them away in her satchel as the carriage rolled to a stop, where carriages like hers, as well as coaches, gigs, barouches, and other conveyances, were directed to disembark their passengers.

A short distance away, Lydia and Sophia jumped from their carriage and raced toward the frozen river with their governess, Miss O'Brian chasing after them and shouting for them to slow down. The adults from the carriage caravan were more circumspect in their movements, but no less joyous in their expressions as they too joined in the festivities.

Madeline gathered her reticle to do the same, worrying about how she could find the duke in the crush of what must be close to hundreds if not thousands of people.

The door to her carriage opened and the man of her thoughts and dreams stood before her. He had transformed from the man who had ridden to save her life to the one who stood before her. He wore a top hat and had changed into a well-tailored, midnight-blue topcoat, cream breeches, and silver waistcoat, with an intricately tied cravat.

He was every inch a gentleman. But it was not his clothes that spoke to her but the way his eyes gazed over her and the way his smile chased the chill from the air and the doubts from her heart.

"I hope my surprise will be welcomed. It is my way of apologizing for the wretched way I criticized your sketches. You are a talented artist, and it is not my place to dictate the subject you wish to draw or paint. I will understand if you cannot accept my apology. You have but to say the word and I will change course."

He had offered her a way out of the dilemma of conscience she faced. She would tell him she could not accept his apology and they would go their separate ways. Nothing more would need to be said. The kiss would be forgotten.

But she could not forget. She had promised herself more time. Life was long, and if she entered into a loveless marriage, she would have the memories of her time with the duke to keep her warm. She shrugged a laugh. How easy it was to reason with a conscience when the heart was involved.

He gently squeezed her hand. "Something amuses you. Have you made your decision? Am I to be forgiven?"

"Perhaps I should wait until I learn of your surprise," she said with a sly smile.

He smiled, laughing. "A talented artist and a shrewd negotiator. I have met my match, Miss Mercer. I will tell you the first half of the surprises needed to prove to you the sincerity of my apology. I have hired a sleigh to carry you, my sisters, and Miss O'Brian over the frozen river."

She laughed low under her breath, and when she did a plume of frosted air swirled around her. "You have me intrigued, Your Grace. You have gone to a lot of trouble to secure my apology. In addition, your sisters and Miss O'Brian will be thrilled, as am I. Yes, I accept your apology."

He nodded for them to proceed along a walkway leading to the shore. "If I am being honest, I would have preferred we were alone."

"You speak aloud my thoughts as well."

She should tell him that they shouldn't be together, but when he offered his hand, and widened his smile, she knew she couldn't say that today. One more day, she told her conscience. She wanted one more day with him. She would tell him tomorrow.

"Milady, would you care to enter a world of wonder and magic?"

Her heart beat faster. He had moved closer, and his nearness took her breath away. He blocked her view of the Frost Fair until all she saw or felt was the warmth of his smile and the intensity of his gaze. The many-layered colors and delights and sounds and smells of the fair faded into the background like a glittering mist. All that remained was the duke and the rapid beat of her heart.

She laughed, taking his hand. "You have read my thoughts, noble sir, for I was thinking of how the Frost Fair reminds me of *A Midsummer Night's Dream*."

He reached for her and lifted her down, holding her against him for longer than was proper. "A perfect comparison, and much like the masked balls we English are so fond of. During the daylight hours, the Frost Fair is a family affair. When night falls over the river, an enchanted version of the Frost Fair makes an entrance. But even during the day, the Frost Fair casts a spell over the river and many feel as though time slows and they are alone with those they love and cherish."

Breathless and lightheaded, she rested her hands on his arms, thrilling that the cords of his muscles flexed under her touch. "But we are not alone, Your Grace. I have never seen so many people together in one place before."

"And yet, the more crowded our surroundings, the more invisible we are. Those in attendance are concerned with their needs and take little note of ours. I find that to be a comfort. A crowd is where I feel the most alone."

Pulled to touch him, as though by an invisible force, she brushed her gloved fingers over his cheek. "I often have felt the same way regarding crowds. Their conversations became like the buzzing of bees in my ears and the images of the people blurred. I felt as though I could disappear."

"You could never disappear," he said, closing his hand over hers. "You would always stand out, even in the largest crowd." He drew her closer until his breath, warm in the frosted air, caressed her skin. "We are of one mind, then, you and I. Come. I have a surprise for you."

"A surprise, you say. It has been my experience that surprises are one of two types," she said as he led her down to the shoreline. "They are either welcomed or feared."

They continued in silence along the path that led to the shoreline as she glanced over the frozen river. Couples glided on wooden skates over the ice. Their movements were like a waltz, fluid and graceful. Hands touched and faces lifted toward each other in rapt attention and awe. She imagined the couples were lovers—or meeting for the first time on this magical night. Maybe their love was forbidden, like in *A Midsummer Night's Dream*. Then she imagined skating in the duke's arms, and the thought brought warmth to her skin.

Madeline shivered, pressing her hand against her waist. If the duke knew the truth about her mother, the budding love between them would be over before it began.

"Are you cold?" he said. "How foolish of me not to

consider you might prefer the warmth of a cozy fire instead of a sleigh ride in frigid weather. I have taken the liberty of arranging accommodations in London for everyone in the caravan. We could abandon the surprise, and I will escort you, my sisters, and Miss O'Brian to yours straight away."

How could she tell him that she could not breathe when he was so close? She could not reason. She had not wanted to fall in love and experience the emotions that banished all reason and left a person spinning out of control.

"Nonsense," she said, forcing a smile. "I love the idea of a sleigh ride. I was lost in thoughts of no consequence."

"If your thoughts are distressful, then they are of consequence," he argued.

"We are so different," she blurted. "There is no future for us."

There, she had said the words that had haunted her from the first moment she had seen him ride alongside her carriage to return the blunt she had given Lord Dumont. Had some part of her known even then that she would fall in love with him? She should tell him now that she was a fraud. But she held her secret all the closer. Not yet, she cautioned. Not yet. She did not want to break the spell.

He reached for her gloved hand, brought it to his lips, and kissed her fingers. "It was your differences that drew me to you. You are unlike anyone I have ever met. You challenge me, my world, and my way of life. You have a way of throwing open the windows of my heart and letting sunlight into my very soul. At first, I was grateful, but that feeling grew. Now I cannot imagine my life without you in it."

His words chased around her like snowflakes caught in a winter storm. Could she believe them, trust that they would be enough? "You quite take my breath away with your words."

The duke grinned. "That is exactly how I feel when I am around you."

He drew her under a copse of trees whose branches disappeared into the frozen depths of the water. Beneath the tree's canopy was a horse-drawn sleigh on wooden runners, and William was helping his sisters and Miss O'Brian into the sleigh.

The duke waved to his sisters and chuckled. "It looks as though my brother is joining us. It is common knowledge that he does not care for the cold. First a snowball fight, now a sleigh ride? I am pleased with his transformation. He was always a serious young man."

"I believe Miss O'Brian might be the cause of this change," Madeline said with a smile.

"Ah," the duke said, shaking his head as he smiled. "Well now, that is interesting. My brother never ceases to amaze me. Miss O'Brian is a wonderful person. We should join them before they invite others in our place. I was unsure if you knew how to skate," he said, changing the subject, "so I hired a sleigh to take us all to where I had a place constructed for us on the river."

"You are a contradiction. You are a serious and proper gentleman, yet romantic at heart. Women must find you irresistible."

"It is my family's wealth and position that women find irresistible. You are the first lady I have sought to impress with such a grand gesture." He held out his hand to help her into the sleigh. "Will you join me on an adventure?"

"I would be delighted," she said, positioning herself beside Sophia and Lydia. "I will have you know that I do know how to skate, and quite well, in fact."

He grinned again, sitting beside his brother and Miss O'Brian. "I am not surprised. There is no end to your accomplishments. You are rare indeed."

She returned his smile, feeling the warmth of a blush from his compliment.

"Is the ice covering the River Themes strong enough to hold us?" Miss O'Brian asked.

"Quite safe," William said. "One of the London merchants led an elephant across the ice to prove its strength. Every day, Londoners and merchants travel back and forth or up and down this river in sleighs or on skates. But I know my brother and he would have made sure it was safe for us to travel across."

"My brother is correct. I would never risk the safety of those I hold most dear."

Madeline laughed softly at his response and his vow to keep them all safe. This man was easy to love. From her vantage point from the carriage a short time ago, she had compared the area over the frozen river to a small city. Her assessment had been only partially correct. It resembled a city, that much was true, but it was unlike any she had ever seen.

In Boston, New York, and London, the cities were overcrowded, and their buildings were tall and gray, constructed of either stone or smoke-darkened brick. The Frost Fair, in comparison, was bursting with color, laughter, and joy. Bright, colorful fabric in oranges, purples, greens, yellows, reds, and blues draped over the tents that lined the narrow spaces on the frozen river that served as roads where sleighs and people could travel.

There were restaurants, taverns, and vendors, selling everything from secondhand clothing, hats, shoes, and ribbons to jewelry of all types and shapes. There were also bookstores and a printing shop that sold photographs and prints of past and current Frost Fairs. Most surprising were the puppet shows, street jugglers, and acrobats. There was even a stage with actors performing a play.

The sleigh glided over the ice to the sound of bells tinkling on the horse's bridle. It was a quiet tune that soothed her nerves and lightened her mood. She wished this day would never end.

Chapter Thirty-Four

"We have arrived at our destination," the duke said."

The duke's announcement was met with a round of applause and cheers. The joyous mood was infectious. Madeline could not decide if her voice or the children's voices were loudest.

On the journey across the frozen river, the duke had confided that he and Jeremy had found and captured Devonshire and his men at the Frost Faire early in the day. The duke had not gone into great detail other than to say that Devonshire and his men had been arrested and were awaiting justice.

A sense of profound relief washed over her. She had not realized until that moment how much she feared that Devonshire would continue to seek his revenge. It felt as though she could breathe again and looked forward to the duke's surprise.

Snowflakes drifted down like bits of lace as the sleigh pulled alongside a massive white tent. There was a wooden mural panel, painted with images of forest creatures and scenes from *A Midsummer's Night Dream*, attached to the tent walls. Footmen dressed in gold and silver livery held torches on either side of the entrance, while a third footman drew back the flap of the tent.

Sophia and Lydia jumped from the sleigh and rushed through the tent's opening as Miss O'Brian called out words of caution. "Children! You must show decorum! What would your mother say if she knew you were running about willy-nilly? Ladies do not scamper about like puppies!"

William chuckled, offering his arm to Miss O'Brian after helping her down from the sleigh. "The duke and I will keep this a secret from our mother. Let's pretend, if only for tonight, that we are not governed by the rules of the *ton*."

As Lord Oswyn and Miss O'Brian followed the twins inside, the duke helped Madeline from the sleigh. "Your brother is as romantic as you are, Your Grace," she said as she and the duke entered the tent.

White fur rugs covered wooden floors. Jewel-toned pillows in emerald green, ruby red, and sapphire blue were arranged to resemble lounging chairs and sofas. A wide variety of sweets and a decanter of red wine and crystal goblets were spread over a low table. The inside of the room reminded Madeline of stories in the book *One Thousand and One Arabian Nights*. In that book, the woman, Scheherazade, read to Shahryār, the fictional ruler of India and China, a collection of medieval folk tales. The stories were filled with adventure and romance and the possibility of a happily-ever-after ending, which gave Madeline hope that such a conclusion might happen for her as well.

Robert nodded to the footman, who placed a torch in an iron stand and left, closing the door behind him. The glow from the torch bathed the inside of the tent in golden hues that further enhanced the enchanted-seeming atmosphere.

William, the twins, and Miss O'Brian, had circled around the low table on pillows, sampling the sweets displayed on golden trays.

"This place is like something out of a dream," Madeline said. "How did you accomplish so much in such a short amount of time?"

He laughed softly. "I could tell you that for the Duke of Conclarton nothing is impossible, but that played only a small part. It is because of your reputation that these preparations came together so quickly. As you might imagine, hundreds of merchants and vendors are in need of workers to construct their buildings for the Frost Fair. When word spread that I wanted to surprise Miss Madeline Mercer, workers flooded to my aid."

"I do not understand. I am no one of consequence."

"Spoken like a true Angel of Mercy. Many would disagree. You are the woman who saved a village."

"That is not true. I suggested that a few wagonloads of food and clothing be donated to help the villagers. Anyone would have done the same."

"It amounted to twenty wagonloads, with more promised. The village is surrounded by wealthy estate owners who felt that a few baskets of bread or a butchered pig during the holidays was sufficient to ease their conscience. You were not satisfied with pretty words of empathy. You did not suggest, as you would have me and others believe. You demanded action. You exposed the *ton*'s neglect and made it impossible for them to ignore the need. You were the only person who decided to do something about helping those less fortunate with an amount of charity that would make a difference. You have a kind and generous heart and are beloved."

"You have given me too much credit. I did not act alone. I may have suggested we help the village, but your mother found the resources."

"True, my mother was generous. But you and your mother contributed far more. You and your mother donated enough blunt to assure that the people in the village would have full bellies and warm cottages to last through the winter months and into the spring. Speaking of food, I am reminded that if we do not join my brother, sisters, and Miss O'Brian soon, they will devour every crumb." He held out his hand toward her. "Will you join me?"

Chapter Thirty-Five

Late the next day, the sky was overcast as the carriage caravan returned from the Frost Fair and rolled across the bridge and through the gates of Conclarton Castle. The inclement weather did not bother Madeline. She had rarely felt this happy. She, the duke, and his family had shared a wonderful evening together. They had treated her like part of their family. She had never had sisters or brothers, and although her mother had surrounded her with love, Madeline had felt lonely at times. If Madeline was blessed with the ability to have children, she made a vow that she would have as many as three or more.

The return trip had been serene and without incident, and as a result it had been deemed not necessary to overnight at one of the posting inns along the way.

Sophia and Lydia were sleeping like angels next to their dozing governess, Miss O'Brian, on the cushioned bench seat opposite Madeline's. The twins had begged the duke to allow them to travel on the return trip to Conclarton Castle with Madeline.

Robert had initially turned their requests down, whispering to Madeline that he had plans for them to share a private carriage ride home. She had felt the heat in his gaze sear through her from the top of her head to the tips of her toes. Her face had warmed, and she was convinced that the color matched the rose-red ribbons on her bonnet. She was on the verge of allowing him to ride with her unchaperoned when Miss O'Brian intervened, saying that the twins would be disappointed, as they had longed for another drawing lesson.

Miss O'Brian's tone had been gentle but firm. The message behind the thinly veiled art lesson excuse had been clear. It would not be proper for Madeline to share a carriage with the duke unchaperoned. For once, Madeline had been thankful for the strict guidelines that governed women. She knew the duke would not force his attentions upon her, but she also knew she would welcome his kisses and was concerned where that might lead. She finally understood what her mother must have felt all those years ago. Her mother had said she loved Madeline's father and believed he returned her love in kind. The consequences of their lovemaking had produced a child. Madeline's mother had been thrilled when she learned she was with child. Madeline's father had not.

Even so, Madeline had wanted to say yes, and Lord help her, if Robert's sisters had given her pause to reconsider, she might have given in. She harbored little illusion where the long ride on the return trip would have led. She had promised herself that before she allowed her relationship with Robert to continue, she would reveal her and her mother's subterfuge. Until then, it was wise to spend as little time alone with him as possible.

She leaned back against the carriage seat. "What a fine kettle of fish I've gotten myself into. Well done, Madeline."

She glanced over again at the sleeping children and their governess. Sophia and Lydia, even in their sleep, clung to the sketches they had drawn during the long carriage ride. Madeline was pleased at their progress and their eagerness to learn. Sophia had drawn a mischievous rabbit nibbling lettuce in her mother's garden, and Lydia a pony racing over a field of wildflowers.

All and all, Madeline was glad she had chosen to return with the children. She had a wonderful day and the time had sped. The time with the duke would have been fraught with too many complications.

The caravan of carriages crossed beneath the castle's arched gate into a whirlwind of what could only be explained as chaos. Wagons of every imaginable size and shape vied for space to unload food, Christmas decorations, plants, and furniture. Horses whinnied and pulled at their bits as drivers struggled for control. Footmen shouted orders and directed the wagons toward a side entrance of the castle.

Madeline's driver reined in his team of horses, and the carriage came to a full stop. The driver leaned down from the box. "Miss Mercer, Miss O'Brian," he shouted over the din of activity in the courtyard. "My apologies, but this is as close to the entrance as I'm able to get. I'm assured someone will come along to help you disembark the carriage. But until then, please keep inside the coach till it is sorted." He tipped his hat to Madeline and resumed his position on the driver's box.

Miss O'Brian yawned and nudged the two sleeping girls awake. "Did I hear the driver?" She glanced out the window and yawned again. "We have arrived, children. We are a long way from the entrance steps, but a walk will do us good after the long journey. Please gather your belongings."

"Mr. Welsh said we should stay inside the carriage until a footman arrives," Madeline said.

After their last driver had died without Madeline knowing the man's name, she had made it paramount to learn the name of their new driver and as much about him as he was willing to share. He lived outside of London with a wife and family and seemed pleased that Madeline had taken an interest. Mr. Welsh had known their former driver and agreed to give Mr. Tinker's widow the drawing sketched of him before he had died.

Sophia rubbed her eyes, yawned, and leaned on the coach's windowsill as though trying to gain a closer look outside. Her eyes widened in wonder and disbelief. "Is that a peacock?"

Her sister, Lydia, slid from her seat and joined Sophia with a squeal. Her eyes as wide as her sister's, she turned toward Madeline. "I saw an ostrich!"

"Swans!" Lydia shouted. "What do you think it means, Miss O'Brian?"

Madeline and Miss O'Brian crowded to the window, as awestruck as the children. Cages containing swans, peacocks, and ostriches were being unloaded from one of the wagons.

"I do believe the duchess plans to host the grandest Christmas Ball Conclarton Castle has ever seen," Miss O'Brian said, smiling as broadly as the twins.

A short distance away, the duke and Lord Oswyn turned their horses around and cantered over to Madeline's carriage. A ripple of desire caught her off guard as she watched the duke ride toward her. The man rode a horse like he was born to it. They dismounted, but it was the duke who reached the carriage first and opened the door.

"I apologize that your carriage is unable to make it closer to the entrance. Do you mind walking?"

Lydia and Sophia scrambled out of the carriage. "We saw swans and ostriches," they said at the same time.

"Is it true?" Lydia said. "Is Mama planning the grandest Christmas Ball we have ever had?"

"All true. I just met with Winfield, and he believes our mother has gone quite mad." He winked. "Do you know what I think?"

They both bobbed their heads at the same time as he knelt before them. The duke glanced over at Madeline before turning his attention back to his sisters. "Our mother believes, as I do, that our new visitors from America have swept the old cobwebs from our castle and brought us the chance for a fresh, new start."

"Sophia and I agree," Lydia said. "We are glad Miss Mercer is here. She taught us how to draw. I made this for you," she said. "Miss Mercer showed me how. It is a pony."

The duke smiled. "And a very fine pony it is. Well done."

"I drew a bunny eating lettuce in Mama's vegetable garden," Sophia said.

The duke accepted the drawings and examined them closely. "We must show these to Mama. She will want to frame them and put them in her gallery. My two sisters are exceedingly talented."

Laughing, he held them close. "I am such a lucky man to have sisters like you. Cook has prepared her ginger biscuits and…"

He did not have time to finish his sentence. Lydia and Sophia took off running toward the entrance.

The duke laughed again and held out his hand for Madeline as Lord Oswyn rushed to help Miss O'Brian down from the carriage.

"How was your time with my sisters?" the duke asked as Madeline rested her hand on the arm he had offered. "They can be little terrors."

"On the contrary, they are adorable and very talented. I am very fond of them."

He nodded, as he leaned toward her. "As am I. Every day I learn more about you that endears you to me, Miss Mercer."

Chapter Thirty-Six

With Madeline's hand resting on his arm, Robert entered the main entrance, viewing the spectacle, not quite sure how to proceed. He had never seen his mother in this light. His father had abhorred parties of any sort, but it was not only the elaborateness of the party that was planned that drew his attention, it was also the person in charge. His father had been the one directing the servants to their tasks and his mother regulated as a bystander. That was not the case here. It was evident that his mother was in charge and doing a fine job of it. She stood in the center of the activity, directing traffic as calmly as a general directing his troops.

A continual procession of workmen and servants swarmed the entry of the castle as the duchess, her hair slightly out of place and the sleeves on her black crepe dress rolled up past her wrists, gave instructions to the servants. But while the generals of Robert's acquaintance barked out orders, his mother instructions were given as though she were talking to old friends.

Her voice was gentle and respectful in tone. As a result, the servants smiled, and a few hummed. Behavior the old lord would have marked as disrespectful. Robert admitted that he very much liked the change.

His mother glanced toward him as he entered with Madeline. "Robert. Miss Mercer. Your timing is perfection itself. There is so much left to do." She paused as Winfield dipped his head to ask her a question.

"We have a chance to escape while my mother is occupied with Winfield," Robert said to Madeline.

"Not a chance," Madeline said. "I love to decorate and always helped my mother during the Christmas season. Besides, I have a feeling that if we tried to escape, your mother would find and scold us."

Robert laughed softly. "I believe you are correct."

"Please carry the tables and chairs into the assembly room," his mother said in a cheery tone to servants carrying boxes into the entry. Please arrange the fir and pine trees in groups that reflect how they would appear in the forest. Candlesticks should be…" She paused her instructions mid-sentence, interrupting a parade of servants carrying boxes. "Daisy, are these the costumes I ordered from Mr. Potter?"

"Yes, Your Grace," Daisy said. The young woman with strawberry-blonde hair tucked inside her cap bobbed a curtsey as she held the box in both arms.

The duchess instructed the boxes be set down for her examination. "How exciting," she exclaimed as she knelt and opened the box nearest to her. "I am anxious to see how the costumes I ordered for the guests attending the Masquerade Ball turned out. I was beginning to fear I had not given poor Mr. Potter ample money to hire the staff he needed to finish my order. He assured me, however, that I had, and was confident he could meet the deadline. But I worried, nonetheless."

The duchess flipped the lid open, gently removing the tissue paper as she examined the contents. Her shoulders rounded as she sat back on her heels and shook her head. "These are all wrong. I specifically ordered that the costumes were to be lined."

Wringing her hands, Daisy bobbed another curtsey. "I am so sorry, milady. I am sure Mr. Potter will be happy to make the adjustments to the garments at his cost."

"Nonsense. This is not your fault, nor is it Mr. Potter's. Mr. Potter has always been most dependable. I'm sure the fault lies with me. Mr. Potter is a lovely man with a wife, five children, and another child on the way. I do not want to trouble him. I am sure we can find a solution."

"Your Grace," Mary said, approaching. "I overheard that something was amiss with one of the deliveries. May I be of help?"

"The costumes Mr. Potter delivered were not as I had hoped. But perhaps they are not as troublesome as I suspect. Let's have a look, shall we?" The duchess lifted one of the costumes from the box and held it up—the ribbons of light that streamed through the windows shone through the dress.

Mary gasped and clapped her hand over her mouth. "Oh, my stars. Without lining, the garment is as transparent as glass."

"My fear as well. The ladies can wear a chemise underneath, and the men—well, they can decide. Actually, both men and women can decide what is proper. This will be better." She winked. "Certainly, more scandalous."

"Mother!" Robert said as he approached with Madeline on his arm. "What you are suggesting is scandalous. The costumes are…"

"Lovely. I quite agree."

"That is not what I was about to say."

His mother rose and patted him on the cheek. "Son, I am fully aware of what you were about to say. Now, to more important matters. You and Miss Mercer have arrived at an opportune time. We have much to do and I value Miss Mercer's opinion."

"Father would…"

"…would have disapproved," the duchess finished. "Yes, I am well aware of your father's opinion on such matters. I love you dearly, and I grew to love your father very much. He was a good man and treated me with love and kindness. But he was stuck in the past and wound as tight as his father's watch. You have a choice. Take on the rigid mantle your father and his father before him wore, or forge your own path. I look on the Masquerade Ball as a way to move this family out of the stodgy past and into a new world with new and wonderous possibilities." She patted his cheek again and resumed her task of examining the costumes with Mary and Daisy, as Madeline knelt beside them.

Robert stood in silence, mulling over his mother's comments. He did not recognize this version of his mother. Before his father's death, his mother had always been in tight control of her emotions, her hair perfectly coiffed and her demeanor and the tone of her voice modulated. In the past when his mother addressed the servants, her words were clipped, efficient, and distant in much the same manner as his father's had been. She never inquired about their day or how they felt. While his father was alive, his mother would not have concerned herself with a shop owner's expense or circumstances. Or perhaps she would have but knew she would have been overruled by his father.

It seemed this new behavior of his mother's reflected her true nature, one Robert heartily approved.

His mother had asked him to choose. Would he

continue with his father's stringent rules that reflected those of the crème de la crème of society, or would he develop more tolerant ones of his own? He already felt a change. It had begun while he was in the military, where he witnessed inequality of treatment due to a person's station in life. But he knew that, as the Duke of Conclarton, he might have resumed his pampered life if not for his encounter with Miss Mercer, who challenged him at every turn.

The world was changing, and like in nature, those who did not adapt risked extinction. England was no longer the power it once was. The United States had defeated England, in not one but two wars. As a result, America's new ideas and world views were taking root in Europe.

He watched as his mother, Mary, and Madeline, sorted through the costumes as though they were old friends. They oohed and aahed at the sheer silk Greek-style costumes, the gold-colored jewelry, embroidered fans, headpieces, and gilded masks.

He remembered the day he had returned after serving in the military. His mother had hugged him, and with tears of joy brimming in her eyes, she had insisted he share with her everything that had happened to him. At the time, he had been taken by surprise, not knowing how he should react. If he was fortunate to have children of his own, he wanted to emulate her behavior. Yes, he liked the change in his mother very much.

"Mother," Robert said, as he knelt beside her. "May I be of assistance?"

Startled, she looked up and focused as though only just noticing him. Her gaze drifted toward Madeline. Then she smiled a brilliant smile. "We welcome your help, dear boy. And Madeline, I will need your advice. I could not stop thinking of the portrait *Triumph of Bacchus*, by Michaelina Wautier, that your mother owns."

Robert glanced toward Madeline. "*Triumph of Bacchus*?"

"In Greek mythology, Bacchus was the god of wine," his mother interrupted before Madeline could respond. "The painting depicts a Greek-style orgy. Very unusual for a woman to paint such a scene. The artist bowed to the pressures of her time as her other works were mostly religious subjects, such as *Saint John the Baptist,* and *The Annunciation...*"

"I am aware of the god Bacchus," Robert said. "What surprises me is that Madeline's mother would have such a portrait in her home."

"She lives in America," both Madeline and his mother said at the same time, as though that was all the explanation needed.

"Ah," Robert responded as though he understood. Which he did not. From all accounts, America was considered a progressive country. Still... Wouldn't the subject of the painting be considered scandalous even in America? He very well knew what an orgy was. What was unclear and disturbing was how his mother, who according to his father had lived a proper and sheltered life, knew about such things. And how was it that a proper lady, like Madeline's mother, hung in her house a painting such as the one his mother described?

He scrubbed both hands through his hair. Yes, becoming more tolerant would take time and patience. But as he watched his mother and Madeline, both in a joyful mood, he vowed it was worth the effort.

"These are our costumes for the Masquerade Ball. I know it started out as a Christmas Eve Ball, but then I thought—how boring. That is when I remembered the portrait, the *Triumph of Bacchus*, and decided we must hold a masquerade. And because this was so last minute, we will provide costumes to those who would like them."

"Have you told His Grace and Miss Mercer about the other changes Madeline and her mother inspired?" Mary said with a gleam in her eye.

"Oh, my! You are correct. They do not know. I sent out invitations to our guests, advising them that in the spirit of Christmas there had been a few changes. Those attending the Christmas Masquerade will buy tickets, with all proceeds donated to help not only our village, but those in the surrounding area throughout the year. The goal is for this to be an annual event. Attendees were instructed to arrive early tomorrow morning. We will have a glorious day. Changing rooms have been prepared as well as arrangements for those wishing to spend a night or two at the castle. We have hired additional staff to help cook the meals, and wine has been brought from the cellars. We can't have a masquerade honoring Bacchus without wine."

Robert stifled a groan, envisioning guests, foxed on free wine, running half naked through the hallways. His imagination took a turn. At private men's clubs, he had had occasion to see women dressed in the type of clothing his mother had provided for the Masquerade Ball. His muscles tensed as blood surged through his veins. He visualized how Madeline would look with her full, ripe breasts pressed against thin, transparent silk…

His mother reached over to him. "Dear boy, are you well? You look positively flushed."

"A little warm, is all," he said, loosening his cravat.

Her son forgotten, she turned toward Madeline. "We will suggest that people dress like gods and goddesses. The women will all want to identify as Aphrodite, the goddess of love. How boring."

"I have an idea," Madeline said. "I will be happy to sketch images of Artemis, the goddess of the hunt, Athena, the goddess of wisdom, and the nine muses. I feel confident that once they see other options, they will be inclined to dress according to the goddess that best fits their wishes and dreams."

"Excellent idea," the duchess said. "We can include a description of each to help people make an informed decision."

"If you approve," Madeline said, "I would love to dress as Calliope. The Greeks never identified that a muse was needed to inspire painters or sculptors. The Greeks considered that type of work more on the order of manual labor. Calliope, one of the nine muses, is connected to the written word, however, and therefore associated with the arts."

"Quite so, and extraordinarily short-sighted of them. The Greeks had some of the most brilliant minds the world ever created—Socrates, Plato, and Aristotle—and yet did not consider painting and sculpture to be art. Tragic. But I love your choice. As you say, Calliope was the protector of the written word. According to myth, Homer asked her to inspire him while writing the *Iliad* and the *Odyssey*."

"There is also Clio," Madeline continued with a smile. "She is the muse who discovered history, and Euterpe, who is responsible for music, Thalia, the protector of comedy, Melpomene, who invented tragedy and speech, Terpsichore, the protector of dance, Erato, the protector of love and poetry, Polyamine, geometry and grammar, Urania, the stars and therefore the inventor of astronomy. Someone should be Apollo. He watched over the muses."

Both his mother and Madeline looked over at Robert. He felt uncomfortable under their steady gaze until he realized their intentions and shook his head slowly.

"Absolutely, not. I am not dressing as Apollo."

Chapter Thirty-Seven

Madeline was still smiling over the duke's reaction to his mother's suggestion that he dress like the Greek god Apollo as she viewed her image in the cheval mirror in her bedroom. She had finished dressing and felt as though she had stepped back in time. She loved the gown, especially since she did not have to wear a corset. For the first time since she had arrived, she hadn't been required to wear that constricting article of clothing.

The gown the duchess had chosen for her was exquisite. Embroidered images of gold and silver butterflies, their wings encrusted with emeralds and diamonds, were sewn into the silk layers of fabric of her white Grecian-style gown. A matching mask was included, as well as gold ribbons for her hair. She felt every inch the part of the Greek muse Calliope.

Her mother had mentioned that she planned to attend as well, but Madeline had not seen her since this afternoon. Hoping to find her mother and the duchess, in case they needed her help with the ball tonight, Madeline left her room in search of them.

The transformation in the hallway that led to the main staircase was nothing short of a miracle. It reminded her of the enchanting atmosphere the duke had created in the tent at the Frost Fair. Candles and wall sconces lit the way, silver and gold decorations hung in archways and doorways and looped around banisters. It seemed the duchess, after the tragic deaths of her husband and son, wanted to create a feeling of hope and gratitude.

Madeline felt humbled by the gesture. She had been quick to judge the noble women and men of the *ton* as arrogant and unfeeling. A number of them fit that mold, but at Conclarton Castle, at least, the people here felt deeply for those around them. When her stay ended, and she was prepared that it would when she confessed her secret to the duke, she would miss them all very much.

"You look lovely, Miss Mercer," Mary said with a curtsey as Madeline rounded a corner.

Startled, Madeline paused, then smiled in return. "Thank you. You also look lovely. I have never seen you wear such a beautiful dress."

Mary smoothed her hands over the silver-and-blue embroidered gown. "It is a gift from the duchess. She made sure that all the women working at the castle have new dresses to wear tonight." She giggled. "I mentioned that our fine clothes might confuse the guests, but she only laughed harder."

"The duchess is certainly more than she seems. I would love to thank her and locate my mother. Have you seen either one of them?"

"I believe they are in the rooms at the end of the hall. Shall I announce you?"

"No need. I can find my way. Thank you."

The quarters belonging to the duchess were marked by double doors covered with carved images of forest creatures. Madeline opened the main room, only to discover it was empty. This room reminded Madeline of spring, a stark contrast to the old lord's study. Murals of a rose garden, with a gazebo and fountains, covered the walls. The furniture was painted white and green, and vases of silk flowers stood on every table. She recognized her mother's laughter and followed the sound to a door on the far side of the room.

As she was about to open the door, Madeline heard the duchess mention her name.

"You should tell Madeline," The duchess was saying. "She has a right to know."

Madeline edged closer to the door. The duchess's words came through as clear as if the door were made of tissue paper.

"I disagree," Roseline said. "This is your secret to tell, not mine."

"We are connected, and she grows suspicious. Your daughter is intelligent, a tribute to you, not that good-for-nothing father of hers, God rest his black soul."

Madeline froze. How did the duchess know about her father? She moved to press her ear to the door. The voices came through the thin panel clearly.

"I do not want to speak ill of the dead," Roseline said.

"I will if you won't. Dangerously handsome, and a notorious rake. He was the son of an earl, and you had just turned seventeen and thought yourself in love. If it weren't for your mother's jewels, God knows what would have happened to you and your unborn child." She paused. "His brother learned you were here and has made inquiries about you. I would not be surprised if he came courting. I have heard he is not at all like his elder brother and has a respectable income."

"He has already reached out to me in a letter. I intended to meet with him in the village but changed my mind. You and I have had this conversation before. I am content with the single life. My choice in men has been abysmal, as you well know. It is the reason I wrote a letter to Madeline's father before she was born, although I never mailed it. I wanted to never forget what had happened, how I felt, and the events that led to his deserting us. I keep it with me always. But what about you? You are still young enough to find happiness. Is there a man you fancy?"

"None that I would trust would love me for myself and not my fortune."

Rosaline laughed softly. "We share the same dilemma, you and me. I too do not trust that a man would not love my money more than he loved me. But isn't that what you are asking from your sons and daughters?"

The duchess heaved a sigh. "It is true. In my defense, I thought by adding wealthy heirs and heiresses from outside the titled classes of Europe, my children would have more options."

"And when will you tell your children that you have money to burn? That this ruse that they need to marry a person with vast wealth is a lie?"

"I had my reasons."

"Those reasons died with your husband."

There was a long silence, and Madeline held her breath, concerned that their conversation had ended and they might burst into the room where she was hidden, and discover she had been listening. Their conversation opened up more questions than answers. It was clear that her mother and the duchess had known each other for a long while. Why hadn't her mother shared that information?

"Would you like more tea before we continue our conversation?" Roseline said. "I could ring for Winfield or Mary,"

"This conversation calls for whiskey," the duchess said with a chuckle. "I have a feeling we are in for a long night."

There was the sound of a cabinet door opening and glasses clinking, followed by laughter and a second clinking of glasses.

"It has been so good to see you again," the duchess said. "It is as though time rolled back and we are childhood friends once more."

Madeline sucked in a breath and covered her mouth with her hand to stifle another. Not only did her mother and the duchess know each other from when they were children, her mother was drinking whiskey. The most Madeline had seen her mother drink was the occasional sherry.

"Did you hear something, Roseline?" the duchess asked. "No, it must be only the creaks and moans of this old castle," she continued.

"Your plan might not have worked when your husband was alive," Roseline said. "He would not have approved of my daughter, regardless of how much money she offered as a dowry."

"How true. My husband was obsessed with a person's pedigree. He made a list for me of acquaintances he approved. He said my choice of friendships reflected on him."

"Then he never knew his mother's origins?" Roseline said. There was the sound of rustling fabric, and Madeline presumed her mother walked across the room.

The duchess laughed again. "Lord, no. He would have died from the shame of it. Or perhaps he was aware and that was the reason he was so obsessed with titles and lineage. On the reverse of it, his father was good and just, always kind and generous with his servants and treated them well. As a young man, he frequently visited the ladies of the night in London. One lady in particular caught his attention. Rather than keep her as his mistress, as I am sure his parents would have desired, he married her, and they had a son. Her name was Caroline Tinsworthy, and after I married her son, she and I became good friends."

"Why would she tell you her beginnings and not tell her own son?"

"That is a question I have long wondered. But knowing my husband as I did, the only conclusion I have come to was that his mother might have feared he would cast her out when his father died. I do not want to believe he would have, but I guess we will never know."

"But I am confused at your announcement that you have money. The servants say you never miss payments to vendors or their wages, but they still have the impression that it is a struggle. How ever did you manage it?"

"Something my husband's mother taught me. Although Robert's grandfather was a good man, he spoiled and indulged his son and only child. Even before he died, my husband's mother, foreseeing what might happen, taught me how to squirrel away large sums of money. I kept the impression in motion that the Conclarton family needed money. In my mind, it changed the dynamics of the marriage market. Instead of marriage-minded mamas swarming like locusts to snare a man of wealth, they would arrive at the castle secure in their own wealth. My hope was that these women would be more independent and stronger, better choices for a healthy and happy union." She clinked her glass. "And then I discovered you were alive."

"Miss Mercer," Mary said entering the room where Madeline stood eavesdropping. "Did you find the duchess and your mother?"

Startled, Madeline turned and did the only thing she could think of to do. She fled, with only one thing on her mind. She needed to find the letter her mother had written to her father but never mailed.

Chapter Thirty-Eight

Ivy twisted around banisters, and fir trees, decorated with apples tied to the limbs with red and gold ribbons, framed the entrance of the castle's great hall and spilled out into the transformed assembly room. Kissing boughs of holly and mistletoe hung from the ceiling, archways, and doors, while rosemary and potted rose bushes joined the fir and laurel trees, creating a winter wonderland forest.

Thanks to his mother's decorating talents, Christmas at Conclarton Castle was a glorious triumph. Robert planned to add to the joyous occasion with the announcement that he and Madeline were engaged.

He stood at the entrance to the great hall, his hand holding a black velvet box, as he waited for Miss Mercer to descend the stairs. He was as nervous as a schoolboy. At the Frost Fair he had made his decision. He would ask Miss Mercer to marry him. They enjoyed each other's company and the kisses they shared gave him confidence that she would say yes.

His feelings for her since she had given him coins to help a weary traveler had only intensified. He thought she was kind then, and when he galloped to thank her and saw her face and was gifted with her smile, he added beautiful to the growing list.

Somewhere behind him in the great hall he heard the orchestra begin the melody *Joy to the World*. His heart beat in kind.

He saw Miss Mercer at the top of the stairs. Even from this distance, he detected a shadow pass over her features. She heaved a sigh and descended, only to pause on the center landing, where the two staircases joined as one.

He fingered the velvet box in his hand. Her expression troubled him. Had he waited too long to declare himself? Her expression turned thoughtful as her gaze searched the crowd that proceeded into the ballroom. Even as he sensed the moment she became aware of him standing at the base of the staircase, her mouth curled up at the edges and her gaze became focused on him. He let out a breath of relief. He had obviously misinterpreted her mood.

She was a vision in gold as she reached for the banister and descended the stairs. He had envisioned how she would look in the Grecian gown. His mind had wandered into lust and heat at the thought of soft, sheer fabric over her womanly curves. He was aroused, of that he had little doubt. But his feelings for her went deeper than carnal desire. He wanted long nights filled with making love and days filled with discussing the children they would have, and the plans they would make together.

He went to meet her before she took the last step, and he reached for her hand, to press it to his lips. "You are the most beautiful woman I have ever seen in my life."

She pressed her hand against his chest. "You exaggerate, Your Grace, but I accept the compliment. You look quite handsome as well." She laughed softly. "You are dressed as Apollo. I distinctly remember you saying that you would not."

He led her down the remaining stairs and entwined her arm around his. "I did research on Apollo and discovered that he revered the nine Muses and watched over and protected them."

"So he did." She turned to view the decorations as they entered the great hall. "This room has been transformed."

He turned her in his arms. "As am I because of you. Come."

The orchestra had finished *Joy to the World* and begun *O Come All Ye Faithful*. Male servants, in embroidered green-and-gold long coats, carried silver trays filled with sparkling wine. Guests had arrived while he waited for Madeline, and their glittering costumes and festive masks added to the celebratory atmosphere. Many wore the Greek and Roman styles his mother had provided, while others had brought their own costumes.

Knights, kings, and chimney sweeps mingled with queens, princesses, and ladies of the night. As everyone wore masks, it was difficult to discern the person's identity—which was, of course, the whole goal of a masquerade ball. Robert had had reservations, but his mother's instinct had proven correct. Everyone appeared to be having a wonderful time.

But the crush of so many people, although gratifying that so many had accepted his mother's invitation, was not to his liking. He wanted Miss Mercer all to himself and led her toward an alcove near a balcony overlooking the gardens. A ball of holly and mistletoe was suspended from the ceiling. He nodded toward it with his head. "This is a kissing-bough. From ancient times people have kissed beneath its greenery."

"Odd. So a man kissing a woman who is not his wife or betrothed is considered scandalous, but it is permissible to kiss under a ball made of leaves?"

The shadow had returned to blemish her expression, and once again he grew worried. "You do not wish to kiss me?"

"You misunderstand," she said, glancing out the windows to a darkened sky. "I had thought to make a jest, but because my thoughts are in a jumble, my comment sounded harsh. I apologize."

He took her hands in his. "I believe I know the cause of your turmoil. It is I who should apologize. This is a question I should have asked long before now." He retrieved the velvet box and knelt. "I have loved you from the moment I first met you. I denied my love because I believed the emotion an invention of poets and fools. Poets claim that love makes men and women dizzy with desire. That it can fog their thoughts and cloud reason and good sense. What I feel for you is not a clouding of reason, but a clearing of the mind. I see more clearly when you are near. I am not in a fog. I am not dizzy. I am strong and feel as though I could move mountains and tame raging rivers." He held the ring box higher. "Madeline Mercer, will you do me the honor of becoming my wife?"

Tears brimmed in her eyes and traveled down her face. "I must speak with you…in private."

Chapter Thirty-Nine

Back in her room, Madeline stood beside her desk. Her conversation with the duke had not gone well. Today should have been the happiest day of her life. Instead, she felt as though the world was spinning out of control.

She had told him her mother's history, including what she had learned about her father in the conversation between her mother and the duchess. She had ended with her mother's plan, and her agreement, to marry a man with a title.

Robert had listened in silence and then made some remark about being the eighth Duke of Conclarton, and with the title came responsibilities and obligations. His response hurt her more than she cared to admit. In her heart she had wanted him to say it did not matter that she had masqueraded as an heiress. She had wanted him to say all that mattered to him was that he loved her. But he had not.

Madeline felt drained and no more substantial than a silk dress left out in a soaking rain.

For her part, only the hurt remained. He was willing to offer for her hand in marriage when he believed her a wealthy heiress from a respectable family. When he had learned the truth, he had rejected her.

She loved the duke, but love wasn't enough. She no longer blamed him for his unwillingness to see past how she was raised. How could she? She had lied to him.

Everything she had told him about herself had been a lie. She was not a wealthy heiress. She was the daughter of a woman who owned and operated a brothel. It wasn't only the lies that the duke could not reconcile. It was the scandal. And in the duke's world, appearances were everything.

She blinked back a swell of tears. She hadn't lied about everything. She had not lied about her feelings for him. She loved him...which was not enough. Her mother had made that abundantly clear. It had not been enough for her mother. How could she have forgotten that lesson?

Madeline ran her fingers over the lettering on the missive she had found in her mother's drawer. It was right where her mother had told the duchess it would be. It was a letter that had never been sent, a letter her mother had written to Madeline's father before Madeline was born.

At times the words sounded angry and reproachful, and other times they were loving. Much of it Madeline had already overheard when listening in on the conversation between her mother and the duchess.

Each time Madeline reread the missive, the sting of betrayal grew until a numbness set in and would not subside. Her mother had kept the dark character of her father from her. In her daydreams of her father, Madeline had imagined him as heroic and brave. Her mother had told her he had been thrown overboard in a storm and drowned. His manner of death had not changed. He had drowned while sailing on a yacht owned by a married woman with whom he had been having an affair. The duchess had called Madeline's father a rake and worse.

Madeline's legs gave out and she collapsed into a

chair by her desk. What a fool she had been. Her father hadn't cared about her mother. She was a conquest easily won and easily forgotten. If it hadn't been for the jewels, Roseline, and her unborn child likely would have died on the streets of London. They never would have had the money to buy passage to America and start a new life.

When Madeline first read the letter, she had been angry with her mother for keeping the truth from her. Her anger had then turned toward the real villain—her father. Then at herself for clinging to a fantasy of a father that had never existed. She felt drained and disillusioned. Her emotions rocked back and forth like a ship at sea.

Conversation in the hallway broke the silence as her mother's voice carried through the door. "Please inform the duchess that I have changed my mind and will join her for dinner." Her mother entered, shutting the door behind her as she removed her gloves. Her eyebrows raised as she viewed Madeline and then the suitcase near the bed. "Have you and the duke decided to elope to Scotland's Greta Green?"

Madeline lowered her head, folding the letter in her lap. "There will not be a wedding. I am traveling alone. I am packed and have arranged with Winfield for a carriage. I leave for London in the morning and will book a passage to America on the first available ship."

Roseline tossed her gloves on the bed. "What in the devil are you talking about? You and the duke are to be married. The entire flock of guests at the Christmas Masquerade Ball witnessed the duke getting down on one knee and proposing."

Madeline shook her head slowly. "I had to tell him the truth." She lifted the letter toward her mother. "All of it."

Roseline covered her mouth with her hand as she gazed from the letter to her daughter. "How did you find…" She blinked away tears that had gathered in her eyes. "I am so sorry. You were never meant to learn… Let me explain."

Madeline let the letter drop into her lap again. "What is to explain? My father was a monster."

"Your father wasn't a monster. He was human, with human flaws. He made mistakes."

"Mother. You do not need to defend him. I overheard your conversation with the duchess earlier, and then I discovered the letter you wrote but never mailed."

"I am so sorry. You deserved to have a father you could be proud of."

"You wanted me to come to England for the purpose of finding a husband. I found something better. I realized that I may not have had a father in my life, but I have an extraordinary mother. I am so grateful that you are my mother. But what I don't understand is why you and the duchess conspired to match Robert and myself."

"In the beginning, it wasn't about a match between you and Robert but an opportunity to give you a better life. Dorothea said she had had Robert in mind for you all along, but when Donald died, and Lady Montgomery claimed Donald's dying wish was for Robert and Lady Montgomery to wed, that changed. It is extraordinary that Lady Montgomery suspected Devonshire murdered Donald and the old lord in order to get closer in line to inheriting the title of the Duke of Conclarton. Horrible man, Devonshire. We heard Robert and Lord Dumont captured him and he is locked up and awaiting trial. The man has brought so much heartache to this family! Have you heard when his trial is scheduled?"

Madeline shook her head. "I am sure the duke will know."

"Oh, my! I apologize for prattling on and on, when you look as though your heart is breaking. I wish…"

"Please, do not apologize. You did what you needed to do to keep me safe. I was angry, not at you but at myself for making excuses about the life we had, when what I wanted to tell the duke was that I hope I have inherited half your strength of character. I was angry because I realized I was trying to convince the duke I was good enough for him, when I should have been saying how proud I was that you were my mother. If he can't accept me for who I am, then his words of love were empty and meaningless. Against all odds, you not only survived, but you thrived. I love you, Mother."

Chapter Forty

Christmas morning, Robert stood in the Green Room that overlooked the entrance to the castle as he clenched and unclenched his fists. He hadn't slept a wink. Outside, a footman was helping Madeline into the carriage. He felt the sudden urge to rush out and try to stop her. But what would he say? He had behaved abysmally. He seemed to do that around her.

The sky was ice blue, and the forest surrounding the castle glowed in shades of green, the same color Madeline wore the first time he had seen her. Was he always to compare all of nature's glory to images of the woman who was riding out of his life? He had spent the night pacing his quarters, putting his thoughts on paper, only to tear up the pages and toss them into the fire.

What could he say to Madeline that would reverse the damage he had done? It felt as though a part of him were leaving with her as the carriage disappeared from view. She had opened her heart, and he had met her confession with stony silence and a heartless speech he now regretted. Why had he done such a thing? Was it shock at her revelations? Was he scandalized that her mother owned a brothel?

He had spent the night examining those issues and more. His father's argument would have been that if Robert married a woman with that sort of background, it would reflect poorly on the Conclarton family. His father would have also said that the consequences of marriage to a woman whose mother owned a brothel might tarnish his sisters and brother's chances of a suitable marriage.

During a sleepless night, Robert discovered a counter argument. It was apparent that Madeline was well educated and a kind and caring person. The result of an equally kind and caring mother. Those same attributes weren't always present in members of the privileged and pampered *ton*. If he were to wish for a wife, and a mother for his children, it would be someone exactly like Madeline.

The greatest example and gift he could give his brother and sisters was to teach them that a person's character was more important than their wealth and title.

But he had realized the alternative argument too late. He should have arrived at that conclusion the moment Madeline had poured out the truth about her mother. Madeline had said she did not want to begin a life with him based on a lie. Honesty. It was yet another admirable quality possessed by the lady of his heart.

He did not blame her for wanting nothing to do with him. "Bloody hell."

"Good morning, Robert," his mother said, joining him by the window. "I do not approve of that sort of language, but for once I concur. My question to you is, will you stand still and allow that wonderful woman to slip through your fingers?"

"I have no choice. She abhors the sight of me."

"Dear boy, we always have a choice."

Was it his imagination? Had the sky darkened and plunged the world into shadows of gray? He shook his head. No, there was not a cloud in the sky. It was his mood. "Madeline told me…"

The duchess interrupted his words with a lift of her hand. "Robert. I know it all. Roseline and I were childhood friends and I love her like a sister. Roseline fell in love and thought her gentleman loved her in kind. Her life has not been easy and yet she raised a brave, intelligent, and thoughtful daughter." She shrugged. "Perhaps it is best that you let Madeline go. She deserves a man who appreciates the woman she has become."

"You mock me." He cleared his throat. "I was a fool."

"Most men are."

He did not know the story of how his mother and Roseline had become friends. Perhaps he never would, and in truth it did not matter. People had a right to their secrets. Her mother was also good friends with the servant, Mary, and cared about the fate of the villagers. She, like Madeline, did not judge. They accepted.

"How is it that women tolerate us, then?"

"My darling boy, because the majority of you are good of heart, and when you love, when you truly give yourself, it is forever."

"How could a woman like Madeline forgive me?"

"You will never know unless you try."

He kissed his mother on the cheek. "I'll saddle my horse. She could not have gone far."

"Your horse is saddled and waiting for you."

"You knew I would come to my senses."

"I had hoped," she said with a laugh. "Now, off with you."

Robert descended the stairs to the courtyard two at a time. True to his mother's word, Trinity was saddled and waiting for him. Robert nodded his thanks to the groomsman, took the reins, mounted, and spurred his horse in the direction Madeline's carriage had gone.

What would he say to her?

When Madeline had told him her mother's secrets and their expectation for Madeline to marry a man with a title, he had responded with some nonsense about being the eighth Duke of Conclarton. She had merely shaken her head when he had made that declaration. And rightly so. A title did not speak to a person's character. It was not who they were. What a person did with his life, the people they cared for, those they loved, how they treated people, those were the things that mattered.

His horse's shod hooves churned up mud and debris as it closed the distance. The first time he had chased down Madeline's carriage seemed a lifetime ago. His heart had known even then that she was his soulmate. He had wanted to ignore his feelings. Thank goodness he had family and friends who knew him better than he knew himself.

He ducked under a low-hanging branch, and it occurred to him that he was forever chasing a carriage that contained Madeline. He had done so on their first meeting, and then again when her driver, Mr. Tinker, had been killed. The first time was to thank her for her generosity in helping someone she had assumed was in need of help. The next had been to save her life. This time it would be to beg her forgiveness and plead with her to marry him.

Poets wrote sonnets about what happened when love was spurned. They claimed a person could die of a broken heart. He would not die if she refused his offer, of that he was certain. But neither would he live a full and happy life. Life would hold little meaning. It would be something to be endured, as each day blended into the next in an unending chain of events.

Nothing had been the same since their first meeting. She had unsettled his world and tilted it on its axis. Building on his changing perspectives during the war, she had challenged him to see things and people in a new light. Before Madeline, he had spent his life adhering to the rules of proper behavior, and of who one should love. He would not go back to being that person who walked through life as though wearing blinders.

Her carriage appeared in the distance. He spurred his horse into a gallop and closed the distance. Within minutes, he reached her carriage and Trinity galloped alongside the coach, matching the team stride for stride. But she might refuse him again. Nothing was certain about Miss Madeline Mercer. She had refused him and had every right to do so again.

But as he had told his mother, he had to try.

"Madeline," he shouted, as he drew abreast of the carriage. His heart thundered to the beat of his horse's hooves. "There is something I wish to ask."

Mr. Welsh leaned from his bench seat to investigate the commotion, then turned toward Robert. Eyes wide with recognition, he pulled on the reins to slow down the team of horses.

Madeline leaned out the window. Although she was a vision in green and gold, her eyes were red-rimmed as though she had been crying. "Mr. Welsh. Please. Do not stop. There is nothing I wish to say to this man." She ducked back inside as though the matter had been settled, and the carriage resumed its original pace.

She was hurt, and he was the cause. He was the worst sort. But her refusal to speak with him made him more determined. Even if she refused him again, he must beg her forgiveness.

He shouted again. "Please order Mr. Welsh to stop!" He would not give up as long as breath remained in his lungs.

She leaned out the window again. This time her lips were a thin line of pent-up anger. "You are the Duke of Conclarton. Order Mr. Welsh yourself. I am quite sure your lofty position would override my unworthy one." She moved back into the shadows, disappearing from his view.

He deserved her rebuff and more.

Robert leaned over to the side of his horse, reached for the carriage's door handle, and pulled. The door swung open. "This is going to hurt," he said under his breath.

Feet loose from the stirrups, he leapt from his horse, propelling his body into the carriage, where he hit the floor with a thud. "Ow!"

"Are you mad?" Madeline eyed him as though he truly was a madman. "What if you had missed? You would have fallen to the ground and been pulled under the wheels of the carriage and trampled to death! And what about Trinity? Will he be all right?"

"I did not miss." He winced, rolling his shoulder as he pulled himself onto the seat opposite hers. "You are more concerned with my horse than with me?"

"I like Trinity."

Robert winced again under the steady glare of Madeline's gaze. "Trinity will be fine. He knows his way back to the castle."

"What were you thinking?"

"I was thinking that I was a fool and that I owe you another apology."

She leaned back against the padded seat and folded her arms over her chest. "I am listening."

He counted her remark as a sign of hope. At least she hadn't ordered him to jump out while the carriage was still moving. "I love you. Will you marry me?"

Her voice quivered. "We are not suited. You made that clear. You are a duke, and I am the illegitimate daughter of a woman who owns a brothel. I am not worthy to marry a duke, and the *ton* will make your family suffer. We would be shunned by polite society. Your family…"

"Do you love me?" He held his breath. He had not considered that she might not love him as much as he loved her. He would not blame her if she had lost faith in him. "I know I have much to atone for. You confided in me, and in the first test of trust and love, I failed. If you give me a second chance, I will spend the rest of my life earning back your trust. Do you love me?" he repeated.

"I do love you." She glanced toward the open window. "I wish I did not." The sadness in her voice broke him, strengthening his resolve. He wanted only happiness for Madeline, and he wanted more than ever to make her his wife. "I am aware that if we wed, the consequences for your brother and sisters might be severe. The *ton* can be very cruel."

He reached across the space that separated them to take her hand in his. "My family will survive. It is true that the *ton* will gossip, as they have little to amuse themselves these days. In time, they will discover another scandal that will draw their attention. The Conclartons are made of sturdy stock. But as to you and me being unsuited, I must disagree. Vehemently. You make me want to be a better person. It is I who am not worthy of you. Will you marry me?"

"Your Grace…"

The carriage came to an abrupt halt, launching Madeline from her seat and into Robert's arms. He laughed, pulling her close. "I will make sure to give Mr. Welsh a raise. His timing is perfect."

The most adorable smile teased the corners of her mouth as she settled beside him. "You are mad."

He kissed her on the forehead, tilting her chin and leaning toward her until their lips were a heartbeat away. "If by 'mad' you mean madly and impossibly in love with you, then, yes, madam, I am mad and wish never to recover from this state. Will you marry me?"

"You keep asking me that question."

"And I will continue until you say yes." He kissed her mouth softly and whispered, "I am most determined."

"Then my answer must be 'yes.' "

Mr. Welsh pounded on the door of the carriage. "Is everything all right?"

Robert drew back, keeping his gaze on the woman he loved. The woman who held his heart in the palm of her hands. "Everything is as it should be. If you would be so kind, please turn the carriage around. Miss Madeline Mercer and I have a marriage to plan—and please return as slowly as possible. We are in no hurry to reach the castle."

Chapter Forty-One

One week later, it was Madeline's wedding day, and she could not stop smiling. She sat on the bed in her room while a flurry of activity swirled around her. She wore only her chemise as she looked over the selection of Conclarton family necklaces, earrings, bracelets, and tiaras. The selection was stunning. Diamonds, emeralds, rubies, and sapphires shimmered on their bed of velvet like stars in a midnight-blue sky.

When Robert explained the number of guests and preparations who were expected when a duke married, Madeline suggested she would need until spring or perhaps even the following Christmas to prepare. Robert said that would never do, and expressed the alternative solution that they procure a special license and elope.

But when their mothers learned of their intention to elope, the mothers forcefully disagreed and offered to make all the arrangements in a timely fashion. A special license was secured. Then, since most of the family and friends were already in residence because of the Christmas Masquerade Ball, the solution was simple. The duchess extended the invitation for the guests to stay and attend the wedding.

Madeline's first impression was shock, and she waited for frustration to settle in, at their mothers' involvement. It never came because she realized that she loved how much they cared. In addition, when Madeline examined her feelings on the matter, she realized she was in as much of a hurry to wed as Robert. No doubt her feelings were the result of having a chaperone always present, which made for stilted conversations and for frowns and interruptions when Robert so much as reached for Madeline's hand.

But even then, she found humor and gratitude in their mothers' interference. Their mothers wanted everything to be perfect. Madeline had never seen her mother so happy, and it was obvious that she and Lady Conclarton were good friends. Madeline wondered if she would ever learn their whole story.

The mothers enjoyed planning the wedding and left nothing to chance. Additional staff was added to prepare the wedding day feast, menus were discussed, and invitations written and rushed out to those few who were not in attendance. Fresh boughs of greenery were cut to decorate the castle, and more candles displayed on every possible surface.

And then, in what seemed like the blink of an eye, Madeline's wedding day arrived.

The maids in the room discussed options for Madeline's hair. One suggested that a curling iron be heated in order to create a crown of curls. Another option was a long braid down her back, and another was to pull her hair into a tight chignon to better show off one of the tiaras. Madeline vetoed any suggestion that ostrich feathers be used.

"You look like a fairy princess," her mother said with a sigh.

Her mother had entered from the adjoining room and looked lovely dressed in a royal blue silk dress with a lace ruffle at the sleeves. The only jewelry she wore was her mother's feather brooch, that she wore like a pendant attached to a gold chain.

"Mother, you look beautiful, and I am so grateful to you and the duchess."

As one of the maids directed Madeline toward the chair in front of the dressing table, Roseline smiled back at Madeline in the mirror's reflection. "Did I tell you the duke asked for my permission for your hand in marriage?"

"He mentioned he might," Madeline said, as the maid began to arrange Madeline's hair.

"Well, and that is not all the good news. It seems that love is truly in the air. This magical Christmas season brings joy and the promise of good things to come in the New Year. Robert's brother William expressed his love for Miss O'Brian, and they intend to marry. The duchess was thrilled but asked if they could wait until she recovers from the preparations for your wedding. They agreed, but only if they do not have too long a wait. The young are always in such a hurry!" Roseline laughed.

"Will you stay and help the duchess with the wedding plans for her son and Miss O'Brian?" Madeline said. "I know she would love your help."

Her mother took a chair beside Madeline's. "You know, I believe I will stay a little longer in England. Liam has things well in hand in Boston and writes that I should extend my stay if I so desire." A maid tapped Roseline on the shoulder, whispering something in her ear. Roseline nodded, then turned to her daughter. "As much as I am enjoying our time together, you must hurry. Your groom awaits."

****

Robert stood in the church by the vicar, waiting for his bride to appear. William stood next to him as his best man and kept glancing toward Miss O'Brian with love in his gaze. Robert was happy about his brother's engagement to Miss O'Brien and approved wholeheartedly.

The church was decorated for the Christmas season and filled with family, friends, and people from the village, but the only person Robert cared to see was Madeline…and then the music started, and she appeared.

It was as though he and she were the only people in the church. She glided toward him as though she were a dream. She was radiant, wearing a white dress of silk, overlaid with lace. Instead of the diamond tiara, she wore a forest green bonnet with a matching ribbon.

His Lady in Green.

She joined him, and time slowed. Holding Madeline's gaze with his, he heard the vicar's words as though coming from a great distance away. Robert vowed to love and cherish Madeline and heard her repeat the same vows. They exchanged rings and were pronounced man and wife.

Madeline was his wife, his love, his world. He kissed her as wedding bells tolled, and he felt her tears on his face—or were they his?

"I love you," he whispered against her lips. "Now and forever."

"Now and forever," she whispered in return. "I love you."

A word about the author…

Pam Binder lives in the Pacific Northwest and has traveled to twelve countries around the world with no plans to stop adding adventures and countries to her list. She is an award-winning Amazon, *USA Today*, and *New York Times* Bestselling author. Pam is President of the Pacific Northwest Writers Association, and a conference speaker. Pam writes historical fiction, time travel, contemporary fiction, Regency, young adult, and fantasy.

http://pambinder.com